STAY AWHILE LONGER

 This book is a work of fiction. Names, characters, and events are a product of the author's imagination and any resemblance of any person, living or dead, is coincidental.

Printed in the United States of America.
First Edition Printing, 2022

Published by Melissa Powell Gay, LLC
Graphic Design by Inkwell Book Co.
Edited by Well Put, LLC

ISBN print 978-1-7350582-2-1
ISBN e-book 978-1-7350582-3-8

www.MelissaPowellGay.com
www.InkwellBookCompany.com
www.WellPutLLC.com

BOOKS BY MELISSA POWELL GAY

MT PLEASANT SERIES:

When Are You Leaving

Every Now & Then

Stay Awhile Longer

Parkland Tales: Stories for 3 a.m. Readings

Talking to Herself

STAY AWHILE LONGER

A Mt Pleasant Novel

Melissa Powell Gay

DEAR READER,

In his newspaper column, Virginia journalist Charlie McDowell created imaginary characters—Reliable Source, Aunt Gertrude, Mr. Bumbleton—who reacted to his social commentary. He referred to these essays as "contemporary folklore." As an avid reader of Mr. McDowell's columns, I suppose this writing style seeped into my storytelling psyche. The Mt Pleasant books are stories about common folks dealing with modern-day happenings.

Stay Awhile Longer is the third installment of the Mt Pleasant stories and inspired by two recent events.

The first was the death of my brother, Henry Lewis Powell, in June 2020. And, yes, when I created the character Louie Pyle in the first Mt Pleasant book, I was thinking of my tall, handsome brother who watched *The Andy Griffith Show* reruns and appropriated Goober Pyle's corny jokes for his own use. My brother could be serious when a situation called for sincere reflection but, in his natural state of being, he was a funny guy. He relentlessly bombarded friends and family with jokes and funny stories. He'd learned at an early age that humor numbs misfortune's pain. His family certainly wishes that he could have stayed awhile longer on this earth. This story is my eulogy to him.

The second spark of inspiration came from a discussion my creative editor and I had about the coronavirus pandemic and past-century plagues. In the fourteenth century, a young scholar Giovanni Boccaccio penned *The Decameron*, a fictional account of Italian life after the Black Death of 1348. Young Florentine survivors retreat into the countryside to "social distance" themselves from the ravages of the plague. To give their minds respite from the devastation, they entertain one another with stories ranging from morality tales to family yarns. Like Boccaccio's characters, Mt Pleasant's Louie Pyle and his small circle of family and unlikely companions make it through the 2020 pandemic by telling one another stories to escape from their modern-day worries, albeit for a short while.

I hope *Stay Awhile Longer* lifts your spirits in some small way.

Melissa Powell Gay
Spring 2022

For the guys

FALL **1985**

Bench sitting was a popular pastime in Fallam County, Virginia. Louie Pyle, owner of Gas N Go Enterprises, had bought a wobbly chestnut pew, at auction, when the old country store Booker T's closed down for good. He placed the bench, its slick seat polished from decades of cotton twilled backsides, by the main entrance of his first store for his idling customers.

Henry Lee and Donnie Tyler sat on the well-worn perch as they watched their young friend help a customer at the gas pump.

Louie had his head under the opened hood of a shiny new compact. Gas N Go wasn't a full-service car repair shop but Louie helped stranded motorists whenever he could.

"That's the third time this month that lady's been here and asked Louie to look under her hood," Donnie explained to Henry.

"You'd think she'd learn the boy doesn't work on cars, he just sells gas and oil to put in 'em," Henry said as he chewed on the plastic tip of his cigarillo.

"I don't think she's here to have her car serviced," Donnie

said. He guffawed as he slapped his knee. "Maybe some *other* kind of service. Know what I'm sayin'?"

Louie dropped the hood back into place. The woman trailed behind him as he walked toward the store. "I don't see where it's leaking fluids, Sandy," he said, wiping his hands on a paper towel.

Donnie and Henry watched as the woman tipped-toed in her high heels after the lanky, dark-haired store owner. Louie's down-home, dimpled-cheeked charm seemed to capture the lusty heart of any woman he met—a nuisance he managed with a country gentleman's grace.

"I'll take it by Hodge's garage," she said. Stepping closer, the sprite Sandy reached up and tousled Louie's movie star-like mane and said, "You need a trim. Why don't you come over to my house and I'll give you a cut and style?"

"Lisa cuts my hair now," a blushing Louie said, letting the woman know that his hairstyling, and other needs, were now seen to by his new bride, who was ten years younger than he. Louie and Lisa had tied the knot last spring and had a baby on the way.

The woman insisted, "In my opinion, she's falling down on the job. And you can tell her I said so."

The two entered the store, leaving the bench sitters to speculate.

Henry asked, "Why is it that every woman who meets that boy finds it necessary to look after him? Like he's a homeless pup on the side of a busy highway. Every one of them is compelled to rescue him and take him home."

Donnie added, "Wash and iron his clothes and fix him a nice pork chop supper."

Henry went on with his ode to a Fallam County prince,

"Come to think of it, I've never met anybody who didn't want to be his friend."

"'Cause he's the kind of man who'd give anybody the shirt off his back," Donnie said. Adding, "Or the last dollar in his pocket if they needed it."

Henry pushed his everyday fedora to the back of his head and concluded, "I expect so."

EARLY SPRING
2020

CHAPTER **ONE**

Parked in one of the visitor spaces in front of Elder Home, Louie Pyle stared at his truck's radio as he listened to the latest news report on the global pandemic. He was having a tough time understanding what he was hearing. The governor was saying folks wouldn't be able to visit with their loved ones living in places like Elder Home in Mt Pleasant until the pandemic subsided. Nobody knew when it would end. The government scientists were projecting that without an effective vaccine the virus could take quite some time to mutate into a harmless bug.

How was he supposed to check up on his mama every day if he couldn't go inside the building to see her? This pandemic was just another inconvenience piled on top of his already complicated family situation. Betty Doris Shively Pyle had become an Elder Home resident after Lisa convinced Louie that his mother shouldn't be living alone while insisting she couldn't live with them. Louie had to admit that Betty Doris and the Fallam County Fire Department were spending a little too much time together at her home on Elm Street, what with Betty Doris lighting up her kitchen every time she decided to fry something.

A loud thunk on the passenger side of his truck pulled Louie's attention away from the radio and his musings. Some old coot had parked too close to Louie's brand-new truck and was banging his rusty car door against the Super Duty's Race Red side panel.

"Yo!" Louie called as he got out of his vehicle and walked around to the passenger side to confront the other driver.

A senior citizen was yanking on a large denim sack wedged in the back seat of his car. Each time he tugged, his car door smacked Louie's truck. Bump. Bump. Bump.

"Can I help you?" Louie asked, holding his anxious irritation inside.

"What?" the white bearded man asked as he stretched to a height that almost matched Louie's six-foot-one frame.

Louie recognized Earl, a cattle farmer, as "a pack of Camels and the daily newspaper." That was how Louie connected with people, by what they purchased in his convenience stores. Almost every weekday morning Earl came into Louie's Gas N Go East and bought cigarettes and the local newspaper.

"Let me get that for you," Louie offered.

"I'm taking some things to Edith," Earl explained.

Together, Louie and Earl walked to the entrance of the county's only assisted living facility for the convalescing, infirmed, and disheartened. Standing on the rubber mat, they waited for the automatic doors to open. Nothing happened. Louie pulled at the door handle. Nothing happened again.

Checking the time on his phone, he asked, "Did they change their hours?"

"Edith says they let people in by eight most days," Earl replied.

Inside, a man in pajamas shuffled by with the aid of a walker.

Earl pounded on the door and shouted, "Open the door."

The resident stopped and waved at the pair like a child watching a Christmas parade.

"The door's locked," Earl yelled, signaling to the man to open it. He ignored him and continued on his stroll. Earl pulled at his beard and said, "That ain't right."

"Hang on," Louie said. He dialed the center's main number and received the general greeting telling him how important his call was. He pressed zero to speak with an operator, except the operator wasn't answering his call.

"I can't let y'all in this morning," came a voice from behind them.

Louie turned to see Plinkus Young, the center's director, approaching. She swung her oversized handbag to the front of her body with enviable hip action then rummaged around inside it while managing not to spill her coffee. She pulled out two individually wrapped disposable face masks and handed them to Louie and Earl.

"Why not?" Louie asked.

"'Cause the governor says so," she replied. "Don't you people ever watch anything besides the weather report?"

"Channel 7 Weather says there might be some rain this afternoon," Earl confirmed.

"Earl, the governor has mandated that all health-care facilities be closed to the public on account of the virus. We got to keep everybody safe."

"But Edith needs her things," Earl said. "She said to bring her brown britches with the gold stripes."

"Edith's recovery is going fine. Doctor Bowman says she can

go home in a day or so. We'll call you when you can come and get her."

"But what about her britches?"

Louie interrupted by placing himself between Earl and the director, "Plinkus, you're gonna stand there and tell me I can't see Mama?"

"I'm telling you we're closed to the public. If you want to know how her day is going, call her on her cell phone." The director flashed her key card against the magnetic lock and went inside.

Louie dialed Betty Doris's number. "Mama? This is Louie. I'm outside. They won't let me in to see you today."

"I know, son. It's the coronavirus. They got us on lockdown. I feel like a convict in here. And everybody is coughing and you know how I can't stand to be breathed on," Betty Doris said.

Louie sensed the slight strain in her voice. "Let me see what I can do. I'll talk to you tomorrow. Bye-sickle." He slapped his flip phone shut and slid it into his jeans' front pocket.

Louie wasn't having it, none of it. Rubbing the other car's rust and red dirt from the side of his truck, he swore to himself about people butting into some more of his business. When she was in high school, Jessica, his second child, used to laugh at him, saying he got upset whenever somebody moved his cheese. He never quite understood what dairy products had to do with people meddling in his business but then he rarely understood his daughter. With good reason. She was just like her mother. Louie and Lisa had officially divorced a year ago after many years of on-again, off-again separations.

Adjusting the visor of his Gas N Go cap, he put the truck in gear and drove over to Fallam County Community Bank.

Yesterday's deposits for all the stores needed to be made. What if Richmond decided to close the banks, Louie worried. Artie English's boy would tell him what to do. Louie called Artie's son Artie Three on account he was the son and grandson of Arthur English, Jr. and Sr. But the rest of the town called the bank's president by his given name, Travis.

The bank's front door was locked, too. After using up his daily allotment of swear words, Louie got back in the truck and headed for the drive-thru window. Cabbie Jones, a mask with the bank's logo covering most of her round face, waved and said, "Morning, Mr. Pyle."

Louie placed the deposit bags in the drawer and said, "Morning, Cabbie. Is Artie Three in today? I need to talk to him."

"Mr. English is sheltering in place at his house. You can text his assistant and schedule an appointment with him. Will that work for you?"

He pushed his cap back on his head and said, "Are you saying I have a choice?"

Cabbie laughed. "Mr. Pyle, you're a nut."

"I know I am but what are you?" He joked then smiled at the teller. "Let him know I'll catch up with him later." He drove to his third stop of the day, his bookkeeper's office, before heading out to Gas N Go West. Adding the geographical direction at the end of each of his store's names, east, west, south, and at the Shops in town was his ex-wife's idea. Lisa Pyle fancied herself a marketing genius. In spite of Lisa's many harebrained ideas, like one free bunny or chick at Easter for every fill-up, Louie and his bookkeeper Lupita Quinn managed to keep Gas N Go Enterprises in the black most years.

Rolling into the parking space in front of Lupita's office in The Shops of Mt Pleasant, Louie half expected the door to be locked like the bank's and Elder Home's. He watched as Lupita's daughter-in-law Ludie and Ludie's son Tommy came out of the office.

"How y'all doin'?" Louie waved as he got out of his truck.

Ludie, a girl so thin a puff of March wind could blow her away, waved back in that over-excited way of hers. "Hello, Mr. Pyle." She squeezed the shoulder of eight-year-old Tommy.

"Hello, Mr. Pyle," Tommy mumbled.

On the sidewalk, Louie asked, "What? No school today, Power Ranger?"

"It's Easter break," Ludie offered. "But they may not go back until May."

Louie faced Tommy and said, "Are you behaving? If you are, I'll give you a reward."

The boy leaned into his mama.

Grabbing the boy's hand, Louie slapped a Hamilton in his palm and said, "A man's handshake tells you everything you need to know about him. A wise man named Mr. Henry told me that once. He said if a man's handshake is tight and firm, he's a good man and you can trust his word." Louie felt a slight squeeze from the boy's hand. Tommy's eyes lit up when he saw the money.

"What do you say, Tommy?" Ludie asked.

"Thank you, Mr. Pyle."

In Lupita's office, Louie sat patiently while she argued in her native tongue with someone over the phone. Based on the speed and tone of the words flying around, she sounded pretty sore at the individual.

"Aye-ya-ya," Lupita exclaimed as she tossed her cell phone

on her desk. "That man is *loco*." Fluffing her thick tresses with her long fingers, she held her head back and gave it a rigorous shake. Then she said, "Excuse my outburst, Louie, but sometimes I get," she snapped her fingers rapidly, "I get frustrated when speaking to idiots."

"I hear you," Louie said. "Idiots can be hard to take on most days."

Louie secretly fell for this lively woman the first time he laid eyes on her. There she was, commanding the center of attention with her noisy gold bangles and all those dark curls cascading down her back, acting like the Queen of Sheba, and handing out Cuban cigars to her ex-husband's wedding guests. The cigars weren't to celebrate Ethan Quinn's nuptials to the town's most prominent lawyer, Jonnie Bailey, they were to celebrate Ethan and Lupita's son Vinnie and daughter-in-law Ludie's announcement of having a baby. This dark-eyed goddess was celebrating becoming a grandma. When Lisa found out their oldest, Ken, and his wife were expecting, Lisa cried for two days, belly-aching about being too young to be an old woman. Louie had never traveled outside of his own country, but meeting Lupita Quinn confirmed that he'd probably like living south of the border.

"Here's last week's vendor receipts," he said to Lupita. At the beginning of their business relationship, she'd insisted that he could simply text a photocopy of any paperwork with his cell phone. There was no need for him to come into the office. Not having any desire to own a smartphone, he told her it wasn't any bother coming by her office. Visiting Lupita Quinn was always the brightest spot in his week.

"I need you to sign off on your workbook so we can get started on last year's returns," she said. "More importantly, I need to show you something."

He nodded for her to continue.

"Brad, my new bookkeeper, found some discrepancies in expenses when he did the year-over-year analysis." She handed him a copy of Brad's report.

The scent of her perfume wafted up from the paper. He pulled his readers from his shirt pocket and followed along.

"Remember how we grouped your suppliers and listed them from the most profitable down to the least? Profit margins for the last calendar year are down in the top ten categories." Waffling her hand in a sideways motion, she continued, "Most quarters they'll float up and down, based on seasonal merchandise." Then she turned her thumb down and stuck out her tongue. "But now, overall, they are in the dirt. Across all these categories."

"Our sales are up, wouldn't that mean cost of goods would be higher, too?" Louie asked.

"Some. But even after he adjusts for the cost increases, the margins are not comparable to previous years."

"And this means?" Louie asked.

"It means someone is stealing from you, Louie."

He cupped his hand behind his ear and asked, "Did I hear you right? You say someone is stealing from me?"

She nodded.

He was dumbfounded. Never in his thirty-some years of business had he heard those words. On occasion, the summer hires would nick a case of beer or wine. He expected it and built it into the budget. He squinted. All he could think to say was, "What do you mean, stealing?"

"We're not sure how they're doing it but someone is definitely taking money that doesn't belong to them. A lot of money."

Lupita stood and said, "Join me outside for a coffee."

He followed her to the coffee room where she filled two of those itty-bitty cups that she called espressos and handed one to him. Outside, in the back of the office building, she motioned for him to sit on one of the plastic benches in her makeshift courtyard. She lit up one of her apple-scented cigarillos, her favorite scent, and blew out a blue plume.

"I hate thieves," she said.

"Not as much as I do," Louie said, trying to look cool while holding the espresso cup.

Blue vapor swirled in front of her. "I promise you. We'll find them and get your money back."

CHAPTER **TWO**

Later that night Louie sat out on his broad deck and watched daylight fade. He used this time of day to contemplate what came next. But that wasn't always the case. Right after Lisa left for the last time, he'd sit on the deck and drink until he fell asleep. Only his own snoring awakened him. Dr. Bowman had warned him about his high blood pressure and cholesterol, hinting that Louie, at his age, shouldn't be drinking like a college freshman.

The wake-up call came the day he blacked out at Gas N Go at the Shops. Lisa was at the store giving him the what for about the insufficiency of her monthly support check for her and their third child, Alex, who lived with her. One minute her face was all up in his, then, the next everything was black. When he awoke, Lisa was still there along with the lead EMT for Mt Pleasant's emergency medical unit. That day had shown him the error of his ways. He stopped drinking, cold turkey. Now, at sixty-five, the strongest drink he sipped was caffeinated coffee or iced tea.

Tonight, he decided to make a list of the potential somebody, or somebodies, who might be stealing from him. As the evening shade cast a shadow over his notepad, the list remained empty. He couldn't imagine anyone who would want to steal from him. Everybody knew that he'd help if asked. And many had. He donated his time and money to about every local cause that asked for his help. On top of that, he was a sucker for those adorable kids on the children's hospital TV commercials and sent them a check every year from his personal earnings. Lisa hated him for it, saying he spent more time and money on hopeless causes than on his own family. His nondiscriminatory charity was one of the reasons she told the judge that she wanted a divorce. Her saying such a foolish thing was why, Louie suspected, the judge gave Lisa her mama and daddy's three-bedroom brick rancher in town and Louie got the much bigger log cabin on the lake.

Louie turned his thoughts back to the problem at hand. In his book, a thief was the worst kind of criminal, the surliest form of human ineptness there ever was. He sat up from his slump. Scratching at his graying beard, he considered his situation. Maybe instead of listing potential suspects, he needed to set his mind on *how* to catch the thief. Plans for this new strategy were interrupted when he heard footsteps.

"Hello?" A voice called out from the other end of the darkened deck.

"Over here." Louie waved his arms above his head, attracting the attention of the motion detection lights.

"Oh, Mr. Pyle," the voice said. The glaring deck lights revealed the guy who operated the pizza parlor at Lake Village, about a mile from Louie's house. Still in his chef's whites and apron, Sal Contento balanced a pizza box on his forearm. "I want to drop on your house and have a talk."

Louie smiled at Sal. Even though the guy had lived in America most of his adult life, his English was as crooked as an old man's pinkie finger. But who was Louie to criticize? He'd lived in America *all* his life and his English wasn't too good either.

"Pull up a chair. My friends call me Louie. What's on your mind?" Louie asked, silently wondering why the owner of The Happy Pizza was here and not at his restaurant spinning dough.

Setting the pizza on the deck table next to the offered chair, Sal sat and placed his hands in his lap. Clearly, the man was struggling with what he was about to say. Louie waited patiently.

"I come to ask your help." Sal's voice was shaky. His high olive-brown forehead gleamed with sweat.

"How's that?" Louie asked.

"Mr. Pyle, er, Mr. Louie, I come to ask for a job."

"A job? Not enough customers ordering pizza to keep you in the black?" Louie asked.

Sal's dark eyes darted everywhere. "The building owner, he's shutting us down. We have no place to make our pizza."

Louie knew the building owner. Augie Young was the first generation of the Young dynasty to own a legitimate business. The man's great-granddaddy, granddaddy, and daddy had been notorious moonshiners and bootleggers. Now, the family business was headed in another direction of financial opportunities. Augie was a county supervisor and considering a run for a spot in the state House of Delegates.

Sal continued, "I must find more work. For my family. I'm the only one who cares for my grandfather." He was wringing his hands, winding up his jobless jitters.

"Hold on, Slick," Louie said. "We'll get you squared. Let me talk to Augie. Maybe we can work something out."

"I can cook for you, Mr. Louie," Sal suggested.

"I got a chef. She works out of the store over in town," Louie said. Angel Branch, a Marine veteran who rose to the rank of sergeant, was an awesome kitchen manager. What she didn't make herself, she contracted out to Fallam County's farmers—things like cakes, pies, jams, and sauces.

"No, no. I don't explain good," Sal said. "I cook for you, privately. For you and your family. In your home. Yes?" He grinned at Louie, exposing coffee-stained teeth.

Louie wasn't sure what this guy was going on about. Besides his three-legged outside cat Possum, he was the only person in his family home at the moment. After the two oldest kids left for college and their own lives, Lisa packed up most of the Lane and La-Z-Boy furniture and moved back to town. She also took Alex, their youngest, with her. Louie wondered what the Italian New York transplant meant by cooking for his family. He offered, "I usually eat at the store," and left it at that.

"But Mr. Louie, a man, his family, they need good food. Good made, how you say? Made from scrape?"

"Scratch?" Louie asked.

With a nervous grin, Sal said, "Yes. From a-scratch."

"What's really on your mind, Sal?"

Sal looked past Louie. "Mr. Young. He says we have to leave."

"Who's 'we'?"

"My baba and me. We live in back of the store. Mr. Young kicks us out."

"Your baba?" Louie asked. He was confused.

"Yes, baba. This is what I call my grandfather," Sal said, acting like a gun shy pup ready to bolt off the deck and sprint through the woods.

"So, you're looking for a place to live?"

"I think," Sal hesitated then went on, "we live with you. In your basement?"

"Why would you want to do that?" Louie said, not getting the connection.

"When I deliver pizza here, before, for your son and his friends, I notice you have apartment in basement," Sal said.

"You mean the rec room?" Louie asked.

After the retirement of a major loan from his mentor Henry Lee, Louie and Lisa found themselves flush with cash. So, they built their once-in-a-lifetime dream house: a seven-bedroom, 6,200-square-foot log cabin mansion with a lakeside view. As they were moving in, Louie got nothing but eye rolls and groans from Lisa and the kids when he said, "We're in log heaven now. Get it? Instead of *hog* heaven?" In spite of the family's disregard of Louie's bad dad joke, the name stuck. For Christmas one year someone gave them a wooden etching of the manor's name. Log Heaven. After everyone left, Louie hung the etching over the mammoth stone fireplace in the great room. The place had a walk-out basement and boathouse where the family entertained year-round. The basement was divided into bedrooms for guests, a rec room, and a kitchenette with a bar. Louie supposed that someone could live in his basement. But why would they want to?

"I'm gonna have to think on that one, Sal," Louie said. He hated turning people away, especially when he had the means to help them. But having a man, whom he barely knew, and that man's kin move in and live underneath his feet didn't seem right. "Did Augie say why he was chasing you out?"

Sal shook his head and said, "No."

Louie reckoned Sal was afraid to say why Augie Young was throwing the guy to the curb like a sack of flour.

"But if I live here, Mr. Louie, I cook for you. My grandfather can cook, too."

Louie didn't need another cook, or two for that matter. But a maid sure would be nice. The dust and cobwebs were getting pretty thick since Lisa had stopped coming over to clean and run the vacuum. "Does your granddaddy clean house?" As Louie's flip phone vibrated in his pocket, he signaled for Sal to hold his response. Judging from the look on his face, Sal didn't like the suggestion of his family's patriarch doing domestic work.

"What's up?" Louie said, answering his phone.

"Hey, Stinky," his ex-wife said. Stinky was the nickname she'd given him the summer before they were married. By the time they were saying their "I dos," Louie had grown tired of the put-down. He couldn't help it if he had overactive sweat glands in his feet. Yet, still she persisted, "Stinky, my car won't start. Can you come over and see what's wrong with it?"

That question was code for could he come over and fix it.

"Isn't that what mechanics are for?" he asked. Inspired by the advice of Betty Doris, he was working hard on trying not to be so available to his ex and her unending calls for a man's assistance.

"Louie Pyle, stop it. You know I can't afford to take my car to a garage."

He reminded himself that no good came from starting an argument with her but he couldn't help it. "Well, Sugar Britches," she hated it when he called her that, "I reckon you must have spent the money I gave you for a tune-up on something else." He slapped the phone shut and said, "Sal, like I said, I'm gonna have to think on your problem and get back to you. But I will get back to you."

Louie wasn't the smartest guy in his high school class but he kept his promises. Louie Pyle was a man of his word.

CHAPTER **THREE**

The next morning, instead of visiting Betty Doris, Louie turned onto Court Street and parked in front of Town Hall then walked around the back to the public safety building. He wanted to have a chat with Mt Pleasant's chief of police, his deer-hunting buddy, Ethan Quinn. He found Quinn next to the coffee station.

"Ethan, can I have a word?" Louie asked as he removed his Gas N Go cap and shook out his hat hair.

"Sure," Quinn said. "Come on back."

Louie followed Ethan into his office, where the chief motioned for Louie to have a seat in the visitor's chair.

"Since we're both busy guys, I'll get right to it. Can you keep this to yourself?"

"Of course. What's going on?"

"Don't say anything to anybody, not even your ex. *Especially* Lupita," Louie whispered loudly.

"What is it?" Quinn asked as he eased his large frame into the chair behind his desk.

"I went to see Lupita about my tax returns and she says somebody is stealing money from the stores. A lot of money."

"You have any idea who it might be?"

"Your guess is as good as mine," Louie said. "I been racking my brain and I can't for the life of me believe somebody would want to do this to me."

"You're too trusting, man," Quinn said.

"Me and the managers keep up to date with all the inventory and cash audits. And, 'course you know about our 'no hesitation' policy where we fire anybody on the spot who's caught taking from the till and one of your guys or the county law arrests them."

"So, you don't think it's somebody in the store?"

"No, we've got a solid crew. Most of them I've known all my life. Or theirs. Alex and his friend Thor took over the South store. No, the way I figure it, this ain't no inside job. And it don't matter about the *who* right now," Louie said. "I've moved on to the *how*. How can I catch the sumbitch?" A small ball of hot ire burned in Louie's throat.

The lawman aligned the two pens on his neat desk. "Maybe you should consider hiring a forensic accountant."

"A what?" Louie asked.

"Someone who catches crooks by analyzing digital transactions," Ethan said. "When I testified on a case over in Roanoke, I met one. This lady's sharp. She nailed a guy for stealing from his boss by tracking his internet purchases. Dangdest thing. And the judge ruled against him. But, on second thought, why don't you just use Lupita? She's smart. She could figure it out in no time."

Louie bugged his eyes out at Ethan.

"Oh," Ethan said. "You're right, you can't trust anybody.

But I don't think Lupita would do anything like that."

"Just keep this on the down-low." Standing, he asked, "Can you get me in touch with this lady. This accountant?"

Ethan scrolled his phone's contact list then scribbled a number on a sticky post-it note he'd retrieved from the desk drawer. "Her name is Talia Baskerville. She's based in Richmond."

Louie wasn't sure how to approach a woman with such a fancy job title so he asked, "Can we call her now and you explain the situation?"

After listening to Ms. Baskerville's automated greeting, Ethan introduced Louie and explained his situation and asked her to call him.

THE STORE AT THE SHOPS was Gas N Go Enterprises' crown jewel. Located next to a strip mall across from the community hospital in uptown Mt Pleasant, the newest shop was Louie's favorite and most profitable store. His phone rang as he pulled into the parking lot. It was Betty Doris's number. "What's up, Mama?"

"I need you to come and get me. I'm not staying another night in this place. Nurses breathing all over me. They're going to give me the virus."

Having listened to his mama every day of his life, except for the two weeks he and Lisa and the kids went to Myrtle Beach for their summer vacations, Louie recognized her current tone as her bossy voice. She was full on ordering him to drop everything he was doing and come to her aid. Taking a cue from her own advice to Louie about his relationship with his ex, Louie decided to make himself less available. "Mama, I'll stop by when I can. But now I gotta go. Bye-sickle." His phone rang again. Betty

Doris's number scrolled across the display. He ignored it but not without a tinge of guilt. He was brought up to respect a mother's authority. If that made him a mama's boy that was alright with him.

Inside the store, Chunky Brown was stocking the hot dog steamer. After Chunky's Early Riser Café burned down, Iris Lee, the landlord, built him a brand-new restaurant, Chunky's Place. But, to Chunky, and, apparently to most of his customers, the new place just wasn't the same as the original. Somehow the post-Lost Cause ambiance of the café's co-existence vibe didn't translate well with the shiplap décor and seven-dollar micro-brew beers that smelled, to Chunky and his faithful patrons, like skunk spray. He shut his place down and came to work for Louie, supervising the Gas N Go at The Shops' staff.

Chunky wasn't cut out for retail merchandising. Louie was always on him, reminding him that the convenience business was cash and credit card only. Buying things on account was not an option, especially lottery tickets. But Louie knew Chunky to be honest and loyal, even if he smelled like hot dog water most of the time.

"Morning, Chunk," Louie said.

"What's so good about it?" Chunky wasn't exactly a morning person.

Louie checked the cash receipt totals from the previous day. They looked in line with totals for this time last year. Having a photographic mind when it came to numbers, he knew, to the penny, his financial status. Comprehending words was another matter. He struggled with business contracts and the newspaper's editorials. He knew his numbers but the betrayal Lupita had brought to his attention had set him on edge. How had he missed it? He'd have to go over his income and expense statements from last year to see if he could discover where things had started falling off the tracks. A forensic accountant sounded expensive, probably cost as much as a divorce attorney, and he knew what *they* charged. Louie didn't pay for something he knew how to do himself. He knew how to add two and two. "I was born at night but not last night," he mumbled.

"What's that?" Chunky asked.

Not wanting to alarm employees of Lupita's discovery, he ordered, "Let's put all the baked goods on sale today. Clear all this out."

"But we do that on Thursdays and it's only Tuesday," Chunky protested.

"Just do it," Louie said. The pizza man's proposal was gnawing at him. Just like it had at breakfast and again while driving over to see the chief of police. Maybe Sal could make take-away pizzas for his stores. If all the fast-food chains closed because of the governor's orders, Louie reasoned, he could earn a lot of dough in pizzas to-go. "Earn dough in pizzas to-go," he chuckled. "Sometimes, I amaze myself." To Chunky, he added, "Call the other managers and tell them to put everything on sale today."

"OK, but it's your bottom line," Chunky said.

Chunky wouldn't know positive cash flow if it walked up and bit him. Louie didn't care what Chunky advised, that was some more of his business and Chunky should just do what he was asked to do.

While at his desk in the cramped office behind the checkout counter, Louie called Sal and asked if he'd be interested in considering a partnership. Sal was intrigued. He countered with an offer that included him and his grandfather boarding in Log

Heaven's basement. Louie said he'd get back to him on that one. Somehow the notion of someone not blood kin living with him just didn't seem to fit into his view of the world.

He glanced at his phone and noticed that Betty Doris had called two more times.

On his way over to the county offices to attend a public hearing about a new road enhancement that would have an impact on his East store, his phone rang. This time it was Plinkus Young calling.

"Ah'ite," Louie answered.

"Louie, call your mama. She's 'bout wore everybody out over here. She threw a shoe at one of the aides and the aide walked out, quit. She's upsetting other residents, too, telling them that the day of reckoning is upon us. I've never known your mama to quote scripture but she's doing a fine job of it today."

"She ain't sick, is she?"

"She's fine. It's everybody else I'm trying to keep sane over here."

"Can't you make her stay in her room?"

"We can't do that, it's against policy to lock someone in their room."

"You know, if you guys would shut down that 24/7 news brain rot you blast on the big TVs, it would calm her and everybody else down. Listening to those cardboard cutouts would drive anybody to think the world's ending."

"I agree. That's why I've limited their TV time to an hour a day. But now they all believe some conspiracy group is blocking the programs and that's why the broadcasts are only for an hour. Lord, give me strength." Then she let out one of those laughing goose squawks of hers.

"Tell her I'll call tonight when I get off work. Thanks for calling."

"Just do something to make her shut up, will ya?"

Louis tossed his phone on the passenger seat and grinned. Ain't nobody in their right mind gonna tell Betty Doris Shively Pyle to shut up. The consequences would be dire for everyone involved.

CHAPTER **FOUR**

The pizza man surprised Louie. In one day, Sal had laid out a business proposal complete with a cost and profit projection calculator. Plug in the number of pizza slices sold and the spreadsheet's calculator spat out how much the partners would clear. How 'bout that. Sal was handy with numbers, too.

But Louie worried about the part where Sal wanted to move himself and his granddaddy into Log Heaven's basement. What if Sal was a night owl and played loud music at two in the morning, that screeching *I-talian* opera or, worse, that bump and grind European techno noise his son Kenny liked? Besides, he was getting used to his own company. The solitude of the evening stillness on his deck brought his aging mind some peace. If the Contentos moved in, he'd have to move his cheese indoors, as his daughter Jessica would most likely put it.

MT PLEASANT'S COURTHOUSE, bank, and hospital sat atop the highest hill in the county. At the bottom of the hill, and to the north, was last century's retail center and referred to as downtown. Today, half of downtown was boarded up with rotting plywood scrawled with faded graffiti promising a brighter future. In the early 2000s, Gus Young, Fallam County's national baseball hero, converted the old grist mill into an office building and rented to business types needing desk space. The building was across the street from the renovated but defunct train station, now home of Mt Pleasant's History Center.

Gus's son Augie had been dodging Louie's calls about Sal's situation so he decided to drive over to Grist Mill Offices and have a face-to-face word with the boy. Louie suspected Augie of acting above his raising and fancied himself as too important to bother with a convenience store owner.

Inside, ancient grain dust still danced high up in the light beams generated from expansive skylights. Ordinary sounds of a busy office echoed off the towering walls. An assistant, one of Augie's many cousins, escorted Louie to the man's office. Wearing earbuds, Augie sat at a large, circular desk positioned square in the middle of the room, which was once the grain silo. One wall was decorated with pictures of Augie shaking hands with various local and national politicians.

Augie stood and offered his hand. "Louie Pyle. What brings you here, sir? Can we get you anything? Cup of coffee?"

Waving Augie off, he said, "Already had my legal limit for the day."

"I heard about your scare at your store. But you look fit, man," Augie said as he pulled at the front of his too-tight button-down.

Placing his hand on the back of a swivel chair, Louie said, "I'm here to see if I can help you and Sal Contento work out your differences."

Augie's smile disappeared. He sat back in his chair.

"He came to me looking for a job. Said you were kicking him out."

"Not that it's any of your business to know, but Mr. Contento and I had a disagreement that has resulted in his decision to not renew his lease."

"I'm afraid it is my business. The man wants me to hire him. I'm having trouble understanding why he left such a prosperous situation to come work for me." Louie looked down at Augie.

Augie lobbed one of those eye rolls popular with his generation. "He wasn't happy with some changes I made in the lease. It's complicated. But I'm happy to give him a five-star review as a tenant. The guy pays his rent on time."

"If he's such a good tenant, then why are you kicking him out?"

"All I can say is that he's opted not to renew his lease."

"What were the changes to the lease?"

"I'd rather not say." Something on Augie's computer caught his attention.

Talking to Gus's son was like talking to his own son Alex. Louie tried, "Is there anything I can do to help settle your differences?"

Still looking at his computer, Augie said, "You could ask him to sign the lease."

If that didn't beat all, Louie thought. He changed the direction on the conversation. "If you don't mind me askin', what are your plans for the space when Sal leaves?"

"We've got a few folks interested. My cousin Edie is looking for a bigger space for her vape shop. How about you? You need a store on the lakefront?"

"Gas N Go East and South cover that part of the county

pretty good," Louie said. "You know Alex and Thor Mosley are running the South store now. In fact, I'm on my way over there. I'll tell 'em you said 'Hey.'" Louie was done with Mr. Smart Aleck. Something wasn't right about the situation but Louie supposed it wasn't much of his business. The way he saw it, Sal and Augie needed to work out their differences.

Louie parked his truck in the back of Gas N Go South and caught Thor Mosley taking a smoke break. Just out of high school, Thor Bear was a friend of Alex's and was so big he needed a size 4X Gas N Go work tee. Thor Bear was Alex's guardian angel and the two were inseparable.

Theodore Edward Mosley attained his first nickname, Thor, at age three when his older sister could not pronounce his given name. The Bear part was added when, at five, Alex tried to hug him at Sunday school and proclaimed, "You're my Thor Bear." The name stuck until his high school years when the teenage giant proclaimed in the online yearbook that he wanted to be called "just plain Thor." That did it for the homies, from that time on, his friends called him Just Plain or J.P. His mama never used anything but Theodore. But to Alex, he was Thor or Thor Bear.

Louie pointed at the smoking giant and deadpanned, "You know that's how the dinosaurs became extinct?"

The boy grinned at hearing Mr. Pyle's dad joke about smoking for, like, the thousandth time.

Stepping up to the kid, Louie said, "Let me ask you something. You and Alex like the pizza over at the Village?"

"It's ah'ite, I guess," Thor said shrugging his Montana-size shoulders.

"What is it you don't like about it? They don't put enough

pepperoni on it?" He poked at Thor's stomach.

"Their all meat-all day specials are to die for. Plate of pork chops and chicken and homemade sausages." The Bear licked his lips.

"So, the food's good?" Louie asked.

"Yeah, food's good," Thor said, grounding out his cigarette butt on the bottom of his sneaker.

"Is there anything about the place that doesn't work for you?" Louie asked.

"Besides they don't serve Mountain Dew?" He played with the blond downy on his upper lip, a sign that the Bear was thinking. "The owner's partner is kind of a butt-hole."

"How do you mean?" Louie asked.

"Last time I was in there the old guy was going off on a customer, screaming at him in some language that wasn't English, then he took his shoe off and threw it at the poor s.o.b." After a pause, he added, "Stuff like that."

"Did you ever see him do that to other customers?" Louie asked.

"Naw. But he gives me the stink eye every time I go in there to pick up an order. He's always sitting at the table closest to the kitchen reading the paper and playing with a gold lighter. He comes in here from time to time and buys those cigarillos we started carrying."

To increase his chances at a personal relationship with the mysterious Lupita, Louie had upped the variety of his cigar and cigarillo stock for her smoking pleasure. The plan worked better than expected. Not only did he see more of the Latina vixen, other tobacco aficionados from as far away as Washington had discovered Louie's exotic tobacco selections and their purchases generated an increase in Gas N Go's overall tobacco sales.

Louie and Thor joined Alex behind the counter as a swarm of hungry lunch timers cued a line to check out. In appearance, Alex was all Louie, a slender build, chocolate brown eyes and a mop of dark hair. Unfortunately, he'd inherited his mother's penchant for nagging at his dad for something until he wore Louie down.

"Dad. Dad," Alex said. "Mom says we need to wear masks at the store." Then he joked, "I'm wearing my Batman mask."

Louie laughed. The boy had a sharp wit that few people appreciated.

"Dad. Dad. You can wear my Superman mask I got last year for Halloween. We already decided that Thor Bear will be Thor of Odinson." Then in a worldwide wrestler announcer's voice, he added, "Goooooodddddd of Thuuuunder."

Thor flexed his chubby biceps and said with all the seriousness of a Marvel comic devotee, "These are my hammers," then he kissed them. The boys laughed as did the customer waiting for his change.

After the midday rush, the boys stocked the stand-up coolers while Louie checked the register for sales history totals and saw no inconsistencies from the previous year. He wasn't seeing what Lupita had seen. The numbers looked fine.

"Must be on the cost side," he mumbled.

"Dad. Dad," Alex interrupted Louie's number noodling. "Seriously, are we all going to get the coronavirus and die?"

"What?" Louie raised his head from his notepad.

"Gran Betty said we were all going to get the virus and die."

"No, son. You get that thought out of your head right now." Louie gripped Alex's shoulders, forcing the boy to make eye contact. "Ain't nobody here going to die. Gran Betty is just a little confused is all."

"But she said people with the virus are breathing on her and she was going to get it and die."

Damn virus, Louie thought. Just another excuse for his mama to use to break out of the old folks' home. Ever since Lisa moved out, his mama had a daily excuse for why he needed to take her out of Elder Home and move her stuff into Log Heaven. But that wasn't happening. Louie loved his mama, would do anything in the world for her. Well, anything except live under the same roof. "Tell you what, let's call her tonight. You'll see she's safe."

"I talk to her every day, Dad. We video chat on our phones," Alex said. "If you would get a smartphone, you could talk to her, too."

"I talk to her plenty," Louie said.

"Mr. Pyle," Thor joined in. "Are me and Alex going to lose our jobs on account of you closing down the Gas N Go?"

"Nope. The store's not closing and you and Alex ain't losing your jobs. Governor said we're just like a grocery store. We have things people need, like gas and toilet paper."

"And cigarettes and lottery tickets," Thor added.

"And hot dogs and pork rinds," Alex played along.

"That's right, guys. This world can't operate without Slim Jims and Ho Ho cakes," Louie assured them. However, inside, Louie was worrying plenty. He dialed the number Ethan had given him for the forensic accountant. The lady's voice mail answered so he hung up.

CHAPTER **FIVE**

Thor had given Alex a ride for their shift at Gas N Go South, but he had to leave early for a doctor's appointment. Louie stayed to give Alex a lift home. They rode in silence for the first mile or so before Alex said, "Thor Bear snores. That's why he's going to the doctor's. He's getting a mask to wear on his face when he sleeps at night."

"I see," Louie said.

"His mama says he snores like a Mac truck hauling logs," Alex reported.

"Let's let Thor tell it, buddy. He may not want other people to know that about his-self," Louie advised. Louie worried about how Alex had no social filters when it came to repeating things he'd heard. One time, Alex repeated Lisa's assessment of his schoolteacher's mental state and Louie received a call from the principal. Alex told the woman that his mother said she was neurotic and he proceeded to define the condition and its cures. Alex was assigned to another class. Louie grinned at the memory. Then he turned to worrying, as he always did, about who would be Alex's social filter when he and Lisa were gone. "Does Thor still go with you to Sunday school?"

"No, he says it's for babies."

"But you don't think that, right?"

"I drive myself. Mom says she hates being stared at by all the haters," Alex said. "I sit with Marsha Ann and her aunt."

"That's nice," Louie said. When the kids were little, the family attended church regularly and with open hearts, or so Louie thought. Upon entering their teen years, Ken and Jessica, with the support of their mother, launched a united stay-at-home coup, boycotting all church-affiliated events. For a while Louie attended with Alex. But when he and Lisa split up and Alex moved in with her, what was the point? "You like Marsha Ann?"

"She's nice. She has Down syndrome," Alex said.

Each time Alex spoke of Marsha Ann, he included her genetic pedigree. Louie waited for the rest of it.

"She's got an extra gene," Alex added.

"That makes her extra special then," Louie always replied. Talk of this kind made Louie uncomfortable so he changed the subject. "Your mom's car is giving her trouble?"

"When she was coming home from Larry's, the check engine light came on," Alex said.

Larry was Lisa's latest. He seemed a nice enough guy, if a bit dimwitted. "Did she take it in to Hodge's for them to have a look at it?"

"I don't know," Alex said. "Dad, Dad, can we get this for the store?" Alex planted his smartphone in front of Louie's face.

"I can't look at it while I'm driving. Tell me about it."

"It's a whole kiosk for gummy bears and worms. I love gummy bears."

"Read what it says," Louie said.

"It says for your customer's high times we guarantee high volume sales with high margins," Alex read. "I'd like to have a special candy isle in the store and call it the 'Candy Lane.'" He laughed.

Louie suspected the ad was click-bate for cannabis displays, which, for now, happened to be illegal in Virginia. He was doing everything he could to keep Alex away from that whole scene. Given the medication Alex took for his anxiety, there was no telling what illegal drugs would do to his mind. But, as a new product line for his stores, he was looking forward to attending a convenience store conference in Las Vegas in June and learning about potential cannabis opportunities. The conference's keynote speaker was a successful marijuana dispensary owner. Louie wanted to be ready when Virginia allowed the legal selling and recreational use of marijuana. "We're always looking for new ideas to make money to put beans on the table, Champ," he said as they approached Lisa's house. "Maybe you can go with me to Las Vegas this year and get some ideas for the store. Would you like that?"

"I don't fly, Dad. You know what happens to me when I get on an airplane," Alex said. Alex was the reason the family drove to vacation and holiday spots. His fear of flying couldn't be explained, in spite of the thousands of dollars and hours they had spent on doctors and experts. "Oh, gosh, Larry's here," Alex added loudly as he unhooked his seatbelt.

Larry's showroom shiny Hummer was taking up most of the driveway, so Louie parked in front of the house.

"Maybe he's here to look at your mom's car," Louie said, trying to be positive for his son. However, the combination of Larry

Baldwin and car repair tools was like a snowman and Florida sunshine. Louie supposed owning a brand-new military style SUV to haul around groceries and a soccer ball was one of the perks of being the thirty-something son of a car dealer king.

Inside the house, Alex avoided eye contact with everyone and beelined to his room.

From the skunk odor, Louie guessed Lisa and Larry were up to no good. A bong was tucked next to Alex's TV chair, smoke curling up from the mouthpiece.

Louie motioned for Lisa to follow him to the kitchen, out of her guest's earshot. "Really, Lisa? Smoking weed around Alex? What the hell!" he exclaimed. He threw his cap onto the kitchen table. "You're violating our agreement." Pointing his finger in her face, he said, "Stop doing it or I'll report you to the judge."

Swatting at his finger, Lisa went on the offensive, "Where's Thor? He calls when he's on the way."

"I ain't Thor."

"Duh!" she snapped back. "Larry gave me a ride home and we decided to have an afternoon toke. Don't make such a big deal of it." She busied herself with retrieving groceries from a bag and storing them in the small pantry next to the back door. Holding a can of black beans in each hand, she said, "Why am I explaining myself to you? You're supposed to call whenever you come over."

Louie saw she was getting frazzled and things went sideways when Lisa got this way. He took a deep breath and swallowed his frustration. "Thor had a doctor's appointment so I gave Alex a ride. Excuse me for not calling."

Lisa rolled a chair from the kitchen table and slid into it. "What do you want?"

"You said you was having car trouble," he reminded her.

"Larry met me at Hodge's and gave me a ride home. They said they'd look at it tomorrow." She swept her blond curls up and readjusted her pony tail.

Feeling guilty about the disagreement they'd had over the telephone about the check engine light, Louie said, "Tell Hodge's to send me the bill."

Hearing a panicked Alex, Lisa and Louie returned to a hazy living room. Alex and Larry were playing tug-of-war with the smoking water bong.

"You're not supposed to do drugs. It's bad for you," Alex yelled at Larry.

Seeing Lisa and Louie, Larry raised his hands in surrender. The bong flew into the air as Alex fell backward onto the sofa. They all watched as the bong flipped end over end, spewing putrid water everywhere before landing on the carpet.

A few seconds of dead silence passed as Lisa pulled at the front of her soaked Van Halen T-shirt. "Get out!" she screamed. "Get out, get out, get out!"

All three men stood motionless, unsure as to whom she was directing her order.

She stomped her foot and screamed, "All of you. Get out of my sight!"

Sheepishly looking over his shoulder as he picked up the bong, Larry said, "Lisa, I'll talk to you tomorrow," and walked out the front door.

"Alex, go to your room," she ordered.

"But, Mom," Alex whined.

"Now!" She pointed in the direction of the bedrooms.

"Let me help you clean …," Louie began.

Now pointing at him, Lisa shrilled, "You. Out!"

Louie did what he was told.

AT SUNSET, LOUIE DOZED in his deck rocker. A wispy breeze ruffled the newspaper trapped under his crossed arms. Familiar scents of orange and nutmeg cologne and aged leather rode on the breeze. Then he heard him. "Ace?"

Henry Lee appeared in front of Louie dressed in his leather car coat and beat up fedora. An unlit cigarillo was tucked behind his ear, right where Louie had placed it the last time he visited him in the hospital.

Louie tried to speak but it was as if his tongue had been unplugged from his brain. The weight of his body was too great for him to move or to stand.

"Ace, you having a tough time?" The old man asked as he bent to get a closer look.

The old man's face was vivid with its deep vertical creases on each cheek. His small black eyes searched Louie's face.

Louie was conscious, aware of where he was but unable to move. He tried to say the old man's name but his tongue wouldn't budge. Real or not, Louie was excited to see his dearest friend. He tried to extend his hand for a shake but it wasn't cooperating.

"You know you can talk to me," he assured Louie.

Louie watched as Henry Lee turned and walked down the long deck, disappearing around the corner of the house.

CHAPTER SIX

Louie checked his phone for missed calls after he parked in front of Lisa's house the next morning. Ethan's accounting detective still hadn't tried to reach him. He massaged the back of his neck. Somehow he had managed to sleep through the night in his deck chair and his neck was reminding him, at his age, that was probably not a good idea. The vivid dream about Henry Lee still lingered. What had made him think about the old man? Henry Lee had been dead for years. But not long enough for Louie to have forgotten what he looked like, how he dressed the same way, every day, in a starched white shirt, that one-of-a-kind leather car coat, and a dusty fedora pushed back on his head. The car coat, given to Louie by Henry's daughter after the man died, was hanging in Louie's coat closet at home.

Henry Lee had stepped in for Louie when Lucas Pyle had abandoned his family. He counseled Louie through his teenage years, supported him in his business venture, and encouraged him to stand for town council. Louie felt his presence from time to time, especially when a hard decision needed to be made.

He missed the Mt Pleasant maverick.

Lisa had summoned Louie. And, like the fool he still was for her, he'd obeyed.

Louie found Alex sitting on the front steps atop the family's blue whale, what Jessica called the oversized, hard-sided suitcase Lisa bought the year they went to Disney. His head bent over his phone, Alex was arguing with it.

Louie watched his youngest for a minute. As much as he wanted, he didn't dare touch him, brush the black hair away from his face, or pat him on the shoulder. Alex didn't like being touched. Louie loved that boy more than anything but there were times when he wanted to throw up his hands and walk away from it all, the boy, Lisa, his business, Mt Pleasant. Then he'd talk himself down off the ledge by realizing there was no other place he'd rather be. Once the kids were old enough to look after themselves, he and Lisa traveled some but the sweetest part of their vacations, for him, was returning home and sleeping in his own bed. Mt Pleasant was his life.

"Alex," he said as he stooped to the boy's eye level. "Where you going?"

Alex ignored him. He was in one of his animated game trances.

Louie knocked on the door then tried the knob.

"Your mom gone to work?" Louie asked. Lisa was the receptionist at Girl Curls hair salon two days a week. "Did Sandy pick her up?"

No answer to his questions, only a slight grunt.

Louie'd heard that sound a thousand times, Alex was half-asleep. He wasn't going to bother asking his son why he was sitting on the blue whale on the front porch at seven o'clock in the morning. He wouldn't get an answer.

Louie dialed Lisa's number. The call went straight to voice mail so he left a message. "Leese, you wanted me to come by? You ain't here. And why is Alex sittin' on the front stoop looking like a runaway?" He tried Thor's phone next but it went to voice mail, too. Didn't anybody ever answer a phone anymore?

"Thor Bear's mama's sick. He's not picking me up today," Alex offered.

Louie thought about that. "Is anybody at the store?"

"Thor Bear said Normal was taking his shift," Alex offered. Normal was Norman Stokes and there wasn't anything normal about the kid. In fact, if left alone, he would rob the store blind, not intentionally. Customers took advantage of the fact that Normal had trouble counting change. Wanting to help the boy's family out, Louie had given Normal a part-time job sweeping up and shelving stock.

Louie dialed Gas N Go South. "Yo, Normal, you working Thor's shift?"

"That's right, Mr. Pyle," came the reply.

"Anybody there with you?" Louie asked.

"Nope, just us chickens," Normal said.

"I'll get someone over there to help." Louie slapped his phone shut and said to Alex, "Son, you need to get to work. Normal can't handle the morning shift all by hisself."

Alex looked up from his noodling, squinting from the morning sun.

"Just because Thor can't go to work doesn't give you a pass. Go on," Louie insisted. "And make sure you run the register. You know how Normal is, sometimes he gets his numbers mixed up." Then he added, "It's time for you to grow up and be a leader,

Alex. Go help Normal out."

Alex stood and stuffed his phone in the back pocket of his skinny jeans, a fashion trend Louie wasn't sure why any self-respecting guy would consider. The boy pushed his hair away from his face and said, "Mom said I have to go and live with you."

That explained the suitcase.

"She did?" Louie asked, stalling to come up with a better response. Then he asked, "Where do you want to live?"

"I guess I want to live at Log Heaven," Alex said. He busied himself by stuffing his hand in his hoodie's pocket and pulling out his truck keys.

"Son, no matter what happens, you can always come home and be with me," Louie said. Nodding at the suitcase, he asked, "Is this all you're taking? What about your computer stand and your gamer's station?"

"Mom said you'd move it with your truck," Alex said.

Louie extended his arm over the boy's shoulder and did a side-bump hug. "We'll get you squared away. Take your suitcase and get on to work. Give me your key and I'll get your other stuff."

"She took it off my key ring," Alex said. "She's really sore about me and Larry spilling that gross water all over the new carpet. She said all men live like animals."

Really, Lisa? Louie said to himself. To make the boy feel better, Louie laughed and said, "Well, I guess you'll have to move into the doghouse with me."

"But, Dad, we learned in biology that humans *are* animals. Why does Mom really want me to move out?"

Thinking of Lisa and her new boyfriend, Louie said, "I'm guessing she just needs some alone time." He didn't blame Lisa, being with Alex full time was exhausting. His endless and, mostly, useless questions wore on a person. As soon as she tired of Larry, she'd be calling Louie up and harassing him to bring Alex back to Mt Pleasant. "Get to work before Normal gives away all the cash in the register and starts handing cigarettes out for change."

"He never looks at the display to see how much money he's supposed to give the customer," Alex said.

"You make sure you show him how to do that today," Louie said. "I'll see you tonight."

"But I've already shown him how to do it, like, a hundred times already, Dad," Alex complained.

"I know, but sometimes we have to use our patience with others. Now, git!"

LOUIE SAT IN THE PARKING LOT of Elder Home listening to the latest news about what state officials were calling a novel virus. Cases were beginning to appear throughout the state and the governor was making noise about shutting everything down. What would that mean for Louie and his employees, exactly? Louie thought about Alex and his irrational fear of dying. He hoped the spacious emptiness of Log Heaven would soothe and assure Alex that he was safe, that he wasn't going to die.

Louie reached into his shirt pocket and pulled out his spiral notebook to make a note about seeing what changes he should make to his inventory. Changing his mind, he dialed Boyd Latimer, the manager at Gas N Go West. Boyd enjoyed the extra duty of monitoring inventory levels, saying it kept his mind busy and his body out of trouble.

"Boyd?" Louie said. "You hearing all this stuff about people not being able to leave their houses for two weeks?"

"Crazy, ain't it?" Boyd said. Sounds from a busy cash register filled the background.

"Store doing ah'ite?"

"There was a run on toilet paper this morning. Lady bought all we had on the shelf. Had to restock three times already. Want me to limit one pack to a customer?"

"That sounds like a plan," Louie said.

"And before you ask, I already put in an order for three pallets. That was all Yippies would give me. Want me to call another supplier?"

"Good idea. While you're at it, take a look and see what else is hot. We can decide tomorrow what we need to bump up."

"Already done, Chief," Boyd said. "In your in-box. Check out the display for face masks."

"You're a good man, Boyd. Have a cup of coffee on me," Louie said.

His pocket notebook was opened to the page with Talia Baskerville's number. He dialed it and the call went straight to voice mail. He waited for the perky voice to finish, surmising that the voice was automated because no human could be that happy. He left a message with his name and phone number.

Louie jumped as a pair of arthritic brown knuckles knocked on the truck's window. Leaning against a cane, Donnie Tyler motioned for Louie to lower his window.

"How's it going, Donnie?" Louie asked the skinniest denizen of Elder Home.

"Louie Pyle!" Donnie wheezed. Once he caught his breath, he added his hip cat tag, "What's shakin'? Besides your bacon!" At eighty-seven, Donnie Tyler had lived at Elder Home longer than any of his peers and was celebrated for that fact every year.

He and Henry Lee had been pals and, in some fraternal settings, heralded as brothers from different mothers. Henry used to talk to Louie about Donnie and his large family and how the pair were related. Louie had forgotten the details.

"Are you allowed to come outside?" Louie asked Donnie.

Donnie put a crooked finger to his chapped lips and said, "Shh. I'm busting out for a nice stroll around the parking lot."

Louie watched as the old man wobbled over to the raised curb of the parking lot and veered left, reminding Louie of a windup doll.

He dialed Betty Doris's number and she answered before the first ring could finish.

"Why haven't you called?"

"I did," Louie said

"When?"

Trying to cheer her up, he laughed and said, "Just now." Seemed like he'd spent half a lifetime trying to make the women in his life happy. "Now, what's got you so riled that you have to jam up my voice mail so my vendors and employees can't get ahold of me?"

"I need a new chair for my room and that bossy Plinkus Young won't let Samson take me to Bassett Outlet to buy a new one. I can see your truck in the parking lot. Will you take me to the store?"

"They still won't let me come inside," Louie said. At least the obsession with others breathing on her had passed.

"I keep telling you, they got us on lockdown," she stressed.

A fan for the dramatic, Betty Doris made everything out to be an epic scene in her life's saga. Everything about her life was either too big or too small, or not enough or too much. She always wanted to fix things that weren't broken in the first place. The chair in her room was the perfect example. Louie had taken her to three different stores to find a replacement but when they placed it in her room, she'd decided she didn't like the color, and it didn't match the shabby chic look she was aiming for. After much haranguing, she had decided to keep her old one.

"I saw Donnie Tyler talking to you. What did he have to say?" Not waiting for an answer, she plowed on, "From what they're saying about this virus, me and Donnie won't make it if we get it. I told him he should go to his niece's house but he said he didn't want to bother her. That she was dealing with one of her cousins' kids. I told him that it's times like these when folks should be with their own family the most, but he won't listen."

"I'll get Alex to come over and take you to get a new chair," Louie offered.

"You don't get it, son," Betty Doris said. "They won't let us go out. If I leave, I can't come back."

Attempting to calm her, Louie said, "Let me talk to Plinkus. I'm sure we can work something out." He hung up his phone as he searched the parking lot for Plinkus's car.

CHAPTER SEVEN

Plinkus's car wasn't in the Elder Home parking lot. On his way to Gas N Go at the Shops, Louie spied her in front of the courthouse war memorial conducting one of her Mt Pleasant Historical Society tours for a handful of out-of-towners and high school students. All dolled up in her Victorian widow's mourning dress, she was spouting nonsense about losing her husband and her boy to The Cause, whatever that meant. Lisa told him once that whenever the Society ladies wore those poofy dresses, they were in character and acting out a part in a historical reenactment. Like this world needed another history expert, he mused. Better to let the history stay where it belonged, in the past.

At the store, Angel Branch was stocking the display cases with her latest sheppard's pie creation. It was a hit and he'd asked her to double the production for the following week. And, based on all the fuss about people staying at home, he wanted to up all his ready meals and desserts production. Gotta make hay while you can, he told Angel.

At his desk, he accessed Boyd's recommendations on his computer. After a half hour or so, he felt he had a pretty good handle on what needed to be ordered and sent a reply back to Boyd. He slogged through other emails before declaring that an hour in one day was about all he could stand at a desk. He summoned Angel into his office and asked, "Have you seen the unit sales for the prepared foods this month?"

"We can't keep the seasoned green beans in the case, Mr. Pyle," Angel said. She chewed at a fingernail that hadn't had a chance to grow since middle school.

"Let's get together with Chunky tomorrow and go over the production schedule for the second quarter. I want y'all to come up with more ideas on new ready meals. Looks like folks will be staying home while this nasty bug is riding herd on us all. We want to make sure they can buy dinner while getting their beer and lottery tickets."

"Mr. Pyle, do you think they'll shut us down?" Angel asked.

"Don't know. But don't you worry, just do your job and keep the kitchen clean like it was your own."

Out in The Shops parking lot, Louie watched as Plinkus, who was standing on the sidewalk, wave good-bye to the tourist then float his way. He felt the intent of her determined stare. Seeing the woman decked out in her silly costume reminded him of the time he and Lisa took Jessica and her best friend to Roanoke to see *The Nutcracker* ballet. One of the characters, Mrs. Ginger, wore a huge dress and little tiny dancers swirled out from underneath her skirts. He laughed at the memory.

"What are you laughing at, Louie Pyle?" Plinkus asked, sweat fogging up her thick glasses.

"Nothing, Mrs. Ginger," he replied. "Mama said you was

looking for me."

"You haven't kept your end of our agreement. You were going to talk to her and tell her to stop stirring everybody up."

Louie rolled his eyes. "You know telling Betty Doris what not to do is like telling the wind to stop blowing."

She fiddled with the strings on her tiny handbag and said, "I guess you're right."

"You can't move her to an area where she's not around others?"

"Honey, we tried that a week after she moved in," Plinkus said. She bowed her head and mumbled, "Sorry. I don't mean to sound so disrespectful toward your mother. It's just, well, you know how she can be. Besides, if she was too feeble to get around, we wouldn't be having this conversation. But, you know, your mother is as healthy as a plow mule."

"I would have thought the others would have gotten used to her by now," Louie said.

"For the most part, they have. But this business with the virus has them all worked up. And I don't blame them."

"I don't know what to tell you, Plinkus," Louie said. "I'm all ears for suggestions."

"We need you to take her out of Elder Home for a few weeks. Just 'til this thing blows over. Then she can come back. She can have her old room back."

Realizing he'd been trapped, he blurted out, "I can't. I got a business to run." That statement sounded really stupid out loud. What were his other responsibilities that he couldn't look after his own mother? He was having trouble thinking of any at the moment. Stalling for a better solution than having her lord over Log Heaven, he said to Plinkus, "Can you give me a day or so to make arrangements?"

"Don't lollygag on me, Louie. We're serious about this," she said. "Don't make this harder than it needs to be. We can bring her to you if that works better." She turned and sashayed away, swinging that handbag like she was headed to a Sunday barbecue.

At the end of the day, Louie stopped at Lisa's to pick up Alex's stuff. He found a note taped to the front door with clues on where to find the house key. Against his better judgment, he lifted and carried everything she'd tagged in Alex's bedroom to his truck, making several trips. The last thing to move was Alex's captain's chair from in front of the family room TV. Feeling wobbly, he plopped into the chair to catch his breath. A cold sweat soaked his shirt.

Aloud, he said, "Alex, you're going to have to get this one yourself." He wiped the side of his face with his shirt sleeve, stood, and stumbled out of the house.

The traffic glare convinced Louie to slow down on the highway. This allowed him to think, to worry about what he was going to do with Betty Doris, what he was going to do if he had to lay off his employees, what he was going to do with all the inventory that would spoil if the government shut him down.

He tapped the steering wheel with an open palm and declared out loud, "I'll donate it to the community kitchen."

"That's a smart idea," Henry Lee offered.

Taking his eyes off the road, Louie glanced to his right and felt as much as saw his mentor sitting on the passenger side of the truck. "What the?" Louie pulled the truck over to the shoulder and came to an abrupt stop. Amid the noise of traffic whizzing by, he rubbed his face and then shook his head. When he looked again, the old man was still sitting beside him.

"What the?" Louie repeated. He didn't know what else to say. He'd never talked to a ghost before. "Mr. Henry?" Everybody called the old man "Mr." out of respect.

The old man said, "You're concerned about the uncertainty of the future. But don't be. You have what it takes to face what's coming. I'm sure of it."

"What's going to happen?" Louie wanted to know.

"I never got the chance to tell you how proud I am of you. Starting with nothing and making your life a success. You were like a son to me, a good son." His face shimmered translucent from the headlights of oncoming traffic.

Louie awoke to blue lights violently swirling around inside the cab of his truck. He shaded his eyes as someone beamed a flashlight into his face. Judging from the starched hat, Louie guessed a state trooper. He opened the truck window to a chilly and dark night.

"Everything all right?" the officer asked.

Dazed, Louie patted his chest, feeling his notepad in his shirt pocket. He looked at the truck's clock, 9 p.m., and felt the hum of the engine. Louie summoned up an excuse as fast as he could, "Got a little drowsy, officer. Pulled over for a nap."

"Where were you headed?"

Pointing at the intersection a few yards ahead, Louie said, "Down that road. I live on North Lake Road."

"Sounds like you're almost home. This isn't a very safe place for a nap, Mr.?"

"Pyle, Louie Pyle. I own the Gas N Gos," he said.

"Do I need to give you a lift home?"

"Nah, I'm ah 'ite," he said. He put the truck in gear and pulled away. The ride home was flooded with memories of his visit from Mr. Henry. What did he mean when he told Louie that he was sure he could handle the future?

THE NEXT MORNING ALEX sat across from Louie at Log Heaven's breakfast nook, eating a bowl of that sugary cereal he lived on.

"Dad, Dad, look," he said as he pulled down the newspaper Louie was reading and shoved his phone into Louie's face.

The doorbell rang and Louie said, "You want to get that?"

Alex stood and put on his hoodie, saying, "It's Thor Bear. I texted him that I've moved back to Log Heaven."

"Good," Louie mumbled, returning to his paper.

A minute later, Alex came back to the table and resumed eating his breakfast.

Louie looked up from the paper. "Where's Thor?"

Alex didn't answer.

"Mr. Pyle?" Someone was calling from the front of the house.

At the front door, Louie found it wide opened. Sal, the pizza man, was standing at the threshold.

"Alex!" Louie called. Looking back at a puzzled Sal, Louie motioned for him to come inside. Closing the door, he swore under his breath, wondering where he and Lisa went wrong in the raising of their youngest. He sighed, it was only eight in the morning and he was already tired of the day. Rubbing the back of his head, he said, "What can I do for you?"

The slight man extended a pizza box and said, "I've come to see if you have had a chance to review and consider my offer."

Louie stared at the man. Still groggy from last night's revelation, that he'd talked to a dead man while driving in his truck, Louie rubbed at his dry eyes.

“The single slice of pizza for the Gas N Go shopper?” Sal prompted, smiling nervously.

“Oh, that,” Louie said. “Forgive me. My morning coffee hasn’t taken ahold of me yet. Come on back to the kitchen.”

Before he could pour his guest a cup of coffee, the doorbell rang again. “Alex,” he commanded and nodded toward the front of the house.

“Thor Bear’s late,” Alex complained. He picked up his phone and left.

As he was offering a seat at his kitchen table to Sal, Louie heard Alex’s insistent plea.

“Dad, Dad, guess who’s here!”

Curiosity led Louie and Sal to the front door. Standing in the foyer was Betty Doris, all four feet and nine inches of her. Samson, Elder Home’s most popular nurse’s aide, stood behind her hefting three extra-large suitcases.

“I escaped!” Betty Doris exclaimed. “Samson, take those to the bedroom down the hall and to your left. Louie, before you move your stuff up to Jessica’s room, give the nice man a tip. Is there any coffee? I’d love a second cup.”

She waltzed away, leaving the men staring at her exit.

SUMMER **2020**

CHAPTER **EIGHT**

Within weeks, Louie's life had gone sideways. What with the world shutting itself down, the new shelter in place rules were making him and most folks even more suspicious of the outside world on the other side of the Fallam County hills. They all stayed at home, went to bed early, and hoped that the world would reset itself to its rightful orbit sometime in the night.

The uncertainty was too much for some. Watching endless breaking news reports about a global pandemic, Betty Doris and Alex had become stymied by their fear of an invisible foe. Louie considered canceling the cable service but thought better of it as the pair would just dog him until it was reconnected.

In spite of the great digital inferno, Louie acted on his instincts and made a deal with Sal Contento. Sal held back on signing a contract until Louie agreed to allow Sal and his grandfather to move into Log Heaven on the first day of June on a month-to-month arrangement until Sal found a permanent home for his family. Louie was waiting for the right time to tell

Betty Doris about the new boarders.

Sal's Get N Go Dinner, as they had decided to call it, was an instant hit. Each day around four o'clock lines formed outside every Gas N Go to buy the ready-made meals. Under Sal's supervision, Gas N Go at the Shops added a pizza oven. Sal and Angel worked up new recipes for the hungry herd of county residents who feared their kitchens as much as the dreaded virus. That Sal was a pushy fellow in the kitchen, Louie vowed, but he knew how to spin pizza dough into greenbacks.

Louie's hours at the store had increased when some of the staff took time off to be with their kids. While working a shift at Gas N Go at the Shops one day, Louie rang up two Get N Go panini sandwiches and a liter of water for a young woman. He could tell from the way she dressed that she wasn't from Mt Pleasant. Or, if she was, she'd been away and come home. Either way, she wasn't a regular customer.

"You home for a visit?" he asked as he scanned her items.

She tilted her forehead toward him with an amused contempt reserved for older, total strangers hitting on her. "I'm home visiting my Uncle Donnie," she said as she swiped her bank card.

"Donnie Tyler?" Louie asked.

"You know him?" she asked as she lowered her face mask and pushed a stray braid out of her eyes. She smelled of waffles and maple syrup.

"I expect I've known Donnie Tyler, let me see, as long as I been breathing," he joked.

The smile in her eyes revealed she was somebody special. Light flowed out of her face and onto Louie. He'd be hard pressed to explain it to anyone. Her presence felt like a down jacket on a cold morning, warm and fluffy.

"Tell him Louie says 'hey' next time you see him," he said.

"I'm going over to see him now," she offered.

"How you going to do that? Elder Home is in quarantine," Louie said.

"That's our secret," she said. Then she left the store.

An hour or so later, here came Donnie Tyler and the pretty young woman into the store. Louie watched as she helped him maneuver his way to the counter. Working in the convenience business for so many years, Louie could figure out in a single glance what a person was after in his store. He was confident the two weren't there to buy a pack of crackers. They wanted something from him, something that wasn't for sale on a shelf next to the candy bars.

Donnie's breath was ragged. He struggled with saying, "Louie Pyle, I'd like you to meet Kiara Tyler Moss. She's my sister Karina's grandbaby."

Louie nodded and said, "How'd that sandwich work out for you guys?"

"Tell the chef the pesto was perfect," Kiara said and smiled that warm smile of hers.

Donnie gripped at the handle of his cane, his loud wheezing becoming more regular. Alternating a word with each breath, he said, "She's come home from D.C. Got laid off from her job." He hacked out a long cough.

She gently rubbed her uncle's back and asked, "Are you all right?"

Donnie nodded and signaled with his hand for her to finish what he'd started. "What my uncle is trying to say is I'm looking for work and a place to live. Any leads or suggestions you may have would be appreciated."

Louie scratched at his beard. This wasn't what he was expecting. "I don't know of anything off the top of my head but I'll ask around."

Coming up for air, Donnie bragged, "She's a trained classical pee-anist and she's got her M.F.A. in African American literature."

Kiara laughed and said, "That and five bucks will get me a latte at the corner café."

"She's selling herself short, Louie. She's capable of anything," Donnie bragged some more.

"What sort of work are you looking for?" Louie asked.

"Anything, really," she said. "I was a content provider for the Kennedy Center's performance blog. Along with my performance duties, of course."

"Of course," Louie said, having no idea what this sprite just said to him.

"I'm good with people," she said. Now she sounded desperate. "I volunteered at a family shelter near my apartment complex. Gave free music lessons and helped with the fund drive to raise money for their community garden."

"That's cool," Louie said. "If I hear of anybody needing a music teacher, I'll send them your way."

Later that night while Louie, Alex, and Betty Doris were enjoying one of Sal and Angel's latest dinner packs—chicken gyros with Greek salads, Louie's phone vibrated. As he pulled the phone from his pocket, he recognized Sal's number.

"Dad, you said no phones during dinner," Alex reminded him.

Louie got up from the table and let himself out onto the deck. "Sal?"

"Ah, Mr. Pyle? Er, Mr. Louie?"

Louie had worked closely enough with the nervous little man over the last few weeks to recognize the hesitation in his voice meant bad news. "Just say what's wrong," Louie said.

"It's my landlord. He says we have to move out," Sal said. "I pay rent for full month but he says we must leave by today."

Louie sighed. Why was it always up to him to solve other people's problems? For the second time in one day, here he was, in the middle of somebody else's business. He tried a different approach, one he'd used on his kids. "What are you going to do about it?"

"I was hoping we could move into Log Heaven a few days early?" Sal said.

Louie sighed again, this time loud enough for Sal to hear. "Ah'ite. But like we agreed, this is temporary. As soon as you can find a place of your own, you're out."

Before Louie could resume his dinner and explain to his mother the upcoming change in her residential arrangements, the doorbell rang. At the front door, Louie found Sal Contento and his grandfather looking like the immigrants they were. Each man had one leather valise and that was all.

Louie motioned for the pair to come into the high-beamed living room. His voice echoed throughout the grand space as he called out, "Alex, Mama, I need y'all to come in here."

"Who's that at the door?" Betty Doris asked as she made her entrance. She wrapped her pink sweater, the one with a boa feather collar, tightly across her chest. Seeing the two men, she played with the hair on the nape of her neck and said, "Goodness, we've got company."

"Mama, this is Sal and his grandpa. Sal's the fella who made our dinner tonight."

"Oh?" Betty Doris asked. Seeing the bags, she asked Louie, "What's going on, son?"

"Sal and Mr. Contento lost their lease on their apartment and are going to stay with us for a few days. Until they can find something."

"Where in the world do they expect to stay? In the laundry room?"

"They'll be staying downstairs," Louie said. "In the guest bedrooms."

"Downstairs?" Alex protested. "But where am I supposed to keep my gaming station?"

Facing his new house guests, Louie said, "Excuse me." He then asked Alex and his mother to join him in the kitchen. He commanded, "Sit, both of you." After they complied, Louie continued, "Sal and Mr. Contento are here for a few weeks. We're helping them through a rough patch."

"But, Dad."

"No 'but Dads,' Alex. We're helping these fellas out. Now, get downstairs and pick up all your things in the rec room. Put them in your bedroom."

"I'll move out to the boathouse," Alex threatened.

"Sounds like a plan," Louie said, knowing he'd be back within the hour as the Wi-Fi extender was busted and he'd not gotten around to replacing it. "But you are to treat these two men as the guests they are. You understand me?"

"Yes, sir." Alex stomped down the backstairs to the rec room, leaving Louie to deal with the wrath of Betty Doris.

"Mama, the same goes for you. This is my house and these are my guests. I expect you to respect their privacy by staying upstairs and not going downstairs unless you're invited."

"Well, I never. It hurts me to think you would think I'd do anything different." She stuffed her hands inside the sleeves of her sweater.

"All I'm asking is for you to be polite. Don't go turning your nose up at them just because they talk different."

Caution in her face, she said, "Do you really know these swarthy men? Giving them free reign of our house? They could be Islamic terrorists for all you know."

From gritted teeth, Louie whispered, "Sal Contento makes pizzas. He's *I-talian.* He told me he's been living here and paying taxes since before Alex was born."

Raising an eyebrow, she said, "The 9/11 attacks happened when Alex was two." Clutching at her sweater, she said, "They're a sleeper cell!"

"For crying out loud, you watch way yonders too much of that 24-hour news entertainment crap," Louie said. "Just be nice to them."

"I'm letting them know I have a gun and I know how to use it."

Louie laughed. "Listen to you. You're afraid to be in the same room with a gun, much less use one."

"Well, they don't need to know that."

Lecturing her, he said, "Don't even think about saying such a thing."

Louie led Sal and Mr. Contento down to the ground floor of the house, passing Alex on the way up carrying his laptop and a pile of clothes. Downstairs, the place was a wreck, with junk piled on top of the pool table and Kenny's music equipment sprawled against an entire wall beside the kitchenette. The place was layered with three years of dust and cobwebs and reeked of twenty-something angst. He picked up a damp towel from the sofa, draped it over his arm, then gathered up a dirty glass and plate from the coffee table.

"Sorry for the mess. Thought you was coming later in the week," he said.

"No, no, Mr. Louie," Sal said. "Not to worry. We are the ones who are inconveniencing you and your family."

The expression on Mr. Contento's face didn't seem to agree with Sal's sentiment. Holding his valise, he garbled something Louie assumed was in his native tongue.

"Baba!" Sal said. Embarrassed by his grandfather's words, he added, "English, please."

A disingenuous smile spread across the old man's face. He nodded at his host and said, "You have a lovely home and we are grateful for your kindness."

Louie showed them around. The expansive great room had three sliding glass doors leading to a patio with the upper deck acting as a roof. He pointed in the direction of the guest bedrooms off a darkened hallway and said, "There are three bedrooms back there. Take your pick. Linen closet at the end of the hall has all the stuff y'all might need for bed and bath. I'll get Alex to clear out all the mess in here tomorrow." Upstairs, he found Betty Doris directing Alex as he pushed Lisa's sizable kitchen buffet hutch toward the basement door.

"What in the Sam Hill are you two doing?" Louie asked.

"Close the door then get out of the way," Betty Doris ordered.

"Mama, have you lost your mind?"

"You're the one who wanted to make sure we don't bother our guests." She caught a serving platter before it rolled off the hutch. "Besides, this way it keeps them from coming up here and doing God knows what all," she added.

"If it makes you feel safe, I guess it's a good idea." Turning his back to Betty Doris and Alex, he straightened the hutch, saying, "after we finish eating, Alex, I need you to go downstairs and clean up the rec room, clear out all Kenny's stuff. Put it in the loft." When he turned, they had vanished.

With family back living at Log Heaven, Louie's appreciation for Lisa's housekeeping skills were renewed each time he loaded and unloaded the dishwasher. A picture of Lisa wearing a sparkly paper crown, the words "Domestic Goddess" propped atop her curly head, hung over the washing machine. Each time he did a load of laundry, he wished all over again that she hadn't left him and wondering what had gone wrong with their marriage. But wishing and hoping never got him anywhere except another day older. He needed a change. For starters, he needed a new domestic goddess. Or god. He couldn't care less what the person's pronoun preferences were.

CHAPTER **NINE**

Before leaving for work the next morning, Louie went around to the back of the house to check on his guests. He found Sal sweeping red dust from the patio as Mr. Contento sat at a table reading Louie's newspaper while drinking coffee and smoking a cigarette.

"See you found the smoking section," Louie said. "We don't allow smoking inside the house, by the way." The low growl he caught from the moody elder helped Louie understand why Augie Young and the Contentos weren't on the best of terms. Mr. Contento senior wasn't as genial as his grandson.

Later that day during a slow time at the store, Louie asked Sal, "Why does your granddad act like he's got a double wedgy all the time?"

"He's never adjusted to American life."

Avoiding the obvious question of why the pair left Italy, Louie asked, "How long y'all been here?"

"We came to this country in the nineties to live in New York with my mother's brothers. I was a young boy. My mother and

Baba gave up everything to come here," Sal said as he boxed up one of his popular meatloaf pizzas.

Attempting to lighten the situation, Louie joked, "You mean to tell me your granddaddy's been constipated for over twenty years?"

Sal's face revealed that he didn't like Louie's joking about his grandfather, so Louie let the joke fall flat without trying to explain it. Some people didn't do funny, Louie reminded himself.

THE LATE MAY WEATHER ushered in warmer temperatures and longer days and an explosion of green foliage. Louie encouraged Betty Doris and Alex to join him on the deck one evening for one of Sal's meatloaf pizzas. The pair were becoming hermits and this worried him.

"Did you wipe that pizza box down, son? You don't know where it's been before it came here. I can't afford to get the coronavirus at my age," Betty Doris said.

"We've implemented everything the department of health told us to," Louie said. In fact, his team had gone over and above what was required. He had a good bunch of employees who wanted to stay on the job. He wished Alex had that attitude.

"Reheated pizza again," Alex complained. He pulled out the wrought iron deck chair and sat.

"You be nice to your father. He's doing the best he can," Betty Doris said.

"You know where the kitchen is. How about you fix dinner tomorrow night," Louie said to Alex. Then he said, "Let's pray. *Dear Jesus, thank you for this food and for the hands that made it. Show us how to help each other in these times of uncertainty.*

Watch over Ken and his family and Jessica and her Jumpin' Bean. In your name, amen."

"Excuse me?" Sal was standing at the opposite side of the deck, holding a plate and a glass of water. "May I join you?"

Embarrassed, the Pyles didn't know how to react to such a simple request. The pandemic had deleted the common code of civil interaction without replacing it with a new one.

Louie spoke up. "Sure, pull up a chair and join us."

After Sal sat, all three of them peered at their over-microwaved pizza and then at Sal's chicken Marsala. The creamy wine sauce's aroma drifted its way to their nostrils. Louie licked his lips.

"I'm working on a new version of Uncle Roberto's recipe." Sal cut a piece of the chicken, speared it and a mushroom with his fork, and dragged the bite through the creamy sauce. Lifting the fork, he asked, "Mrs. Betty Doris, would you care to taste?"

Slowly, she moved her head side to side as if Sal had asked her to eat mold from one of the dishes under Alex's bed.

"I do!" Alex volunteered. As the flavors hit his tongue, his eyes lit up. "Got anymore?"

"Downstairs, I have entire pan." He pushed the plate toward Alex and went downstairs to retrieve the rest of the chicken.

Watching the others dig in, Betty Doris couldn't resist the rich aromas coming from the iron skillet, the one that belonged to her granny and she'd given to Lisa. Succumbing to Sal's culinary alchemy, she inched her plate toward the skillet and said, "Maybe I'll try a taste." Like a baby rabbit, she nibbled at the sample. When it was gone, she helped herself to a larger portion. Finishing, she wiped the corners of her mouth with her finger and thumb and said, "Sal, in my book, you're a bona fide chef.

Alex, why don't you get Sal to give you some cooking lessons?"

In response to his grandmother's suggestion, Alex lifted his plate and licked it clean.

"Son, stop that. You ain't a dog," Louie said. "Sal, that's the best dinner I ever ate. You say it's an Italian dish?"

Sal smiled. "Thank all of you for the compliments but I'm just a simple cook. Uncle Roberto was the real chef of the family. He told me he learned to cook to impress a girl."

"Did it work?" Betty Doris asked.

"Sort of," Sal said. "But, he no longer cooks."

"Why's that?" Louie asked.

"Because he is in prison for murdering his wife."

No one spoke.

Using that universal Italian sign for appreciating great food, Sal kissed his fingers and said, "This man made best *bistecca alla fiorentina* in New York City. People from all over the world, even Florence, came to eat at his restaurant."

"Never mind the fancy *I-talian* food," Betty Doris said as she leaned in closer, forgoing her own mandated social distance rule, "You're burying the headline. Why did he murder his wife?"

"That is latest tragedy of my family's long and sad history," Sal said, slumping his rounded shoulders.

After a few impatient seconds, Betty Doris spoke up, "Don't leave us in suspense. Tell us what happened."

Sal placed his hands in prayer to his chest and said, "Roberto loved his brother Emilio very much. Since childhood, they do everything together. They come to America to find their fortune together. They work many hours every day in other people's kitchens until they could open their own *ristorante*. When they do, they called it *Il Pomodoro*, The Tomato. Their patron, a meatpacker, had one condition when he loaned money to start their business. Roberto must marry his daughter and give him a grandson."

"But how could Roberto promise that?" Alex asked. "What if all they had were, like, girls?"

"Shhh!" Betty Doris said. "Go on, Sal."

"Roberto had seen the daughter once when he'd picked up special orders at her father's packing house. He fell in love with her, from afar. The day came for the patron to introduce his daughter to the young business partner. Nervous about the meeting, Roberto asked Emilio to go with him. You see, Roberto, he was a sweater."

"Ha!" Alex laughed. "Was he a cardigan or a V-neck?"

Louie gave Alex his dad look which said, "Don't disappoint me."

"Em," Sal went on. "Let me explain, Alex. The girls, you know, they don't like him because he sweats too much. All the time. Even in winter. The girls don't like his looks so much, neither. His too much frizzy hair. But Emilio, he is a handsome man and ladies buzz like honeybees around him.

"They go to the man's house in Brooklyn to meet his daughter Eliana. And just like that," Sal snapped his fingers, "the girl faints and now it's the *other* brother, Emilio, who begins to sweat. You see, it was Emilio who had captured Eliana's heart. And, yet, at the father's insistence, Roberto and Eliana married. Eliana, she never smiled again."

Betty Doris clutched at the collar of her blouse, "I don't suppose you'd be none too happy if you were forced to marry someone you didn't love."

"Mrs. Betty Doris, it is the way of my family's traditions," Sal tried to explain.

"I hope she told her father what he could do with his traditions," Betty Doris said.

"A child was born six months after the wedding," Sal offered.

"Ain't that an inconvenient truth," Louie said.

The diners were silent for a minute, then Betty Doris said, "That poor girl."

"So then what happened?" Alex asked.

"As Eliana's belly grew, Roberto shared his joy with his customers and friends. He passed out cigars when the *bambino,* Amedeo, was christened. He constantly reminded Emilio of their many blessings of God's love. To share in their good fortune, Roberto sent for his sister and her family to come to America. He finds a place for us to live. He encourages Emilio to go to college to learn business. And, he spent all his time in his kitchen with Ame at his side. In his great happiness, he was a selfless man."

"Sounds like a sap," Betty Doris said.

"His joy for all wonderful things that happened in his family blinded him to Eliana's misery. Every day she goes to Mass to beg her savior's forgiveness for not telling Roberto the truth, that he wasn't Ame's father. This I overheard her say to Uncle Emilio."

Sal cast out a long sigh then continued, "The baby died."

"What?" Betty Doris demanded. "Did Roberto kill the baby?"

"No, never! He loved Ame," Sal said. "The baby, he was always underfoot when he begins to crawl. He finds poison under a table, put there for the rats. No one knew, until it was too late." He bowed his head, mumbling a quick prayer, then continued, "We all watched over Ame in the kitchen but one day was particularly busy. A U.N. dignitary was at the restaurant and Roberto wanted everything *perfetto*."

"Galdarned politicians," Betty Doris muttered.

"Then what happened?" Louie wanted to know.

In a strained voice, Sal continued. "As the days passed, we all felt the weight of guilt. But, Roberto, his grief consumed him. He stopped talking. Offering up the *bambino's* name to any question we had of him. 'Roberto, what is today's special?' and he would say things like, 'Ame's *sorriso*.' This dish I make for you tonight, he called it Ame's Smile."

Alex sniffed, looking into his lap and pretending to read a text on his phone.

"Tears of sorrow dripped into every sauce. The pain of losing little Ame was pounded into every loaf of *filone*." Sal hugged himself, staring past his audience but went on, "On the eve of first anniversary of the child's death, Roberto wept all morning, repeating the words, 'Ame, how I failed you. Ah, Ame, my sweet.'" Sal sniffed.

"Later, right in the middle of a hectic lunch shift, Eliana sat down in the middle of the dining room and sobbed. Baba said that her guilty secret and her own grief had become too much for her. Hearing Eliana's wailing, Roberto rushed from the kitchen with his fillet knife raised, expecting robbers. In front of all the customers, Eliana screamed out to my uncle. 'You have no right to say my *bambino's* name day after day. Ame's not your child. Emilio is Ame's father.' Then she accused Roberto of being blind to her pain." Sal sipped his water, then went on with his story. "My mother saw it happen. She said that in one clean motion her brother Roberto's knife slashed open Eliana's lovely throat."

"Damn!" Louie exclaimed.

"Uncle Roberto's attorney told us he would argue it was a crime of passion. Committed in response to provocation. A fit of instant and uncontrollable rage bought on by a truth too painful for him to endure. But my uncle refused. He murdered his wife, he tells the attorney, just as he had surely murdered his Ame. He must pay."

"What happened to him?" Alex asked.

"He pled guilty and was sentenced to life in prison."

"What happened to Emilio?" Louie asked.

"He and his sister, my mother, went back to Italy. Me and Baba stayed in New York."

CHAPTER **TEN**

The next day after his rounds to all his stores, Louie sat at his kitchen counter and opened his laptop. He'd delayed for long enough the tedious task of reviewing his financial records to find Gas N Go's crook. Lupita had sent him several emails with examples of discrepancies in purchasing reports. After an hour or so of staring at too many numbers, he blew out a puff of air. This task called for someone with experience in thinking like a criminal. He dialed the number of the forensic accountant Ethan Quinn had recommended. She'd not returned any of his calls but he decided to try her once more.

Talia Baskerville answered on the first ring.

Finally. Louie explained why he was calling.

In a jittery voice, as if she'd already surpassed her entire weekly allotment of coffee consumption, the accountant said, "Yes, I seem to recall Mr. Quinn contacting me about your situation. Want to meet up? Do you know Cognito Coffee? It's in The Slip."

"The Slip?" Louie asked.

"Downtown. Richmond," she said.

"I live in Mt Pleasant," Louie said, as if living in one place precluded him from traveling to another. "Can't we just do this over the telephone? I mean with the pandemic restrictions and all."

"Awesome sauce," Baskerville said. "I'll send you a description of my services and a contract. You review and sign it and we'll get started."

"What happens after I sign the contract?"

"You'll give me access to your systems and financial data from the period you suspect the thefts have occurred and I'll work my magic."

"Ethan Quinn spoke highly of you but I'm going to need some references," he said. Giving a total stranger, one who sounded as if she'd just graduated high school, free rein over his financial records wasn't something Mr. Henry would have done. He wasn't yet convinced that Ms. Baskerville was the answer to his problem. 'Awesome sauce,' really?

"No worries. Go to my website. You'll see a list of people I've worked with," she said and abruptly hung up.

Louie went back to reviewing the purchasing reports but was distracted when he heard a car door slam and muted voices in the front of the house. From the front window, he spied Betty Doris talking with a woman who Louie recalled meeting before but wasn't sure where. Someone was sitting in the passenger side of the car.

"Is that Donnie Tyler?" he said aloud. And sure enough Betty Doris opened the car door and helped the old billy goat out of the car. "Keena? Kisha?" he asked himself while knocking on his forehead. "Kiara!" he exclaimed. "What are they doing here?"

Betty Doris, Donnie, and Kiara entered the house and after all the how y'all doings and nice place oglings, Donnie said to Louie, "Thank y'all for doing this for us."

"Doing what?" Louie asked.

"Inviting them to stay with us so Donnie doesn't get the virus," Betty Doris said.

"Mrs. Pyle said we were welcome to stay here for a few days until I can find a place," Kiara said, looking confused.

"Where have I heard that before?" Louie mumbled as he scratched the back of his head. Whispering, he said, "Mama, can I talk to you? In the kitchen." The pair left Donnie and Kiara standing in the great room.

"Before you get all ugly, let me explain," Betty Doris began her defense. "I get so lonely rattling around in this big ole house while you guys are working. Besides, I don't like being here alone with that, that man downstairs. Plus, I took to heart what you were saying about me and Alex watching the TV all the time so I called Donnie to have a visit with him. You know, on the telephone? He said that his niece, well actually she's his great-niece, but anyway, she needed a place to stay and—."

"I know, Mama, I met her at the store in town. She's looking for a job," Louie said as he poured himself another cup of coffee. "But I ain't the CEO of StuffMart. I can't afford to hire someone just because they need a job. It don't work like that. Besides where are they going to stay? In the boathouse?"

Assuming she'd won her son over, she clapped once and said, "I was thinking we'd move you into the loft, put Alex on the sofa bed in the den since he spends most of his time in there anyway, and Donnie and Kiara could have the second floor all to themselves. What do you say?"

"Seems like what I have to say doesn't matter."

"Good, go and move your stuff out of Jessica's bedroom. I'm thinking we'll put Kiara in there and Donnie can go in Alex's old room. Once everybody's settled maybe you and Alex can persuade Sal to whip up another one of Uncle Roberto's recipes for dinner."

Experience had taught him that there was no arguing with Betty Doris once her mind was set on something, so Louie trod up and down the third-floor stairs several times, moving his clothes and personal toiletries, for the second time, to the loft. All the climbing got him a little winded. Feeling dizzy, he tossed the last armful of T-shirts on the narrow daybed and sat in a rickety cane rocker Lisa had used in the nursery when the kids were babies. As he wiped a bead of cool sweat from his brow, he admired the view from the loft's A-frame lookout. This view and this room were why he and Lisa had built the house. Thinking back now, Louie supposed that they had probably spent more time dreaming about the room than they had actually spent in it.

"It *is* a lovely view," Mr. Henry said. He was standing beside the rocker, looking out over the treetops and to the lake and distant hills.

Louie jumped. "Don't sneak up on me like that," he shouted.

The old man shrugged as if to convey how else does a ghost appear. "It's a good deed you and your mother are doing for Donnie Tyler. He deserves some kindness."

Not that Louie would admit it to anyone but he was getting comfortable talking to the old man. If he counted the dream he'd had that night out on the deck, this was Henry Lee's third visit. "Weren't you two close?"

"Like brothers. Known each other since we both wore short pants."

"I had a friend like that once but he moved to New Jersey," Louie said. He chuckled then said, "I suppose there are fates worse than death."

Ignoring Louie's joke comparing the Garden State to the afterlife, the old man said, "We were into all kinds of mischief. When we were chaps, we hid firecrackers under my sister's bed. Then we grew into grown-up games. The romance of our day was bootlegging whiskey."

"I'm glad I took your advice on staying away from that kind of business."

"As we got older, my father advised me to keep my distance from Donnie and the likes of the Tylers. He said that Donnie's father and uncles liked to gamble too much and, by association, I'd be deemed a sinner myself. But in my heart I knew he wanted me to stay away from them because they were Negros."

"That was another time, Mr. Henry," Louie said.

"Yes, it was. But there are certain absolutes we should all abide by," he said.

"Did you show up to preach at me?" Louie asked.

"My father couldn't have been more wrong. Between the two of us, Donnie Tyler was the one with the moral compass. Even though he gambled away any extra money that came his way, he kept me on a straight path." And with that advice, the old man's image drifted away.

The loft's stuffy air helped Louie ease into an afternoon nap.

SAL WAS DELIGHTED TO make a bowl of pasta and meatballs for his new friends. With the day waning, they all gathered around the deck table. Sal dished out the pasta as he explained to everyone that Mr. Contento would not be joining them.

After the prayer of thanks, Betty Doris asked Louie, "Who were you talking to in the loft earlier?"

"Nobody," Louie said. "Nobody living."

"What's that supposed to mean?" she asked.

Changing the subject, Louie complimented Sal on another delicious dish and the others joined in with much excited agreement.

"I never had spaghetti made by a bona fide Italian chef before. It sure has opened my eyes to what I been missing," Donnie said. "Chef Boyardee been lying to us all these years."

"And the meatballs are gargantuan," Alex offered. "Not like any mom used to make."

Silence followed as everyone gobbled up Sal's cuisine. And as they all pushed their plates away, Betty Doris asked Sal, "Do you have another story for us tonight?" Then she filled Donnie and Kiara in on Sal's telling of his family's tragedy.

Sal demurred and suggested someone else tell a story.

"If it's suffering and misunderstanding you want, I've got a story," Kiara said as she gathered up her braids and retied her cotton hairband. "I met Jude my freshman year at college. We both had declared as music majors and shared an eight o'clock music theory class. First day of class, she bragged to everybody about being voted most talented and most likely to succeed at her high school.

"One day in class, Jude kept interrupting the instructor, who was also her voice coach, with negative critiques on an opera diva's performance he was using in a lesson. He asked her to stop interrupting but then she'd do it again. After about six more times, he lost it. Told her she didn't know what real talent was because she had none whatsoever. Told her she was wasting her parents' money and that she didn't need an expensive music degree to sing second chair in a community choir." Kiara paused and played with her necklace. "Said it in front of the entire class."

"That mean teacher," Betty Doris said. "I hope Jude didn't listen to his awful advice."

"He was telling her what we were all thinking. Jude's singing voice *was* pretty weak. Everybody knew it. They just didn't want to say it to her face, afraid it would hurt her feelings. She didn't have that wow factor. You know? When you hear someone sing and you know right away they have the gift? I guess up to that point in her life everyone around Jude had told her she was a diva and could do anything she wanted."

"But then she met Real World," Donnie said. "Know what I'm sayin'?"

"Yeah, ole Mr. Real World set her straight," Louie added.

"That was part of it, sure," Kiara said. "I tried to get her to enroll in an acting class. But she wouldn't listen." Kiara tapped her temple and said, "It was hardwired in her brain. She was convinced she was going to be the world's next singing sensation."

"Once someone makes their mind up about something, they aren't likely to change it," Louie said. "No amount of arguing with them is going to change how they feel."

"I guess," Kiara said. "Anyway, someone posted one of her practice sessions onto the internet. The haters came out in droves. Any normal person would have been devastated. But not Jude. She had been told since she was two that she was a star."

"I hope she proved that mean old teacher wrong," Betty Doris said.

"Oh, she did. But not in the way you might think, like getting the lead in the spring musical or going viral on a music streaming channel. No, no. That wasn't Jude's style. She started interrupting his class at every session. Some of my classmates believe she provoked him on purpose, you know, so he'd lose his temper. And he did. The episodes were recorded on someone's phone and posted on the internet."

"Here we go," Donnie said.

"He was fired. Lost his tenure," Kiara said. "Second semester, she changed her major to women's studies."

Louie laughed. "That'll show them."

"Yep. I guess you could say she traded one type of performance art for another. Right before spring break, she went to a frat party and woke up in the cafeteria dumpster the next morning. She told me somebody had put roofies in her beer and she couldn't remember a thing."

"What is roofies?" Sal asked.

"It's a drug used to treat insomnia. But creeps use it to incapacitate a person so they can, you know, ah," Alex said.

"Do what they will with them," Betty Doris finished the sentence for her grandson.

Kiara continued, "Jude wasn't right after that. She became paranoid, insisting that someone was following her around. She got so she never bathed. I saw her in the cafeteria one day and urged her to get counseling but she just yelled at me. She didn't come back sophomore year."

"That poor girl. I bet that disgusting professor drugged her," Betty Doris said.

"About six months after she left school, the local news reported a story on her. Apparently, she had regained her memory about that night. She accused this guy Loren Stevens of rape, and alleged that with the help of two of his friends, he had tossed her in the dumpster. Loren's friends denied the allegations. Their daddies had good lawyers and they got off. Loren admitted that he and Jude had hooked up at the party, claimed it was consensual. He was convicted and got five years. He hanged himself while in prison."

Betty Doris gasped.

"Loren's sister led an effort to prove her brother's innocence."

"Well? Was he?" Betty Doris asked.

"His family believes so," Kiara said. "I talked to the sister. She said they found witnesses who saw Jude and Loren at the party. She'd stripped down to her underwear, hanging all over him, taking selfies with her phone. In one video someone had made, she was yelling at him to take her outside and, as Betty Doris would put it, do what he would with her. Loren's family took the video to the prosecutor's office but they said it didn't matter."

"I'm sorry but the 'she was asking for it' defense doesn't work for me," Betty Doris said. "I bet he took advantage of her after she fell asleep from drinking too many beers."

"What happened to Jude?" someone asked.

"Loren's sister told me she confronted Jude about the party videos but Jude claimed she didn't remember taking her clothes off. Jude later wrote to her and apologized for the pain she and Loren's behavior may have caused the family."

"That doesn't sound like a retraction of her accusations," Sal said.

"Weasel words. Sounds like something her parents or counselor made her write," Louie said.

"Loren's sister thought that, too. She claimed Jude eventually came to the realization that Loren hadn't raped her."

"Whoa!" Louie said. "Bet that didn't make the six o'clock news." To Alex, he said, "Let this be a lesson. Be careful out there."

"Always be a gentleman," Betty Doris put in.

"Jude overdosed on heroin," Kiara eventually said. "I don't know if she took to drugs because she couldn't accept the painful fact that she'd never be famous or because she had a hand in destroying one man's life and ending another's."

"Shameful," Donnie said.

"Either way, I feel so bad for both families. During the trial they were at each other's throats, wanting blood for vengeance."

"A modern-day Romeo and Juliet," Sal offered.

"A modern-day tragedy, for sure," Donnie added.

CHAPTER **ELEVEN**

Having his morning coffee on his deck, Louie grumbled to himself about his house guests. Mr. Contento had assumed that the paper tossed down the driveway every morning belonged to him. Louie pulled his notepad from his shirt pocket and scribbled a reminder to order a second copy on his account.

Glancing at his to-do list, he was reminded to read the contract information Ms. Baskerville had emailed him the night before. He found the document on his laptop. Over fifty pages of eight-point font legalese greeted him. "Ho, boy," he mumbled. He'd rather read the funny pages or work the sudoku puzzle. But the work had to be done. The first page provided him with tips on how to protect his business records from internal theft. And that was as far as he got.

"Mind if I join you?" With the aid of his cane, Donnie shuffled across the deck, dressed for the day in his polyester pants and a short-sleeved, collared shirt. Sitting in the wrought iron deck chair, he said, "I saw a man taking the paper from the driveway at daybreak."

"Sal's grandfather," Louie said. Remembering Mr. Henry's edict to respect Donnie Tyler, he added, "I'll sign up for another paper for you."

"Don't want to be too much trouble," Donnie said. "But I do feel like I'm in a fancy hotel up in here."

"We enjoy having you," Louie said. "Think Kiara will find a job here?"

Donnie gazed out at the lake. "You know as well as I do Fallam County ain't got no use for her kind of skills."

"What about Mr. Henry's daughter Iris? She might have something for her," Louie offered.

"Aside from working at Food Market, her chances of getting work here are slim and none." Then he grinned at Louie and said, "Unless you got something?"

Louie shrugged. "With all this mess goin' on, I don't know what's going to happen. I might have to lay people off. Don't want to but it might happen." As an afterthought he added, "And that's for your ears only. Alex and Betty Doris obsess over bad news so I'd rather not have them knowing this."

"I hear you," Donnie said. "Your mama is like a pit bull on an ankle when her mind is set on something."

"She'd have global warming solved in ten minutes if she was in charge," Louie added.

"Umm-hmm," Donnie agreed then set into a coughing fit.

Louie closed his laptop and stood. "You ah'ite?"

Donnie raised a hand and waved him off. "Just a cough. Had it since Clinton was president. I'm good."

"I'll bring you a paper tonight. Anything else I can get you?"

Reaching into his pocket, Donnie said, "You know those Sister Addie fried apple pies you sell? I'd love one of those."

TROUBLES GREETED LOUIE at each store. Thor reported that the lottery machine was on the fritz again and the service tech couldn't come until the following week. At the west store, someone had left the doors to the outside ice cooler unlocked. What hadn't been stolen had melted. At noon he found Angel and Sal arguing over the correct way to wrap the pizza suppers. While Louie was in the middle of changing all the system passwords as Ms. Baskerville's guidelines suggested, his phone rang.

"Louie, your house is on fire," the caller said.

"Who is this?" he asked.

"Herb, from across the street. The front door's wide open and smoke's coming out of it," he said. "Thought I'd call and tell you. You might want to call the fire department."

After calling for fire and rescue, Louie raced home. He slowed to make a right turn on Main Street and there was Mr. Henry in the passenger seat, the seat belt snugly strapped across his chest.

"Oh, no. I don't have time for you, Mr. Henry. Not today."

The old man laughed. "As if you control time."

Louie focused on his driving, thinking that if he didn't talk to the old man, he'd go away.

"Slow down. Your house isn't on fire. The man said he saw smoke coming out of the front door, which means someone had to have opened the doors to let out the smoke. Probably someone has burned the toast," Mr. Henry reasoned.

"Yeah, maybe," Louie said as he saw a fire truck in his rearview mirror.

With the neighbor Herb standing in the middle of the road waving his arms like airport ground crew, Louie and Fallam County's Fire and Rescue arrived at Log Heaven's front door.

Kiara, over the noise of the idling truck, said, "We got it under control guys. Mrs. Pyle got a little ambitious with the skillet."

Louie turned to catch Mr. Henry's gloating but he was gone.

Inside, the house was filled with a burnt bacon-scented haze. Betty Doris was sitting in one of the oversized wingback chairs in the front room, shivering.

"What happened?" Louie asked Kiara after the fire truck had left.

"I went to the store to get some things and when I got back, I found the pan in flames," Kiara explained. She leaned close to Louie and whispered, "We got lucky."

"Don't fuss at her, son. I wanted to make us all BLTs for lunch," Betty Doris said. "I left the room for just a minute to check on my soaps, is all."

"Mama, didn't we decide, like, a decade ago, that cooking wasn't your thing anymore?" Louie asked.

"I know, I know. Don't fuss at me," she said as she burrowed into the chair.

Louie and Kiara set about putting the kitchen back in order. And as they worked, Kiara talked about her jobs while in school. "I worked at McDonald's and then I was a bartender at this trendy spot in the Harbor. I cleaned houses and gave music lessons at a community center."

"Great day, you've done a lot of things. Do you plan to stay in Mt Pleasant or are you here just for a visit?" Louie asked.

"What with the shutdowns and all, I don't know." Wiping down the countertops, she suggested, "How about I look after Betty Doris and the house for you. That is, until I can find something."

"I thought that was the plan." Louie said.

Kiara smiled. "I'm a ninja when it comes to dusting and cleaning."

THAT NIGHT, KIARA ANNOUNCED that she would prepare the meal for everyone. A flash thunderstorm rushed everyone inside to the dining room, which had been last used two Thanksgivings ago. After dinner, Betty Doris announced, "Who wants to tell their story tonight? And after Kiara's story from last night, let's have a funny one."

The room was silent for a minute. Then Donnie spoke. "We was clearing out some brush on the back side of Mr. Lee's pastures." He stopped to cough. "We found a moonshiners' camp. It was a right good-sized operation. At first I counted five collector pots."

Betty Doris asked, "Who was 'we'?"

"Me and Hank. When we was young men, Henry Lee wanted to be called Hank. So that's what I called him. But when Bert got old enough to know him, she called him Mr. Henry and it stuck and everybody called him that."

"Who is this 'Mr. Henry'?" Sal asked.

"Young man, Henry Lee was about as good a man as there ever was in Fallam County. He died a few years back. Got a room at the library named after him. He helped us raise my oldest niece, Bert. She was Hank's brother and my sister Vee's love child. You want a sad story, Vee lived one, one of her own makin'. But that's my opinion." Donnie popped an antacid tablet and continued, "Anyway, Hank took it on hisself to look after Bert after Vee died. I reckon I don't know what would have become of that child if Hank Lee hadn't stepped in."

"So you got a story about you and Henry Lee getting into

some mischief with a moonshine still?" Betty Doris asked, attempting to lighten the group's mood. "I remember him coming round our house looking for your daddy, Louie. And for trouble."

"As I recall, Mr. Pyle was usually the instigator when it come to trouble," Donnie said to Betty Doris. He patted his forehead with his napkin and continued, "No, the story I was thinking about was the time Hank and I found a 'shiners' camp halfway up a mountain in the back of his daddy's homeplace."

"What is this 'shiners' camp'?" Sal asked.

"Folks in this part of the country been making and selling whiskey and not telling the tax collector about it, I guess, since before Washington was president," Donnie said. "They hid their stills deep in the woods where nobody could find them and worked by the light of the moon. That's why they call it moonshine."

"Still do," Louie murmured.

"Did you report them to the sheriff?" Alex asked.

Together, Donnie, Louie, and Betty Doris laughed.

"Well, tadpole, in those days, that wasn't the way things were done," Donnie explained. "See, most times, the law already knew where the stills were and expected a sample off the top. If you know what I'm sayin'."

"A payoff," Alex said.

"That's right," Donnie said. "Anyway, Hank was mowing with his daddy's brand-new bush hog and I was building up the brush pile so we could do a burn when I seen a plume of smoke coming up out of the trees on the side of Crook's Mountain. Hank seen it, too. While we worked, we kept an eye on the hill and, sure enough, 'long about midday, we seen two white fellas coming over the crest of the far end of the pasture and head toward the hardtop. We kept at our work for about another hour, then Hank jumped off the tractor and scampered up the hill with me on his heels." Donnie paused to take a few breaths.

"And, Lordy," he continued, "we found a still operation big enough to keep the entire state lit for a right good while. Hank decided we was gonna take some of that illegal whiskey and sell it ourselves. When I tried to convince him that two wrongs don't make a right, he laughed and said, 'True, but when they discover somebody's found them out, they'll move off Lee Farm. We can make a dollar or two and no one will be the wiser.'"

"Did they find out?" Kiara asked.

"You're getting ahead of the story, sweet pea. Every night for about a week, Hank and I watched the comings and goings from a rickety tree stand he and his brother had built in an oak tree in the family cemetery. It was hard to tell who they was but we watched as they killed the lights on their truck on the roadside and made their way past us and on up the hill." All eyes were on him as Donnie wiped at his forehead again.

"On the first night we heard clanking bottles pass us. Hank handed me his Army flashlight and told me to signal him when I heard them heading back to the truck with a load of whiskey. Well, sir, at daybreak, I found Hank standing waist deep in field grass across the road from where the truck was parked. He'd managed to nick several cases. We drove over to Honey's Hut and sold it right away. Got enough money to rebuild the engine on the old Ford coupe his daddy give us and for some new duds." Donnie pulled out his wallet, flipped it open, and showed them a picture of a young Donnie and his friend standing in front of the coupe.

"Cool!" Alex said.

"Did they ever catch you stealing their booze?" Kiara asked

"Patience, Kiara," Donnie said as he shifted in the high back dining chair. "Where was I? Right. We sold the juice to Honey and were up in that tree house the next night, watching and waiting for them to start loading the truck again. This went on for about another week. Then the bartender at Honey's, he started asking questions. Wanting to know where we was getting the stock and could we get more. We learned that our prices was way lower than his other suppliers. One night Hank was late getting to the tree house. When he got there he told me that he finally got a good look at who the moonshiners were. They was two of Pops Young's boys, Gus and Finny."

Louie chuckled.

"What are you laughing about?" Betty Doris asked.

"Pops Young owned Honey's Hut," Louie said.

"So, Mr. Henry and my great-uncle were selling the whiskey back to the guys that were making it?" Kiara asked. She giggled.

Donnie's eyes bulged as he nodded his head up and down. "Yep, we was selling them their own hooch!" He slapped his knee and cleared his throat. "Even after we found out whose whiskey we was taking, we kept snatching it from the truck. Every few nights for the rest of the summer, we'd camp out on the tree stand to see if Gus and Finny was gettin' a haul. As soon as they'd go back for another trip, Hank would sneak into the back of the truck and pick off a half a case or so. We got caught when we tried to sell it to The Lickin' Hole."

"What's this Lickin' Hole?" Alex asked.

"Juke joint in Roanoke. Somebody recognized the bottles as belonging to the Young brothers and we was called out."

"I heard that they used to have live acts there," Kiara said.

"Did you see any live performances?"

"We didn't call them performances like you think of in the fancy music halls. Before the juke boxes come along, there was live music every weekend, gigs we called them. Lickin' Hole was on the Chitlin Circuit. I heard some big names before they became famous and performed on the white people stages. Muddy Waters, John Lee Hooker, Ella, and Fats," Donnie said.

"Uncle Donnie gave me his record collection," Kiara said. "It's where I got my love for music."

"We should get you a piano so you won't get out of practice," Betty Doris said.

"What happened to you and Mr. Henry when you got caught?" Sal asked.

"We got chased out of The Lickin' Hole. A week later the camp got raided by the feds," Donnie said. "I never found out who reported it. But we sure had a time that summer. We was in high cotton. Plus, getting one over on Pops Young was an added bonus." Donnie laughed until his breath tripped into a wheezy coughing fit and Kiara had to help him to his room.

CHAPTER **TWELVE**

Driving into town the next morning, Louie chuckled as he thought about Donnie's story. The legendary tale of the largest moonshiner in the tri-county area being duped into buying his own whiskey had been around for decades. But this was the first time he'd ever heard tell of Mr. Henry being the one who cheated the scoundrel. And somehow, Donnie's version rang true for Louie.

He decided he'd ask Mr. Henry to confirm the claim if ever he appeared in the passenger seat of his truck again. Then he thought, should he see someone about talking to a ghost while driving? The fact that he was even asking himself this question knotted his stomach. Perhaps the visions were caused by his mind having trouble adjusting to all the talk about pandemics, contagions, incurable diseases, and certain death.

At The Shops of Mt Pleasant, Lupita Quinn waved to him as she was getting out of her fancy SUV by her office. Happy to get his mind away from ghosts and death, he waved back. But his own sense of ineptitude reminded him, "Forget about it, amigo.

She's got New York strip taste and you're a pinto bean kind of guy."

In his office behind the checkout counter, Lisa was sitting at his desk, forcefully pressing on the keyboard with her blingy fingers. "Arrrrr!"

"Careful there. You want to beat up on a computer, do it to your own," Louie said. "What's wrong?" he asked as he removed his ball cap and tossed it on its hook.

"This dern thing won't let me in to report my hours," she said. Lisa did what she called Gas N Go's social media outreach, which, according to Angel, was a crucial element of their new Get N Go Dinner line. However, Angel and Sal were the brains behind the new Gas N Go website with its online menu and ordering system. For the past year or so, Lisa's contributions to Gas N Go's successes were like her fingernails, sparkly and veneered. She'd checked out of their life together.

"Let me try," Louie said as he reached for the keyboard.

"No, I'll do it," she said. A couple of swear words and a few more keystrokes seemed to do the trick. She gave him a thumbs up and went about her task. Louie stood by, waiting for her to finish. "Quit standing over me. You're making me uncomfortable," she said.

"Leese, this is my desk. I got stuff I need to do," he said. He wanted to remind her about the computer he bought for her after she'd complained of having to come into the store to do her time report. But he wasn't in the mood to argue with her.

"It'll only take a minute, snarky butt. I couldn't get into my account for some reason. And Alex wasn't around to help me," she said. "How is he by the way? Haven't heard from him. Is he behaving?"

Louie shrugged. "Believe it or not, he's been a big help to his grandma."

"Oh my God, so it *is* true," Lisa screeched. "I'd heard that the she-devil moved into Log Heaven."

"If you're talking about Betty Doris, then, yes, she's living with me for the time being, until the pandemic is over."

Still sitting, Lisa placed her hands on her hips. "Word at Girl Curl has you and Donnie Tyler's niece shacking up together." Saying "Oooo," she reached for his arm to pinch it.

Swatting at her hand, he said, "And when has the gossip of a bunch of ladies who watch daytime talk shows produced anything sounding like truth?" He wasn't going to mention the obvious, that Kiara Moss was too young to have an interest in him. No matter how good looking he was, he'd never make the cut. But that was Kiara's story to tell, and besides, it was none of Lisa's business.

Lisa raised her hands and said, "Just sayin'."

Sitting on the edge of the desk, he said, "You can put an end to people telling lies about me by telling 'em I'm letting Donnie and his *grand*-niece Kiara stay with us until she can get a place. That's all there is to it."

"So, y'all are shacking up," Lisa taunted as she went back to her task on the computer.

"Stop it, Lisa," Louie warned. "She's a nice girl and Betty Doris wanted to help her and Donnie out. We put them in Jessica and Ken's rooms."

She looked up and yelped, "What!" In an annoyed tone, she went on, "You let her stay in my daughter's room, messing with her stuff? You've got some nerve, Louie Pyle. Letting total strangers have free rein of our private space. They're liable to steal everything that isn't nailed down. I can't believe you."

"It's not your house anymore, Lisa. If there's anything you want in it, let me know and I'll bring it to you," Louie reasoned.

She stood abruptly and waved her hands in front of her face. "I'm done. You are unbelievable." She gathered her keys, purse, and coffee tumbler and stumbled from the desk to the door. Over her shoulder, she said, "I used your password to get into the admin, by the way. 'Louieandlisa4ever,' what a joke. I'm done with you. I'm out." She slammed the door.

Louie sat at his desk and asked the closed door, "Does this mean you quit your job?" Man, she knew how to punch his buttons. After changing his password, he clicked the inactive button on her employee status.

WHILE CHUNKY WAS ON LUNCH BREAK, Louie sat on the stool minding the cash register and listening to Sal and Angel bicker over the temperature setting on the new oven. "Would you two cut it out?" Louie said as he looked up from the newspaper and saw Lupita entering the store.

Pointing at the cigarillos, Lupita said, "Two packs of my usual, *por favor*." Her voice was muffled by her gold and red lamé face mask. Her dark brown eyes widened when she asked, "Sounds like they are in love. No?"

"More like two cats fighting," he said. "Will there be anything else?" he asked as he watched her shake her head, sweeping a thatch of silky hair away from her eyes.

"Yes, I'll have one of the Papa Izads chicken kebabs," she said. "You are a genius Louie Pyle to bring ready-made ethnic food to your stores. They're popular, yes?"

"You bet," Louie said, proud to learn that he'd impressed this brainy woman with a centerfold's body.

When Sal handed Lupita her order, she said to him, "*Come stai oggi*?"

To which, he replied, "*Bien. ¿Y usted*?"

"*Bene*," she said and her eyes smiled. Facing Louie, she offered, "Sal and I are practicing our language skills. I talk to him in *italiano* and he speaks to me in *español*."

"Ah'ite," Louie said. "That's Fallam County-eese for 'wow.'" He winked at her, hoping she got the joke.

In response, she rattled off something to Sal, then put her finger to her covered lips and left the store, leaving Louie wondering what she'd said about him.

THAT NIGHT, THE LOG HEAVEN deck diners were down to Louie, Kiara, and Sal. The elders were resting in their respective rooms and Alex was in the den making video war with Thor. Sal had served up leftovers from the day's Mediterranean menu.

"These are so good!" Kiara exclaimed. "What was your inspiration for them?"

Sal hesitated for a moment then said, "Me and *Signora* Quinn talk about foods we loved as *bambinos*. Baba used to make these, only with lamb, but lamb here is expensive so we use chicken."

"*Signora* Quinn?" Kiara asked.

"Ethan Quinn's ex," Louis said.

"Lupita Quinn is Gas N Go's business accountant," Sal said.

"Her office is next door to our town store," Louie explained. "She and Sal here speak their Spanish and *I-talian* at each other. What were you two laughing about when she left the store today? What did she say?"

Sal's face changed and he busied with the dirty dishes. "Ah, she say you are not only a clever man but a funny one."

"Come on, Sal. I'm a grown man, I can take it. What did she really say about me?" But deep inside, he wasn't sure he was ready for rejection, not from Lupita.

Waving his hands in the air, he said, "*Sí*, Mr. Louie, it's true. She said these words."

"What else did she say?" Louie asked.

Sal replied, "She asked me not to say."

"Way to go, Louie," Kiara cheered as she bumped shoulders with him. "She likes you but is not ready for you to know it."

Sal stood and picked up the stacked dishes. "I must check on Baba. See you in the morning."

"How's the house hunting going?" Louie asked Sal.

"I've been too busy getting the food service running. I have no time to search."

"What about your grandfather? Is his leg broke?" Louie asked.

"Excuse me?"

"What's he do with his time all day? Can't he help you two find a place to live?"

"Baba is not comfortable talking to Americans," Sal said. "I've got to go, I hear him calling." Plates rattling, Sal hurried from the deck.

After Sal had left, Kiara asked Louie, "Is he all right?"

"I guess," Louie said.

"He seems nice enough but he's always so fidgety, like a turkey on Thanksgiving eve."

"If you lived with a guy as pompous and rigid as that old man, you'd be strung a little tight, too," Louie said. "You weren't here when he actually told us the story about his uncle slitting his auntie's throat. The whole family seems a little off-center, if you ask me." Louie repeated the recap Betty Doris had made about Sal and his mom and his grandfather coming to live with his uncles in New York and about how one uncle dropped his basket one day and killed his wife on account of their child dying from eating rat poison.

"That makes my story sound lame," Kiara said. "I'll have to up my game at story time."

Louie smoothed down his beard. "She doesn't want me to know that she thinks I'm clever and funny? How does that translate into Lupita liking me?"

"Well, duh! She likes you but she wants to be the first one to make a move," Kiara said.

"It's been awhile since I was in the dating scene. How am I supposed to act?"

"You gotta stay back, give a girl some room. You know, keep being your smooth self but let her be the one asking for a date to the dance."

"I suppose women want to do all the leading these days," Louie said.

"That's right. We lead, you follow," she giggled.

Darkness was settling in so Louie turned on Betty Doris' battery-powered table candle. The two sat content in their silence. Kiara's comment reminded Louie of his dealings with the bossy accountant detective lady. In his way of seeing things, they not only wanted to lead the dance but they wanted to be in charge of the music as well. To get along in this new post-marriage world, he guessed he'd have to learn some new dance steps.

CHAPTER **THIRTEEN**

Upstairs in the loft later that night, Louie grunted as he shoved the daybed to the middle of the room so he'd have a nice view of the sunrise over the lake. Under the sprawling windows, he arranged the petite oak table Jessica had used for studying and an old easy chair upholstered in faded Scottish plaid that he'd rescued from the end of their driveway after one of Lisa's many redecorating binges. Then he rummaged around in the crawl space and dusted off a brass lamp, its shade yellowed and dented. He descended three flights of stairs then back up with a new light bulb. Feeling a tad light-headed and winded, he sat in the chair and slipped off his shoes.

A breeze swirled around his feet feeling like the chill of underwater springs kicked up while treading water in the lake on a hot summer's day. He didn't need to turn on the light to see the old man's image projected on the spanning windows. He was buttoned up tight in his suit with a starched pocket square in his breast pocket.

"Donnie's story," Mr. Henry said. "He left out a few parts."

"Such as?"

"We did steal the Youngs' liquor and sell it back to them. And we did try to sell it to The Lickin' Hole. But once we'd been found out, I wanted to get out. I told Donnie to give the remaining cases to his uncles. The numbskull tried to sell them to the wrong man and landed in a ditch with a busted up face and two broken hands."

"It was you who called the feds about the still on your dad's property," Louie said.

The old man's silence confirmed Louie's guess.

"What's it like where you are?" Louie asked.

Mr. Henry's image rippled like a flag. "Ask me something useful, for crying out loud."

Louie hesitated, confused. The years since Mr. Henry's death had been rough. Upon his family's abandonment, he'd relied on the old man for solace.

Aloud, he heard the old man say, "Clock's ticking. What do you need my help with?"

Louie gulped. "I'm worried about a lot of things," he blundered.

"Spell them out," Mr. Henry commanded, he was losing his patience.

"For one thing, this pandemic business has got me tied up and I can't find the time to figure out who's stealing from the stores or how they're doing it," Louie said. This was crazy, a dead man couldn't help him solve his missing inventory problem. "For another thing, Ethan referred me to this accountant detective lady but I'm having trouble trusting a computer hacker who probably wasn't born before 1999."

"What else?"

"What do you mean 'what else?' Ain't that enough?" Louie cried out.

Mr. Henry waited.

"I don't know why I torture myself over why Lisa left me. I worry about Alex and if he'll be all right when Lisa and I are no longer around." He pushed himself up from the chair and slipped onto the bed. "And, some days, I'm just not sure if there is anything left to do in my life. I feel like I'm done, as if I've done all I was meant to do. Why do I need to get up and put my shoes on in the morning?"

"If I could smack you on the back of that thick head of yours, I would," Mr. Henry said. "It's as plain as the nose on your face, boy. Lisa never loved you for being you. She loved you for the things you could give her. Most of the world's population is wired that way, I'm afraid. And Alex's fate was made the moment he was conceived. He'll be fine. You made it on *your* own, didn't you?"

"I guess I did. But that doesn't keep me from worrying about him," Louie said. "You're wrong about Lisa. She loved me." Rubbing at an arthritic knuckle on his thumb he added, "once."

"And now she doesn't. Stop wringing your hands like an old hag," Henry said. "Move on. The exotic Mexican woman seems interested in a tango around the dance floor."

"You think she's into me?" Louie asked like a sixth-grader.

"See there, you've solved your own worries," Mr. Henry said. "Dancing with the lovely *señora* is a definite reason to get up and put your shoes on."

"But what if she's just being nice and ain't interested in dating me?" Louie asked.

Too late, Mr. Henry had melted into the windows' glassy

reflection of the dark night.

"That settles it," Louie said as he punched at his bed pillow. He would ask Lupita if she would like to go with him to Las Vegas for the Convenience Market Expo at the end of the month, separate rooms, of course.

In the morning, Louie used the excuse of showing Kiara how to operate the washer and dryer to get her alone.

"You know what we were talking about last night. About dating?" he asked her.

Kiara nodded as she took a small sip from her coffee mug.

"I was thinking about inviting the lady, you know, the one we talked about . . . ."

Kiara interrupted by saying loudly, "You mean Lupita Quinn?"

"Shh. The whole house doesn't need to know my private business," he whispered.

She pressed her lips together in a tight grin.

"You're enjoying this, ain't you?" he asked. "I was wondering if you was her, would you like to go to Las Vegas for a long weekend? To the convenience store convention? Separate rooms, of course."

"Convenience store convention, sounds romantic," Kiara teased.

"You know what I mean. If you was interested in somebody, does a few days in Vegas sound like a fun date?"

"Well, if you put it that way," Kiara said. She tapped him on his arm and added, "Of course, you goofball. That would be an awesome date. Except," she held up a finger and said, "that'd be a dicey move for a first-date ask."

"What do you mean?"

Kiara blew a raspberry. "That's a huge commitment for a first date, bra. Besides, with all the pandemic cancellations, are they even having the event?" Vigorously shaking her head, she said, "Nope, nope, nope! All that time together on a long weekend date would be way, way too much. A Vegas weekend is more like a dating anniversary date."

"Come again?" Louie asked.

"What if, like, the two of you discover you're not compatible on the first day? There you are. Stranded in the middle of party town with someone you don't like."

"But we've known each other for several years. She does my personal tax return, I'm an open book to her. And, her, well, if you ever meet her, you'd see she's gorgeous. And nice."

"Good looks aren't everything," Kiara said. "I had a date with this person who was drop-dead gorgeous but when we met up for dinner, in five minutes, I was pretending I had to be somewhere else. He had the table manners of a starving dog. Chewed with his mouth wide open, ran fingers around the butter plate, licked them, did it again. Ugh, drove me crazy."

"But that's not how it is in this situation," Louie protested.

"All I'm saying is to take it slow. Ask her out for a coffee, you know, or a quick lunch. Sort of build up to the Vegas weekend."

"If you think that's best," Louie said.

"Trust me. I'm the closest thing you'll find to a dating advisor in Mt Pleasant," Kiara said.

On the topic of Las Vegas first dates, the universe seemed to agree with Kiara. Checking his email in his town office later that morning, Louie found a cancellation notice for the expo in the spam box, a refund of his deposit for a suite at the Golden Gate Hotel and Casino was forthcoming. The pandemic was affecting every aspect of Louie's life, even his attempt at starting a new one. He considered Kiara's advice of inviting Lupita to lunch.

At noon, Louie brushed his hand down the front of his shirt, pulling on it to check for coffee dribble. He asked Angel to bag up two sandwiches made with those paper-thin slices of salty ham with the funny name then he walked across the parking lot to Quinn's Business Services. He found Lupita at her desk, on the phone rattling off words sounding like English but he wasn't sure.

Their eyes met as she stopped to listen to the person on the other end and motioned for him to have a seat. When the call ended, she removed her sparkly readers and folded them. "*Hola,* Louie," she said. "Did we have a meeting scheduled?"

"No," Louie said. "Thought you might be interested in sharing a lunch with me in your courtyard. Tell me what you think of Sal's latest."

She glanced at her rhinestone-studded watch. "It's lunch already? What a lovely thing you offer." When she stood, her height matched his. Her black skirt wrapped snuggly around the curves of her hips and thighs then fell away at her dimpled knees in a flair. The tinkling of her gold bangles was ever present.

Louie followed Lupita out to her smoking area. The two sat across from each other, eating Sal's prosciutto with watercress paninis. The delicate saltiness of the meat mixing with the contrasted bitterness of the greens awakened all Louie's senses. Each time Lupita tossed her head to free strands of hair from her face, he caught whiffs of orange and rose scents that he knew probably had names. But what did he know of such things? So much he didn't know, so much he wanted to learn but wasn't sure how to begin.

He watched as she broke off each bite-sized piece of the panini, held it between her finger and ringed thumb then raised it to her full lips. She treated each bite as if it were an offering, a precious gift to be savored. He could watch her eat all day and wondered what Kiara would have to say about Lupita's chewing.

"Mm," Lupita mumbled, "tell Sal it's *delizioso.*" Then she kissed the tips of her fingers.

"You'll have to do that yourself," Louie said shyly, "I'm not sure I could say it the way you do."

Brushing hair aside with the back of her hand, Lupita burst into one of her hardy laughs. "Mt Pleasant men, what am I to do with you?"

"Am I that hopeless?"

"You're just like Ethan and others I have met since I've been here," she said. "Afraid to try new things."

Ruffled by her criticism, he protested, "Hey, give me a little credit. I'm trying funny sandwiches on burnt toast and stuffed with duckweed."

She laughed again and popped the last bite of her sandwich into her mouth.

Louie watched as a breeze played with her unruly hair and, for the first time, noticed the smattering of gray strands and the fine laugh lines around her eyes.

She gathered the lunch wrappers and said, "My work won't do itself."

Louie gambled. "Do you tango?"

"¿Qué?"

He stumbled to recover, "I mean, do you like to dance?"

"*Sí,* I love to salsa. But tango? No, no. Too," she paused and brushed at her flowery blouse, "too, eh, involved. But is dancing allowed now?"

Searching for his way out of a subject Lupita clearly had a better command of than he did, he said, "You're right. I forgot. This virus mess has the whole world canceled."

"It does. I'm going *loco* working all day then going home and doing nothing. Thankfully, I get to see my sweet cherub Tommy every night. He sends me kisses from the computer before he goes to bed. Vinnie and Ludie think I spoil him too much." After an awkward silence, she added, "This was a beautiful treat. Tell Sal I like a bit more pesto with my prosciutto," she said.

Without thinking, Louie blurted out, "Why don't you tell him yourself. We meet up for dinner on the deck at Log Heaven nearly every night. Come join us tonight?"

"Log Heaven? I don't know this place," she said as she led Louie back through the breakroom and to the reception area.

"Oh. That's what I call my house. It's a log cabin, sort of. And, it's on the lake so, to me, it's heaven," he said. He felt the need to keep talking because he didn't want to hear her refusal. "We meet up. Sal brings a dish. And we all have supper. And it's safe, the deck's pretty long and Betty Doris, my mama, makes sure we're all separated so we don't sneeze on one another's macaroni." Man, he thought, as she stared at him with those sleepy eyes of hers and saying nothing, she was gorgeous.

After a respectful pause, Lupita explained that she had other plans for the evening, despite her earlier proclamation of domestic boredom. Could he ask her again? Some other time, perhaps.

CHAPTER **FOURTEEN**

After Lupita's rejection of his invitation to join him and his family for dinner, Louie decided to take the afternoon off from his store rounds and go fishing to think about what she had said. Did she mean that she wanted him to ask her to come for dinner on another night or was she putting him off, hoping he'd not ask again? When he got home, he'd ask Kiara for her opinion on Lupita's cool response.

Back at Log Heaven, he found Betty Doris directing Kiara on the rearrangement of furniture in the front room. Pointing at the dusty coffee table, Betty Doris said, "This goes. If it won't fit through the door, cut it up and use it for kindling. Lord-a-mercy, that's got to be the ugliest table ever made. I don't know what possessed that wife of yours to pay good money for such a thing."

"*Ex*-wife. What's going on?" Louie asked.

"We're rearranging so we can get the piano in here," Betty Doris said.

A quick glance at Kiara got Louie one of her amused grins.

"What piano?"

"The free one Lansing Morris said Kiara could have if we moved it out of his house."

"When were you going to ask me?"

Betty Doris dismissed him with a wave of her hand.

"Here," Kiara said and held up her phone, which displayed a picture of an ebony piano. "We drove over and I played it. It's in pretty good condition, doesn't need a lot of tuning." Louie saw the excitement in her face, all lit up like a kid's at Christmas.

"How are you going to get it here?" Louie asked. He rubbed the back of his neck and offered, "I suppose Alex and Thor could move it with Alex's truck."

"That's not how you move a piano, silly," Kiara said. "It's a baby grand. It's too wide and too long to fit in the back of Alex's little truck. It has to be wrapped and secured so the wires don't break. Besides, it weighs, like, five or six hundred pounds. Don't take this the wrong way but Alex and Thor don't instill in me a confidence of managing that kind of weight. But in spite of its weight, it's a delicate thing. One bump and it could be knocked out of pitch and there we'd be with an oversized anchor in the living room." She playfully batted her eyes at him.

"Kiara knows best. That's why Red Carpet Movers is delivering it tomorrow afternoon," Betty Doris said. "I used your credit card for the deposit. You'll have to pay the balance when they get here."

"Y'all do what you want," he said. "I'm going fishing."

Down at the boathouse, Louie swore under his breath when he couldn't start the motor on his john boat. Since tooling around in the small craft wasn't an option, he lifted the aluminum canoe from its hooks and lowered it into the water. The day was like any mid-June day on the lake, mild with clouds drifting in front of the sun creating shadows amid the twinkling lake ripples. He tossed his rod and tackle into the canoe along with his fish cooler and a plastic thermos of iced tea. He slipped on his life vest, letting out the belt from last year's setting, and eased into the canoe. Putting a boat in the water for the first time of the summer season was what Alex called their maiden voyage. On his way home he'd stopped at Gas N Go South to ask Alex if he wanted to take their maiden voyage but Alex replied, "I can't. I'm adulting right now, Dad." Louie was happy to see his baby boy finally taking an interest in the family business.

The pandemic had interrupted Louie's chance to see his oldest son, Ken, and his three grandsons. Every year they'd come from Nashville for an end-of-school-year lake visit. On one such trip Ken adamantly expressed that he wanted no part of the family business or living in Fallam County, as though he was ashamed of his family and his home. The proclamation had cut deep. And then, at her James Madison University cap and gown ceremony, Jessica told her parents that she was moving to northern Virginia. She now had a daughter and no husband, which made Louie sad. Lisa told him to keep his nose out of it, so that's what he did.

He paddled out to his favorite fishing spot, not far from the house and around a spit of land, and secured the canoe to a fallen tree. Before he broke open his tackle box, he pulled his notepad from his shirt pocket and turned to a new page. He wrote "call Jessica and tell her you're thinking about her." He chuckled because he knew the minute he said those words, she'd say something smart-alecky like, "Dad, you could just text me." God, he missed her. What the heck, he dialed Jessica's number and waited for her voice mail to answer.

"Dad? What's wrong?"

"Wow, it's you, live and in person. I'm speechless. I hope your voice mail doesn't get jealous because I'm talking to you instead of her."

"Ha-ha," she said and continued in her serious tone, "Is everything all right? Why are you calling me in the middle of the afternoon?"

"Everything's fine. Sitting in the canoe at our favorite fishing spot and thought I'd check in. How's Jumpin' Bean?" Jumpin' Bean was Jessica's five-year-old daughter Madison.

"Driving me crazy. Since they canceled summer programs and I have to work from home, it's insane. She's growing like a weed. None of her clothes from last summer fit."

Louie listened patiently as his daughter extolled her own virtues of motherly intentions. With all her left-handed bragging on Madison's growth spurts and boundless curiosity, Jessica sounded like Lisa when their three were tots.

Sensing the end of the conversation approaching, Louie asked the question he always asked, "When are y'all coming down for a visit?"

"Oh, I don't know," came Jessica's standard answer. "I've only got a few vacation days left and I want to save them for Christmas."

"You know, Fallam County ain't on Mars. We've got internet. *And* running water," he joked. "We got plenty of room to carve out a place for you to have a remote office."

"That's not what I hear from Mom," Jessica said. "She said that you've got a house full of strangers. I'm not sure I'd want to expose Maddy to—."

"Aww, there's not a stranger here. Maddy would love it. We have a nice meal out on the deck every day. Your Gran Betty is in charge of making sure everybody stays exactly six feet from each other at all times and my new chef Sal cooks for us. What do you say? It would be good for Maddy to spend some time with her Great-Gran Betty," then he quietly added, "and her grandpa. I've got a nice little reading nook set up in the loft. You and Maddy could stay up there." His daughter didn't respond so Louie kept talking. "There's plenty of room. Come on down for a few days. Enjoy the lake. We'll take Maddy out for a ride in the ski boat. Has she had swimming lessons yet?"

"Yep, she's a certified guppy," Jessica said. "Let me think about it," which was always her response to his invitations.

"Don't think about it too long. Summer's only here for a few weeks. Besides, with all the travel restrictions, Log Heaven is the perfect place for a few summer vacation days. Think about it and let me know."

"All right, I will," she said. Then with conviction, she repeated, "I will."

"Love you, Jessica. Give Jumpin' Bean a kiss for me when you tuck her in tonight."

He cast his line into the shadowy waters along the bank and slowly reeled it in. He cast it again and trolled the line. Maybe he'd get lucky and snag a crappie or two for Sal to fry up. Someone was calling him so he placed the rod in its holder and fished his phone out of his shirt pocket.

"Did you hear?" Lupita asked excitedly.

"No, what's happened?"

"*eSpeedy's* is coming to Fallam County!" Her energetic news transcended through the ether and into Louie's ear, causing him to grip the phone tighter. Speedy's was a successful convenience store chain found throughout the Southeast. A Speedy's in Fallam County could mean trouble for Gas N Go. "Louie? Are you still there?"

"Where did you hear that?" he asked.

"On the radio. Just now."

Louie had met Turks "Speedy" McGraw at last year's convention. A short, compact man, McGraw followed Louie around the convention hall asking him questions about things that were, in Louie's opinion, none of his business, like Gas N Go's margins on tobacco products. "Speedy McGraw. I met him last year," Louie said to Lupita. "He'll be a tough competitor. Did he say where he was building his store?"

"No, he just said his team was eager to get started on being part of the community," Lupita said. "Do you think he'll open a store in town?"

"Probably," Louie said, knowing his high traffic store in town was way more profitable than the county stores. "Thanks for letting me know about this. I appreciate it." He stashed his phone back in his pocket as something tugged on his line. Like a pro, he reeled in a good sized crappie and stowed it in his fish cooler. Casting his line again, he asked himself why Lupita would call to tell him this news. Why would she care?

Thoughts of Lupita and her motives were clouded over by images of his competitor's logo—a goofy looking country bumpkin caricature. He'd been considering closing Gas N Go West for some time because, per square foot, it was the costliest store to operate. Foot traffic had flattened and overall costs were trending in the wrong direction. The last of the stores to open, the west store had no emotional ties for Louie but it had an awesome view of rocky pastures and hills on the back side. Maybe he could rent the building to Sal. The skinny Italian could make it a destination restaurant. Folks these days seemed to want to drive great distances to eat the same things they could buy at the grocery store and fix at home. "Yep," he said aloud. He'd mention the idea to Sal.

Another tug on the line produced a second crappie. The third time he cast his line the reel spun madly. The rod bowed as he pulled it back and reeled in the line. This time the hook had snagged a striped bass big enough to feed everybody. With dinner on ice, he kicked back in the bottom of the canoe and sipped his tea, which was sweet and strong, just how he liked it. His fish haul, what Alex called their monumental fishing achievement, boosted his confidence. He decided to try again at asking Lupita for dinner, tempting her with fresh caught fish prepared by her new favorite chef. When he heard her voice mail, he hung up, deciding his luck had been used up on the biggest bass he'd ever caught. Try her again tomorrow, Louie.

Back at the dock, Louie placed the tackle box and cooler on newly painted boards and lifted himself out of the canoe. Grabbing at the sides of the craft, he pivoted around, hoping to lift and hang it on its hooks just inside the boathouse in one turn. As he stepped forward, he stumbled over the tackle box and lost his balance. On instinct, he freed his hands to restore his balance. Free from Louie's grip, the canoe knocked him down as it splashed into the water. On his back, he waited for reports of pain from any injuries. None came so he lay there and watched billowy white clouds as they changed shape. Hearing voices, he turned his head and watched as Mr. Henry and Lupita floated away in the canoe. They were pointing at the clouds and talking about them. Louie closed his eyes, deciding a nap seemed like a fine idea. As their voices faded, he stretched out on the warm dock and fell asleep.

CHAPTER **FIFTEEN**

Thunder awoke Louie from his nap. He watched as high winds swirled through the trees on the bank of the lake and lightning illuminated the clouds overhead. He sat up and pressed his back against a dock pole.

"Hey!" Kiara called out. "Where were you? We were getting worried."

Louie struggled to stand so she offered her hand. He brushed it aside as he avoided her gaze of concern.

"You OK?" Noticing the overturned tackle box, she asked, "What happened?"

Thunder and lightning struck, too close.

"Let's get inside," she cried out.

She tried to take his arm but the speechless Louie pulled away, bending to gather all the stuff that had tumbled out of the tackle box. Lifting the tackle and fish cooler, he stood and searched for his thermos. It was gone. Mr. Henry and Lupita were gone, too.

Fat raindrops, plopping on surfaces, announced the coming

of the downpour. As if God Himself had opened the tap, heavy showers poured out of the clouds. The pair rushed for the cover of the boathouse.

Kiara repeated, "You OK?"

"I'm fine," Louie said. "Tripped over the dern tackle box while I was trying to hang the canoe."

She looked around and asked, "Where is it?"

"It fell back into the water. I'll take the john boat out to look for it later."

Swiping through apps on her phone, she said, "I can post an H Y S on my neighborhood app."

"A what?"

"A 'have you seen' post. You know, for lost dogs, stuff like that." She chuckled and added, "In your case, 'has anyone seen my canoe?'"

They watched and listened to the deluge, barely able to see the end of the dock.

Louie said, "Sounds like something Willie would sing about." He crooned, "'Has anybody seen my canoe? It took my girl away, now I'm blue-oooooo.'"

They both laughed. Kiara pointed at the cooler. "What's in there?"

Louie opened it to show Kiara the fish. "A monumental fishing achievement."

They laughed again, this time not as spontaneously.

"Wow, that's some haul. Dinner's going to be down-home righteous tonight. Got any beer in there?"

"You know I don't drink on the job," he joked. He rustled around in his tackle for his fish scaler. Squatting, he pulled the bass out and plopped it on top of the cooler's lid and proceeded to scale and gut the fish.

"Yuck," Kiara said, "this visual is way too much information for me." She lifted two plastic chairs from the stack in the corner of the boathouse and offered one to Louie as she sat in the other one. Over the noisy downpour, she said, "It sure is nice here. Log Heaven, I mean. I'm truly grateful to have you and Betty Doris come into my life. And for helping out with Uncle D."

"Your uncle has lived a long, hard life," Louie said. "He deserves a little peace and quiet. And I appreciate you talking to Betty Doris all day so I don't have to."

"Aren't we a pair of mutual admiration society members," Kiara joked.

"Can I ask you something?"

"Shoot," Kiara said.

"I asked Lupita if she'd like to come over for dinner tonight," he said.

"You did?"

"Wait to hear it all," he said. "She said she had other plans, maybe another time. But she said this right after telling me she's doing the COVID shuffle like everybody else, working, going home, and doing nothing."

"Your point?"

"It's more of a question. Is she telling me to ask her again some other time or is she really telling me to get lost in a nice way?"

"I see," Kiara replied as she poked a finger into her tight braids to scratch at her scalp. "It won't hurt anything to ask her again, except your pride if she says 'no.'" Watching him cut the fish into fillets, she speculated, "She's not part of your COVID bubble. She may be genuinely afraid to go into other people's houses."

Louie put the pan-ready bass back in the cooler then pulled out one of the crappie. "I get that. But, help me understand this. Why did she call me, while I was out on the lake, on something I would have learned about the minute I saw the latest news?"

"Ah, the fish is nibbling at the bait," Kiara mused. "Remember what I said about letting her lead the dance?"

Frustrated, Louie let out a puff of air and said, "What does fishing and dancing have to do with each other or this conversation?"

Kiara grinned. "She's dancing around the topic of you two dating. Trust me, let her lead the dance."

Louie slammed the lid on the cooler of cleaned fish. He confessed, "I'm getting too old for those kinds of games. At my age, it's just downright exhausting."

Sal appeared ecstatic when Louie delivered the cleaned fish to him at the sliding glass door of the rec room. The chef prattled off something about capers and onions while Louie tried to glimpse at what Sal's grandfather was doing on the floor over in the corner next to Ken's drum set.

"Tell your granddad we'd love for him to join us," Louie said as he pulled a sticky fish scale off the top of his hand. "We'll see y'all at the usual time?"

Sal saw Louie watching his grandfather. Quickly, he crowded Louie out onto the patio, slid the door to a narrow crack, and said, "Baba, he's old fashioned. He doesn't take his meals with, ah, people outside of his family."

"I see," Louie said. "Tell him if he's afraid of getting the COVID, he ain't getting it here. Not as long as Betty Doris has sanitizer wipes." He grinned at Sal. A strange droning sound floated through the crack of the door. "What's wrong with Mr. Contento? He sounds like he's ailing."

"I'll see you at our usual time," Sal said as his thin frame slid through the door before he slammed it shut.

Louie heard the familiar click of the door's lock and mumbled, "Strange little dude."

THE AFTERNOON STORM TURNED the evening cool. Betty Doris buttoned her cotton sweater as she asked Sal, "Why doesn't Mr. Contento ever join us for dinner? Tell him we're fun and we don't bite. I'd love to hear his story."

Sal pretended to look for bones in his fish.

Knowing Betty Doris made Sal nervous, Louie pushed back from the table and announced, "I guess I'll try to tell a story."

"I bet you've seen your share of strange things at the convenience store," Kiara said.

"On the four-to-midnight shift one night two girls came in the store," Alex interrupted. "They were dressed in really tight dresses. Wearing what Mom calls hooker shoes. One of them had a tattoo of Sierra Blue's logo on her arm and her hair was all spiky. The other one had big blue pigtails."

"Who's Sierra Blue? A movie star?" Betty Doris asked.

Kiara and Alex laughed. "Sierra Blue is an emo-grunge rock band, Grandma," Alex said. "Those girls were clearly intoxicated and should not have been buying more alcohol. And I told them so when they came to check out a four pack of IPA. I asked them for IDs and Blue Pigtails got mad and said, 'I'm old enough. Let me pay for the blankety-blank beer or I'll just walk out of here with it.' And Spiky Hair said, 'Don't talk to him like that.' And

Blue Pigtails said, 'I can talk to him any blankety-blank way I feel like.' And Spikey Hair said, 'No you can't.' And Blue Pigtails said, 'F-word I can.' Then they started smacking each other. You know, like boxing kangaroos. Except only *male* kangaroos box, the females don't. Anyway, Blue Pigtails knocks Spikey Hair to the ground and jumps on top of her, takes a selfie, then starts pounding on her head." Excited by his own storytelling, Alex stood and pounded his fist into the palm of his open hand to demonstrate.

Captivated by Alex's demonstration, everyone watched in stunned amazement.

"I dialed the police and told them they should bring EMTs because somebody was going to need a ride to the emergency room," he concluded.

"Son, you never told me this. When did this happen?" Louie asked.

"Dad, you never come to the South store at night. It gets crazy, especially on the weekends. We call it hayseed anarchy."

"Alex, honey, is it safe for you to be there?" Betty Doris asked. Turning to Louie, she lit into him. "How can you let your child work in such horrible conditions? What if he gets hurt? Or worse?" She shivered.

Leveling out his hands, Alex assured her, "Gran' ma, don't worry. I'm prepared. I've got the county sheriff's cell phone number on speed dial and we installed extra cameras." As he sat and leaned into the table, he said, "Plus, Thor's got The Deterrent."

Sal asked, "What is The Deterrent?"

"A pump-action shotgun. Winchester calls it The Defender but we renamed it because we don't want to actually, you know, shoot anybody. Just the sound of Thor pumping a round into the chamber is enough to chase 'em out of the store. And I've got a Taser. Me and Thor practice in back of the store when nobody's around." For good measure, he added, "And there's Sammy Hagar. Thor brings in on weekends."

"Who's Sammy Hagar?" Kiara asked, "A pit bull?"

"No, Thor's pet boa. Sammy hangs out over the chip aisle in a net hammock we made."

Louie smiled ever so slightly, smiled so that Betty Doris couldn't see it. His boy was finally growing up, learning how to take care of himself. "Maybe we can go over to Lee Farm and do some target shooting," Louie offered. "Firing a shotgun behind the store isn't good gun safety."

"I'd like to ride along if you don't mind the company," Donnie said. "Haven't been to Mr. Henry's place in a long while. Is the house still standing?"

"You haven't been there since Iris restored it?" Louie asked. "It's real nice. I'm sure she'd let us come on the property to shoot. She's got a range set up next to the hay barn."

"Dad, can Thor Bear come?" Alex asked.

"I want to come, too," Kiara said. "I've never fired a gun before."

"Why don't you all just make a picnic of it," Betty Doris cried out. And her meaning wasn't hospitable. "Louie Pyle, you know how much I hate guns. What if somebody gets hurt?"

"Don't worry, Mama," Louie said as he pulled a crumpled face mask from his jeans pocket and held it up, "we'll wear protection."

Nobody laughed.

"You know that's not what I mean. Stop acting cute. You're always making a joke of things. What if Alex shoots someone and they die? What if he gets shot at?" Clutching at the front of her sweater, she eked out, "I couldn't bear the thought of some gang rioting and looting the store and killing my grandson. And for what? For a handful of dollar bills and some lousy tasting beer?"

Louie cursed the 24-hour news entertainers and the internet and the outside world, which was turning all their lives upside down. In a matter of a few weeks, he'd seen his feisty, self-confident mother with strong convictions turn frail and scared at every little thing. In these hopeless times, she had become stuck between the despair of living and the fear of dying.

Donnie cut the tension by saying, "The governor did say that outside activities are acceptable where people are six feet apart and wear their masks. The times I've been to shooting ranges, most folks stand at least that far apart."

"When can we go, Dad?" Alex asked.

"I don't know. I'll have to ask Miss Lee if we can use her range," Louie said, regretting that he'd even brought up the subject.

Moving the conversation away from guns and large snakes, Donnie said, "You want to know strange? You all wouldn't believe the goings-on at Elder Home."

"Um-hmm," Betty Doris hummed.

"Should I tell them about the time Plinkus Young lost her wig?" Donnie asked Betty Doris.

"No, let me tell it," she said. She straightened her back, shifted her bottom in the chair and then placed her hands on the table. "First off, that wig belonged to me. But I got tired of looking at that ratty old wool rug she wore with her reenactment costume. I mean, if she's going to make a fool of this town, she should at least dress a little better while doing it."

"Are you talking about the lady that floats around the courthouse looking like the Grim Reaper's widow?" Kiara asked. "That's Plinkus Young? The same lady who's in charge at Elder Home?"

"The one and only," Donnie said.

"What's *her* story?" Sal asked. He was getting into this game he had unintentionally created with his story of family tragedy.

"I'm telling the story, y'all hush," Betty Doris said. "Anyway, where was I?"

"Ratty wig," Kiara said.

"I gave Plinkus my Gibson Girl because I'd just got a new one, the Carte Blanche in silver tones, and I didn't have room for both of them in my closet. And, like I said, if she was going to go around giving tours to out-of-towners and representing us, I wanted to help her look her best."

"And I'm sure she appreciated it," Louie joined in.

"Never got as much as a thank you. Anyway, because of his car accident, Cepheus Bowman was paralyzed from the hips down and got around in his wheelchair. But when Cepheus wasn't using his chair, Tater Head Handy, his roommate, would race up and down the hallway in it. Those two were always up to some kind of mischief. One time they spiked the Jell-O with vodka and the entire first floor of the west wing had Jell-O shooters for dessert. Best fun ever. This was way before they had all those fancy security cameras and added a second guard and made us all feel like we were serving prison time. Anyway, when the front office got new chairs, those two got to arguing in the TV room about which was faster—a wheelchair or an office chair. So they decided to settle the argument by having a race."

"Where was the staff when all this was happening?" Kiara asked.

"Word got around on what was goin' down," Donnie chipped in. "On the night of the big race, folks on the east wing all called for help at about the same time while those two knuckleheads were playing around on the west side."

"And, while Tater Head was in Plinkus's office getting her new fancy chair, he found her costume and her wig."

"No! He didn't," Kiara said, then snorted loudly as she stuffed her hands between her crossed legs to fend off the night's chill.

Sal and Alex were confused. Louie grinned.

"Yes, ma'am, he did. Everybody knows Tater Head lost what hair he ever had when he was thirty-three, so the Gibson Girl was a perfect fit. Here he come, looking like Norman Bates' mother, crab-walking that chair out of the office. Cepheus started laughing so hard T.H. got the drop on him. He whizzed by and headed for the exit door at the other end of the hall. I laughed so hard I peed in my pull-ups."

Sal laughed because everyone else did.

Alex asked, "Who's Norman Bates?"

"Well, sir, Cepheus cried foul and wanted a rematch," Betty Doris continued as she dabbed at an eye with her tissue. "As they were lining up for a do-over, somebody signaled that the guard was on his way. T.H. somehow managed to get the chair back at the desk and tossed the dress back on the coatrack." Controlling her breathing, she struggled to hold back another burst of laughter. "But he forgot the wig!" She howled as everyone watched her swipe at her eyes again. "It was still on his head. We all broke down. We couldn't stop laughing if we had to. Tater Head figured out what everybody was laughing at about the time Officer

Guy turned the corner. T.H. yanked it off his head and tossed it at Cepheus, who managed to stuff it in the side pocket of his wheelchair. After that, every time they came up with some crazy competition, Gibson Girl was the trophy."

"What did Miss Young do when she couldn't find her wig?" Alex insisted.

"She held one of her town hall meetings and got everybody stirred up about respecting personal space. Cepheus spoke out and told her she ought to be ashamed of accusing the helpless of such an awful thing." Betty Doris blew her nose and concluded, "When Cepheus died last summer, his daughter found it in his dresser. I had to assure her that he wasn't, you know, that way."

"What do you mean?" Alex asked.

"You know, that way," Betty Doris said as she waved her hands in front of her. "Fussy. What you young people call a cross-dresser."

"Thanks to the Lord in heaven, and amen," Donnie said.

Everyone reflected on Donnie's proclamation as they watched Possum the cat swat at a moth.

CHAPTER **SIXTEEN**

Before he went to the store the next morning, Louie cruised town to see if any new building sites had signs announcing the arrival of Speedy's. As he drove down Main Street, he saw Iris Lee and Jonnie Bailey standing in front of The Fern Basket—the coffee shop that had replaced Chunky's old place and was across the street from the Fallam County Courthouse. He parked on the street and approached them.

Iris Lee hadn't changed since Louie had last seen her at Jonnie and Ethan's wedding eight years ago. Her hair was a little grayer and she was dressed in those clingy pants, the ones women wore to exercise and shop in, and a fitted neon T-shirt. Jonnie was wearing her lawyer suit. The two had been good friends all their lives but they were as different as night and day. One thing they had in common, Louie thought, they were both smart about business. Ethan told him that Iris ran a consulting firm that helped folks with imminent domain problems. The success of Jonnie's law firm had enabled her to buy all the single-story law offices between her building and the old library on Court Street.

When the county completed construction of the new library, Jonnie purchased the old one, thus owning the entire block. She had restored the old library back to its original purpose—a home. Ethan said it was her daddy's family home with a long history.

"Miss Lee, Miss Bailey," Louie said as he tipped his ball cap.

"Louie, how's business?" Jonnie asked. "Think we'll be able to have the Most Edible Weenie Roast this year?" The Most Edible Weenie Roast was Alex's name for his annual July birthday party. Jonnie and Ethan Quinn were among the guests for the cookout on the dock. As Alex got older the party had waned. The guest list was down to Thor, Alex's Sunday School partner Martha Ann, and Louie's hunting buddies and their better halves.

"A social gathering during a world pandemic? You're the one with the hot line to the governor," he joked, "you tell me. Can we have a cookout in four weeks?"

"Isn't this situation incredible? How are your employees handling this?" She brushed a strand of white hair away from her face then shaded her eyes with her hand, smiling.

Louie believed Jonnie Bailey to be as sincere as a summer day was long but she talked like a politician, never offering anything useful and always fishing for information. He said, "My crew is making things happen. Haven't had to let anyone go. We hired a new chef and we're creating our own kind of happy meals to go."

"I know," Iris said. "Jonnie, have you tried their chicken on a stick four-pack? I bring one to Bert every day." Bert was Iris's cousin, and Donnie Tyler's niece, who had retired from keeping house at the Lee residence on Grove Street, just two blocks away.

"You ladies hear anything about Speedy's coming to Mt Pleasant?"

"I saw that on the news last night," Jonnie replied.

"Mr. Pyle, do you know Augie Young?" Iris asked.

"Sure, but please call me Louie," he said. "What's he got to do with this?"

"He called me a few months back asking about some property I own. The lot where the movie theater used to be?" She pointed in the direction of the vacant lot, a lot mere blocks from Gas N Go at the Shops.

"Listen, you two, I've got court," Jonnie interrupted. She offered Iris an elbow bump and turned to Louie. "Let's hope the Most Edible Weenie Roast can happen this year."

As Louie watched Jonnie cross the street and head for the main entrance of the courthouse, he said to Iris, "Augie Young is a client of hers. Ain't he? And Augie is working with Turks McGraw." He took off his Gas N Go cap and slapped it against his leg. "I'm screwed."

Iris said, "Augie made an offer on my lot and said his client was looking for high-traffic retail spaces. After yesterday's announcement, it doesn't take a detective to figure that out."

On reflex, Louie reached to rub his beard but his homemade Gas N Go COVID mask, the one Kiara had made for him, was in the way. "Handwriting's on the wall," Louie mumbled.

"I've been meaning to call you. You told me once that you'd be interested in the property if I was ever in the mood to sell. Dad would have wanted me to offer you first right of refusal to purchase the lot. You interested?"

He chuckled and said, "That's nice of you. But since my divorce, I don't know if I can afford it. How much you askin'?" When she stated the price, he blew out a low whistle.

"I'd give you the family discount," she said, then grinned. "Mr. Henry really liked you. He told me once that I could rely on you and that I should help you out whenever I could."

"I appreciate that," he said. "But I ain't got that kind of money, you know, to buy something just in case I need it down the road."

"What will happen to Gas N Go if Speedy's comes to town?"

"Like you said, it don't take a detective to figure it out. Since he has a hundred times as many stores as I do, his unit costs are way lower. He can price me out of the market in six months, three if he really tries."

Saying it out loud scared Louie, the demise of his livelihood was unfolding. Either he went full-on offense or Gas N Go was headed for the great recycle heap in the Pacific Ocean. "I am so screwed," he repeated.

"You've certainly got a high hurdle in front of you," she said. She stooped and adjusted the laces on her running shoe.

Slipping his cap back on, he said, "Augie's shut down The Happy Pizza at the lake."

"Ah, man," she cried. "I loved that place. You think he'll lease the building to Speedy's?"

"Maybe? He'd have to gut the building and reconfigure it for a store layout," Louie said. Scratching at his mask, he added, "Probably makes more sense to buy the theater lot and build to Speedy's specs."

While Iris described improvements needed for the lot before anyone could build on it, Louie recalled Thor telling him about Mr. Contento throwing his shoe at someone. It must have been Augie Young. It made sense to Louie now. Augie wanted Sal out of his building so he could offer it to McGraw.

He was screwed.

"WHAT ARE YOU GOING TO DO?" Lupita asked excitedly. She had been waiting for him in front of the store. After tamping out a cigarillo with her high-heeled sandal, she followed him inside, asking again, "What are you going to do?"

"There's not much I *can* do," he said. Louie went over to the coffee service and poured himself a cup of full strength.

"But this guy will destroy you," she said. Frantically, she rummaged around in that oversized carry-on she called a pocketbook and pulled out a piece of paper. "*Mira*! Look!" She shoved the paper at Louie but he didn't take it.

Sipping at the sour coffee, he surveyed the store. Chunky was rubbernecking in their direction. To her, he said, "Keep your voice down. I don't want the others hearing this."

"Are you serious?" she asked. "You don't think they haven't seen or heard about it? You're making it worse by not telling them."

"When I've thought it through and have a plan, I'll share it with everybody," he said.

Lupita followed him behind the checkout counter and into his cramped office. "And when will that be? Time is not on your side in this matter, Louie."

He motioned for her to close the door of the cramped room. "I know the gravity of the situation, ah'ite. But I have to work out what I'm going to do before I tell anybody." His wobbly legs buckled as he eased into his desk chair. His entire body, head and heart, felt it now. He was in the middle of a storm, the storm raging against his life as he knew it. Yet, he hadn't seen the storm coming. He was so screwed.

Lupita placed the paper she'd retrieved from her purse on his desk and smacked her hand on top of it. "I found this interview on the internet. Turks McGraw is a vain man. He likes to talk about his 'golden thumb,' he calls it. In this interview he tells how he destroys his competition." Jabbing at the paper, she added softly, "We know his plan, Louie. We know how he would shut down Gas N Go."

Louie tugged at the paper under Lupita's finger so she raised her hand to release it.

She went on, "I'm sorry about being too loud out there. I'm bold. I get excited, em, emotional when I see things like this happening. I'm not here to pressure you. I want to help." She tugged at her form-fitting dress, the kind the morning weather lady on Channel 14 wore. "And besides, I don't want to lose a client. Can you see poor Sal working at *eSpeedy*'s? I cannot. He would be miserable. Let me help you get in front of this." She fluffed at her hair then clipped it up with a fastener that had been clasped to the handle of her purse.

Louie wanted to trust Lupita. Yet, he had no way of knowing what her intentions were. Was she trying to take his business away from him like McGraw and the inventory thieves? Straight out asking her, he knew would be an affront to her and their relationship. But maybe he should try and trust her just a little bit. So he said, "I saw Iris Lee up on Main Street. She told me Augie Young wants to buy the vacant lot where the movie theater used to be. I suspect Augie Young is working for McGraw."

"See? It's happening," Lupita said. "I don't want to live in a town where my tobacco shop is run by a cartel. I love Mt Pleasant because it's quirky and everybody has a hand in taking care of their own business." Her bangles jingled as she folded her arms across her body.

Louie's head was spinning. First, he'd learned that a behemoth competitor was coming to Mt Pleasant, quite possibly to run him out of business. And, now, Lupita was saying it was a cartel. "Did you just say Speedy's is a cartel?"

"Yes, but," her bangles tinkled, "I don't mean cartel in the way Americans think of cartels, like drugs or sex trafficking. Businesses operate as cartels all the time. Look at Stuff Mart and Anaconda Online. With his distribution network—all his stores—it makes it impossible for anyone to compete against him. If he comes here, we'll pay dearly for our conveniences."

"You think I don't know that?" Louie said. In frustration, he tossed his mask on his desk and scratched the side of his face. "I'll have to look for a co-op."

"That's a good first step," she said, "but it might not be enough. Have you ever been in *eSpeedy's*? I was in one last week and they're offering a one dollar lottery ticket for every gas fill-up."

"They stole that promo from us. That was Lisa's idea. We've been doing it for years."

She looked at her watch and said, "I've got an appointment with another client. Why don't you come over in the afternoon and we can talk about this some more?"

Louie closed and locked the office door after she left. He needed time to think without interruption. He sat at his desk and read the McGraw piece Lupita had left behind. Each sentence worried him. Without warning, the words waved in and out of focus.

The panic attack came on quickly.

Using an anxiety management technique he'd read about on the internet, Louie closed his eyes and breathed in slowly through his nose then exhaled through his mouth. To himself, he counted slowly, one, two, three.

"She's a keeper, that one," the old man said.

"Go away," Louie said. Four, five, six.

"She's what you need right now, son. She's got more courage than I've seen in most men. And business acumen. A rare combination these days."

Seven, eight, nine, ten. Louie blew out a hard breath.

"Stop hiding inside your head," Mr. Henry said. "Look at me."

Louie opened his eyes and jolted back against his chair. Mr. Henry, solidly lucid and smelling of his favorite brand of tobacco and moth balls, stood on the other side of the narrow metal desk. Louie cried, "What do you want from me?"

"Look me in the eye," the old man commanded.

With unease Louie obeyed. The old man was too close. One, two, three. He'd never stared into the eyes of a ghost before. Four, five, six. As he focused on Mr. Henry's black, bottomless eyes, Louie felt his body tense. Seven, eight, nine.

"Stop denying the passage of time. Plan your future now," Mr. Henry advised.

"But this guy is here to ruin my future," Louie argued. He'd stopped counting, stopped his breathing exercise.

"Is his enterprise going to impact where people go to buy their beer and biscuits? Inevitably. Is he going to ruin your future? No. That would be on you, pal. You choose your future."

A knock at the door was followed by, "Mr. Pyle? Everything all right in there?"

"Everything's cool," Louie called out, fearing someone had heard him and the old man talking.

"Let it go," Mr. Henry said. "It's only, what do they call it?

Bricks and mortar."

"But Gas N Go is a place for Alex to work," Louie whispered in an irritated tone. "And the minute it closes down, Speedy's will take advantage of everybody in Mt Pleasant, not just Alex. There are a lot of people, employees and customers alike, that I let slide on things. You think Speedy's would hire a kid like Normal Stokes? He can't read. Will Turks McGraw care about what happens to the people in this county?" He answered his own question, "Hell no!"

"Stop making excuses," Mr. Henry said. "Take it from someone who realized too late that there's more to life than trying to be right all the time."

"What are you talking about? Trying to be right all the time?"

"Do you want to die while ringing up cheese dip and smoked sausages?"

"Huh?"

"Listen to the beautiful Latina," Mr. Henry said. "What does Donnie's Kiara say? 'Let her lead the dance.'"

Someone with a heavy hand was pounding on the door. "Mr. Pyle? I need to talk to Chunky. Is he in there with you? I need to ask him about my work schedule."

CHAPTER **SEVENTEEN**

Lupita, for some reason, had cooled on the urgency of meeting with him to circle Gas N Go's wagons. She had called and asked to reschedule their late afternoon meeting. On his way home, Louie stopped at Gas N Go South to speak with Thor about Alex's account of two ladies wrestling over who had the better manners. The fact that he had no knowledge of Thor keeping a pump-action shotgun on the premises worried Louie.

Before getting out of his truck, he reached for his notepad and scribbled a reminder to ask the other store managers if they concealed guns under their counters, which was against store policy. When he managed a store, he'd kept a baseball bat next to the cash register in case some moron decided to show bad judgment. One of his employees had written in permanent marker the words "The Enforcer" on the bat's barrel for anyone to see when paying for their stuff. No sir, he drew the line at guns in his stores.

This prompted another idea to jot in his notebook. He'd ask Ethan Quinn to conduct a training session on self-defense for his store managers and employees, dos and don'ts in dealing with shoplifters and robbers. That was something they could do while following social distance rules. *Social distance*, he was amazed at how quickly he and everyone else had adapted to the new vocabulary in a matter of days.

A set of pudgy knuckles tapped on his truck window. "Everything OK, boss?" Thor asked as Louie opened the window.

"Making some notes," Louie said as he stuffed his notepad back in his shirt pocket. "I don't recommend getting old, Thor. It causes you to forget things so you got to write them down."

"Are you here about the inventory thing I emailed you about?" Thor asked.

Louie had been so focused on the Speedy's threat that he hadn't bothered with his day's emails.

"Mr. Pyle?" Thor asked.

"Huh?" Louie said. "See there, Thor? My brain broke again. What were you saying?"

"I got something you need to see," he said.

Inside, Normal Stokes was stacking the snack aisle with bags of chips and other munchies. "Hello, Mr. Pyle. Did you get a chance to meet Sammy Hagar?" Grinning, Normal pointed upward. "Awww-wow," Normal sang out like his aging heavy metal band idol.

Louie jerked back at the sight of a forty-pound snake snoozing in a netted hammock, its tail spiraling in the air. "Great Almighty!" he cried out as he backed into a chip display.

Normal laughed. "Sammy just ate so he's a little sleepy. He does that thing with his tail when he sleeps."

"Sammy is a she! How many times do I have to tell you that, Normal," Alex joined them. "Dad, what do you think?"

His hand on his chest and his heart racing, Louie didn't even want to know how many health code violations were being broken. "Take that thing down. Right now!"

"But Dad," Alex protested. "Sammy Hagar is part of our security system. Plus, business has picked up since we started posting videos of her. Chip sales are down a little bit but the soda and beer sales are way, way up."

"I don't care if sales are through the roof," Louie said. "If the health department comes in here and sees this, they'll shut us down. Get that thing out of here!"

The three friends stood in shock at Louie's seemingly irrational outburst. Never before had they, including his son Alex, seen such eruptive behavior coming from their boss.

"Now!" Louie yelled.

"But, Dad, I told you about Sammy the other night. You didn't say get rid of her then," Alex protested.

"That's before I got a good look at it," Louie said. He shuddered. "Not a fan of snakes, boys."

"So, that proves our point," Thor spoke up. "One look at ole Sammy and anybody who comes in here with robbery on their mind changes it real quick-like." Thor smiled with pride at his ingenious security tactic.

"Oh, yeah? What do we do when Sammy here gives somebody's granny a heart attack? It's Louie Pyle they'll come after." He faced Alex and said, "Don't make me ask you a second time."

While Normal and Alex got the ladder out of the men's bathroom so they could remove Sammy from her perch, Thor led Louie to the counter and opened his laptop.

Before he logged on, he said, "It was my idea to bring Sammy up in here."

Realizing the effect his outburst had on the boys, Louie said, "I'm sorry for yelling at you. That was inappropriate." That was inappropriate was one of those two-bit phrases he'd learned at last year's employment management seminar while he was at the convenience store convention. He rubbed his hands together and said, "What did you want to show me?"

"Alex told you about the cameras we installed all around the outside of the building. Right?"

"Sure did. But we already have cameras. Why are you putting up more?" Louie asked as he watched Thor open an application on his laptop.

"Let me show you," Thor said. Five frames with a different view of the building popped up on his laptop. "We can access the new cameras from our laptops via an app me and Alex created." He pointed at one of the frames. "The Yippies Wholesale guy comes here on Tuesdays. Get a load of this." He clicked on one of the frames, activating a video. The Yippies Wholesale delivery van backed up to the loading platform and the driver got out and opened the back doors. Thor paused the screen and said to Louie, "Now here's where it gets inner-resting." He clicked the play icon and the video resumed. A small pickup truck backed in beside the Yippies' van and a man got out, his face covered by a baseball cap and medical face mask. Quickly, the pair filled the back of the pickup with boxes of Yippies inventory and then the masked man hopped in his truck and drove away. Thor pointed at the clock on the video frame and said, "Gone in sixty seconds."

Louie said, "Go back. Can you get a better image of the sum-bitch?"

"Oh, I know who he is," Thor said of the pickup driver. "Comes in here all the time. Gator juice and barbecue chips.

Me and Alex went to high school with him. Kenny Wayne Young, Kenny Young's son, Gus Young's grandson. You know, the baseball player?"

"And Augie Young's nephew," Louie mumbled.

"Yep, that would be him," Thor said. "I got suspended from school for fighting with Kenny Wayne."

"Is he the one who bullied Alex?" Louie asked.

"Same one," Thor said. He pressed reverse on the app and replayed the theft.

Heat rose in Louie's chest. As he looked around for something to throw, Mr. Henry appeared behind Thor.

The old man leaned toward Louie. "Now is the time for a cooler head. Don't go off half-cocked and do something you'll regret. Talk to Quinn. He'll help you sort it out." And he was gone as quickly as he had appeared.

Feeling dizzy, Louie leaned against the counter and focused where the ceiling and wall met. He breathed in and slowly let out bad air.

"Mr. Pyle?" Thor asked.

"I'm fine." He stroked his beard, thinking about Mr. Henry's advice. "Here's what we're going to do, Thor Bear. You keep making these videos." He looked the boy in the eyes and went on, "Don't tell anybody what you're doing. Has Alex seen this?"

Thor shook his head, "Not yet."

"Good. Keep it that way," Louie said.

"I'll try but he looks at these files as much as I do."

"Change the password. Tell him it's a new security procedure or make something else up. It's your job to make sure nobody finds out what you're doing."

"Yes, sir," Thor said.

"And when the delivery truck comes, steer clear. Let them keep at it so they won't know we're on to them." In frustration, he asked, "Don't you guys check the delivery receipts against the actual units?"

Thor lowered his head and fiddled with the keys on his laptop. "I guess we haven't been doing it like you taught us."

Louie put his hand on Thor's hulking shoulder. "Don't beat yourself up. We all make mistakes. But from now on, when they bring the stuff in, make sure you note the difference between what's on the receipt and what they bring in. But don't let them know what you're up to. Ah'ite?"

"Yes, sir," Thor said quietly.

"I'm real proud of you, Thor Bear. Proud of you and Alex for running this store. Now, show me where you keep the shotgun."

Thor's chubby finger wiped tiny sweat beads from his hairline. "What? I ain't got no shotgun up in here," he denied.

"Alex said you had one here," Louie said.

"I…I… it's my granddaddy's. I brung it here for a gag is all."

"I don't want you to have anything like that on the premises. You hear me? Tell me what you do when somebody comes in here and sticks a gun in your face."

Thor lowered his head and mumbled, "Open the register and step away and let them take it all."

"That's right. Just let them have it. It ain't worth gettin' shot at for a couple hundred bucks."

"But, what if the guy acts like he's gonna shoot at me or Alex?"

"No guns on the premises, Thor," Louie said.

Louie and Thor watched while Normal steadied the ladder and Alex climbed up to retrieve Sammy Hagar, who was wearing a teeny Mexican sombrero tied over her eyes. Seeing the snake coil around Alex's arm, a woman dropped her liter of soda and let out a ten-second shriek. Louie looked away to hide his smirk. In spite of things getting so serious, something inside triggered his need to laugh.

"Thor, can you get this nice lady another soda? Ma'am that drink's no charge. I'm sorry you had to see that." He rushed out to the loading area and bent over, propping his hands on his knees. Laughter spewed from inside. No, he wasn't losing his mind, he declared. This crazy-ass world had gone plumb sideways.

Before he left the store, Louie asked Thor to install extra cameras outside of the other three stores. Considering that this could be an inside job after all, he instructed Thor to mount them in inconspicuous places and do it before the stores opened at six in the morning.

On his ride home, Louie dialed Ethan Quinn's cell phone. "Ethan! I think I found out who's stealing from me. Your girl Basket-ville, Basser-ville, however she says her name, gave me some pointers on how to secure the computers but her prices for a full monty analysis are out of my league, pal. One of my employees found something, though. I need to talk with you about it. Give me a jingle. Bye-sickle."

LUPITA'S SHINY BLACK CADILLAC ESCALADE sat in Louie's spot in his driveway. As he approached Log Heaven's front door, Louie heard music. Kiara and her baby grand piano were on display in the wide bay window. Betty Doris, on the bench at Kiara's side, was clapping her hands.

Inside, he found Lupita sitting in the large fireside chair, reigning over the recital, her shapely, brown legs crossed at her ankles. With her eyes closed, Lupita's upper body gently swayed to the rhythm of the music. The melody, something Louie'd heard on the radio but wasn't sure of the name of the artist or the song, floated and swirled around her. Lordy, she was a beautiful woman.

Kiara was definitely riffing on the song's tune.

Betty Doris started crooning and broke the spell of the melody for everybody.

Lupita opened her eyes, amused by Louie's stare.

Kiara stopped playing when she noticed Louie at the door. "Look what came today! Isn't she beautiful?" She ran her fingers up the keys and back with the proficiency of the classical musician she was. "I'm thinking of naming her Betty Sue. What do you think?" She winked at him.

"Son, when you first met Kiara you told her you'd keep your ears to the ground for people looking for a music teacher. Because of you, we're setting up this room for music lessons," Betty Doris said. She crossed her palms over her heart and proclaimed, "I raised a good boy. I taught him right. I'm the luckiest mama in the world."

Lupita raised an eyebrow as a smirk tugged at the corner of her mouth.

Louie agreed with Lupita's assessment. Betty Doris had just served up the sappiest sentiment he'd ever heard. And that was saying a lot since he had served on Mt Pleasant's town council for a good many years.

Over a month ago, he was living alone, with only his reflection staring back at him from that bay window. Now look at him, he had more women in his life than he knew what to do with. Perhaps too many.

"Poppy!" A squeal of excitement echoed off the high walls.

Louie turned and saw his granddaughter Maddy at the front door. Squatting, he extended his arms and cried out, "Jumpin' Bean!" What's one more, he reasoned as she jumped into his embrace and wrapped her little arms around his neck.

"Hi, Dad!" Jessica called out. She was clutching a grocery bag, and her mom, Lisa, was closing the door behind them.

CHAPTER **EIGHTEEN**

The last Sunday night in June, Louie couldn't sleep. He stared into the darkness, thinking about everything he had to do for next weekend's Most Edible Weenie Roast. The ski boat's gas tank needed topping off, all the lawn chairs and the picnic table had to be hosed down. The grill needed cleaning. Food and drinks and decorations set out.

His heart skipped.

The doctor had told Louie that he had an irregular heartbeat, thus, he needed to reduce stress in his life. Except, the McGraw situation was making it hard for him to do that. It wasn't like he could call up Turks McGraw and tell the Texan that this town wasn't big enough for the both of them and demand that he leave.

He breathed out the breath he'd been holding on to.

And, that smart aleck Kenny Wayne Young was stealing stock, literally, out of the back of Louie's stores, in front of God and everybody. Just as bold as a chihuahua's bark, the kid drove up to the back of the stores and took what he wanted. The anticipation of waiting for the right minute to bust the slacker was unbearable. Ethan Quinn and the county sheriff wanted the whole gang so they were following Kenny Wayne around the tri-county area, watching to see who the shiftless dirtbag's known associates were. Louie didn't need an army of overanxious law enforcement ex-GIs to tell him who was ripping off his stores. The Young family had been in the business of relieving people of their property for as long as the county had been in existence. Heck, the younger ones, like Augie, had university degrees on how to do it.

He blew out another hot breath.

Louie pushed away the bedcovers with his feet. Reruns of thoughts about the day Jessica and Maddy showed up for a visit were keeping him awake. The day should have been a happy one. Instead, the barometric pressure dropped the instant Jessica and her mother Lisa came through the front door. For Louie, it was like being locked inside a henhouse twirling around in a Kansas tornado. Betty Doris started in on Lisa, commenting on her ex-daughter-in-law's shirt appearing more snug than the last time she'd seen her, to which Lisa responded with one of her left-handed compliments about Betty Doris's lipstick shade matching those redneck cheesy pork rinds her ex-mother-in-law was so fond of eating. Then Lisa went on, complaining about all the changes in the great room and wanting to know why her coffee table was sitting on the front porch where it would be ruined by the sun and rain. And, over the top of her mother's laments, Jessica jumped in on why she couldn't stay in a house with so many non-family members, fearing her daughter would be exposed to the virus and saying maybe it would be better if she and Maddy stayed at Grandma Lisa's house. Not understanding any of that, Maddy squirmed out of Louie's arms and insisted that Betty Doris move from the piano bench so she could sit on it where she pounded on the keys with her sticky little palms while Kiara patiently guarded the piano and Maddy from hurting each other. After taking her grocery bag to the kitchen, Jessica returned to the great room asking, over her daughter's improvised sonata, why the kitchen hutch was pushed up against the door leading down to the rec room. Lisa caught Kiara's eye roll aimed at Louie and started in on her ex-husband about how his irresponsible actions would cause her children and grandchild to catch the COVID or meet with unknown misadventure.

At the threshold of a brief gap of silence, Lupita stood. The others, Louie noticed, stopped their yakking long enough to admire her timing and her put-together outfit. Taking Louie aside, she whispered that she couldn't stay and would talk to him at another time, perhaps when he wasn't so busy with domestic affairs.

The other women watched, with collective jealousy, as Louie placed his hand on Lupita's elbow and gently guided her to the front door. Louie hadn't heard from Lupita since, not about Gas N Go's business problems or about having dinner with him.

Women baffled Louie. Sometimes, he prayed to God for guidance. But, after a lifetime of living among them, he'd learned that he was on his own when it came to understanding the feminine mystique.

HE PULLED HIMSELF UP and swung his legs over the side of the bed. That's when he heard the sound. Somebody was knocking around downstairs, probably getting a midnight snack, which seemed like a good idea to Louie. Downstairs, he walked silently toward the glow coming from the kitchen.

"Thought you could use a break from all that useless worrying," Mr. Henry said. The bright aura from an outside light outlined his presence.

Louie filled a glass at the spigot and gulped down the water. "I'm worried about the store."

"What about it worries you?" the old man asked.

"Losing it. How will Alex take care of hisself if he doesn't have a job to go to?"

"That boy's going to be fine. But why do you think you're going to lose the store? You've had bigger challenges. Go on the offensive, set the rules for the fight."

Louie turned to get another glass of water.

"Hank? Is that you?" Donnie Tyler was standing in the doorway, barefoot and wearing his faded flannel pj's and a faraway stare. "Have you come for me, Cap?" he whispered in his raspy voice.

Donnie was sleepwalking or so Louie hoped. If Donnie was seeing the old man, too, then Louie had greater worries than a failing business.

"I knew I would see you again. I told Kiara I been hearin' you lately."

Louie's gaze shifted from Donnie's illuminated face back to Mr. Henry but the spirit was gone. He guided Donnie, who seemed slighter than his daytime self, back up the stairs to his bedroom. As Louie helped him into bed, Donnie continued, "Kiara said I was eating too much of that rich food the Persian man's making every night and that's why I was hearing things."

"Probably right. That Kiara's smart," Louie said. "You get some sleep now."

Donnie reached for a framed black and white photo on the bedside table, a portrait of two boys, best friends, with their arms interlaced over each other's shoulders and looking up into the photographer's camera. "Did I ever tell you about the time Hank got in a scrap with one of Elvis's road dogs? We was sittin' out back of The Lickin' Hole and the man, he was drunk, called Hank a prissy-boy. Hank slugged him, broke his jaw." He chuckled then went on, "Times were different back then. We were lucky we didn't get hauled off to jail."

Louie gently took the picture from Donnie and placed it back on the table. "Let's talk about it tomorrow. Right now, you get some sleep."

Donnie grabbed Louie's wrist and said, "That was Hank. I know it was him."

"Get some sleep. Things are brighter in the morning light, Betty Doris always says." Behind the closed door, Louie heard Donnie's low voice, speaking to someone.

A few sleepless hours later, Louie took his coffee out to the deck. The quiet of the morning usually gave him solace. But this morning, his whirring mind wasted the peacefulness. He chewed on a nail as he read from his laptop a complimentary report submitted by Ms. Baskerville as an example of the forensic investigating she could do for Gas N Go. At her suggestion, he had sent her data on the last two years' employee time reports. According to the data analytics oracle of Shockoe Bottom, his ex-wife was double dipping by reporting time as Lisa Pyle and L. Woods, that being her maiden name. There must be a mistake. Why would she do that? Under their divorce settlement, she had plenty of money. He pulled his notepad from his pocket and scribbled a reminder to look at Lisa's time reports when he got a chance. Danged if this didn't set his day moving in the wrong direction.

"Why would she *do* that?" he asked out loud. Even if he'd given up on trying to make sense of her actions, he still cared about her, worried about her. Plus, he reckoned he'd never get over her leaving him. "Ain't going down that rabbit hole. Not today," he whispered.

To get his mind off Lisa, he thought about Mr. Henry's latest nocturnal visit. The old man had said to take an offensive strategy at saving his business. How could his little four-store operation succeed in a market where the most successful venture in convenience store history was about to descend on Fallam County? He wished he could talk to Lupita. But she had made it pretty clear that she wasn't all that into a man with a truckload of lady troubles.

"First off," he said aloud to the trees, "we keep people coming back to the store. And to do that, we got to up our game on offers they can't get anywhere else." He sipped his coffee. "That's the nut of it."

"What's the nut of it?" Kiara asked. Clutching an oversized mug with both hands, she sat beside him. "You didn't sleep last night."

Louie's surprised look asked how she knew.

"I could hear you rolling around on that squeaky bed of yours." She smiled.

"Donnie had some trouble last night, too," Louie said. "Caught him sleepwalking. Claims he's seeing his friend, Captain Hank."

"Hank? Oh, Uncle Donnie's friend Mr. Henry," Kiara said. "Since we've been here, he tells me he hears him every now and then. I'm afraid Uncle D's mind is failing."

Louie tugged on his beard. "When I was helping him get back in bed, he said something. It didn't make sense to me. I figured he was still dreaming. It was something about a Persian making him eat rich food?"

"Oh, he must be talking about the halvah fudge Sal served the other night. It was too rich for him, gave him heartburn," Kiara said.

"So this halvah fudge is a Persian food?"

"Well, Middle Eastern," she explained. "Why?"

"Is Sal Persian?" Louie asked, his head buzzing, anticipating the fact that he probably wasn't going to be too comfortable with her answer.

"Sal's *grandfather* is Persian," she said. Her eyes widened as she added, "But don't tell him I told you. He made me promise not to tell anybody. But it's pretty obvious."

"How's that?"

"Haven't you noticed the dishes he's been making lately, saffron kebabs and ghormeh sabzi? Oh, my God, his kebabs are to die for."

"Gourmet what?" Louie's head was spinning. He wanted to blame it on the lack of sleep. Did Kiara just say Mr. Contento was Persian? He tried to find Persia on a map in his head except world geography hadn't been his best subject in school.

"Ghormeh sabzi. You know that vegetarian stew he served the other night?" She took a sip of her coffee and went on, "I was wondering why he kept calling his granddad 'baba.' But when he told me that Mr. Contento was Iranian, it made perfect sense."

Louie was stunned by the revelation. Never in his entire life on this earth did he think he'd have an Iranian, hiding behind an Italian name, living in his basement. That explained

Mr. Contento crawling around in the corner next to his son Ken's drum set and making those droning sounds. Didn't those guys pray on their hands and knees like five times a day?

He patted her arm and said, "Listen here. Betty Doris does *not* need to know about this. You agree?"

Kiara said, "Oh, I do. Betty Doris has a lot of talents but international diplomacy isn't one of them."

The sound of a vehicle grabbed their attention. A few minutes passed and Alex came around the corner of the house, surprised to see Louie and Kiara sitting at the deck table.

"Hey, Dad. What's up, Kiara?" he said.

"Late night, bud?" Louie asked.

"I went by after work to see Jessica and Maddy at mom's and fell asleep on the sofa," he said. "I'm hungry. What's for breakfast?"

"Whatever you're fixin'," Louie said.

"I'm going for another cup of coffee. Want one?" Kiara offered. He waved her off.

Alex opened the sliding glass door for Kiara and then sat next to his dad. One knee bobbing up and down, Alex pulled his phone out, then shoved it back in his front pocket. "Dad, Dad," he was nervous about something.

"What is it, son?" Louie asked.

"It's Mom. She's smoking weed with Maddy in the house."

Louie leaned in to ask, "Is she doing it in front of her?"

"No, but when I tell her she shouldn't be doing it at all, she gets all mad at me and cusses. Then she starts cussing about you."

"About me? What have I done this time?"

"She says she's going to report you to the immigration police for harboring illegal aliens."

Worried about how his ex-wife's escalating unpredictable behavior might affect Alex, Louie tried to defuse her claims. "Son, you know that ain't true, don't you?"

"Yeah, but, is Kiara Jamaican? Mom said she is."

Louie guffawed. "Kiara was born and raised in Fallam County. So were her mama, and her grandparents, her great-grandparents. Your mom knows that."

Taking in what his father said, Alex cracked his knuckles. His brow wrinkled in confusion when he asked, "Then why is she saying that about you? I mean, why is she so mad at you all the time?"

Louie replied, "Some people just can't be happy, son. It's just not in them. They believe 'cause they can't be happy, then nobody can." He pulled his notepad out of his shirt pocket and wrote underneath the line about checking Lisa's time report history: Ask Sal for his father's identification papers.

CHAPTER **NINTEEN**

On his ride into town Louie obsessed over his uninvited house guests: the ghost of a long dead friend, an eighty-seven-year-old Black man who claimed to be hearing and seeing the long dead friend, and a reclusive Iranian. He wasn't sure how he got himself into playing host to a house full of unlikely confederates during a hundred-year pandemic but here he was. In spite of the situation, he laughed out loud and said, "I'm so funny, I amuse myself."

Chief Quinn had called and asked Louie to stop by his office so he could give him an update on Fallam County law enforcement's surveillance of Kenny Wayne Young and what the county sheriff called his known associates. Before going to the chief's office, Louie stopped at his town store to get a box of Sister Addie's fried apple pies for the folks in blue. Behind the deli display counter, Angel was slamming around pots and pans and mumbling underneath her server's mask.

"What's got you riled?" Louie asked.

"That lady was in here again flashing a badge and asking

for her free coffee and doughnut again this morning," she said as she wiped sweat from her brow with the hem of her paper baker's cap. "Mr. Pyle, I know she don't work for no child services agency, she's using somebody else's badge to get free food."

"Did you ask to see her ID?"

"Yeah, and she got an attitude and accused me of profiling her. I told her, 'Lady, that doesn't make any sense.' She got all huffy and walked out." Angel pulled the strings on her apron and took it off as her early morning baker's shift was ending. "I mean the things people get up to these days. It's like nobody's got any shame anymore."

"You did the right thing," Louie said. "Just keep asking for an ID."

At Mt Pleasant's Command and Safety Center, Louie left the fried apple pies at the front desk and found his way to the chief of police's office. Ethan and the Fallam County sheriff were speaking in low voices.

"Close the door, Louie, and take a seat," Ethan instructed.

"Well?" Louie asked as he sat. "Y'all takin' the sorry rat down?"

Sheriff Jones cleared his throat and stared straight ahead.

"Louie, you need to see something before we move on," Ethan said.

"What is it?"

"I need you to see some of the video we've captured." Ethan swiveled his computer monitor around for Louie to watch. "After hitting three of your stores last week, we followed Mr. Young to a warehouse by the old rail station on the road to Roanoke." The video showed Kenny Wayne transferring boxes from his truck to a white van in broad daylight. The driver of the van helped with the loading. The guy looked familiar but Louie couldn't quite place him. Fast forwarding the video, Ethan said, "Our second team followed the white van, which proceeded to Roanoke's farmers market. After parking, the driver got out of the van then got in this vehicle a few blocks away," Ethan enlarged a still of the video, "a late model Hummer with dealer tags. The Hummer is registered to King's Auto Mart."

Suddenly, Louie realized where the trail was headed.

"Roanoke Police have been watching this guy for about a year. He's doing the same thing at other stores, stores in Roanoke and up into the Shenandoah Valley. Playbook's the same, pulls up beside the Yippies's delivery van, snatches stuff off the back, then is gone before the store clerk sees anything. We've identified two employees in the Yippies organization that are in on the scheme. Your friend the forensic accountant is working with Yippies's owner, Pete Gilly. They're thankful for the surveillance work your employee turned in, by the way."

"When can we get the S. O. B. Kenny Wayne locked up?" Louie inquired.

"Not so fast," Ethan said, "Mr. Young is small fry. We want the big fish."

Sheriff Jones picked up the story, "This operation, we think, is multistate. We're asking the state crime unit and the FBI for assistance. That video your employee made broke this case wide open. We weren't sure how they were taking possession of the stolen items."

Ethan attempted to calm Louie's agitations by showing steady hands and placing them on his desk. "I can assure you, we've got enough from these videos to convict Mr. Young. He'll be a special guest of the governor's for a while when this is all over. But for now, we need to wait and see how the state police need us to proceed."

"And what am I supposed to do? Sit on my hands?"

Ethan gave Louie a few seconds then, as he tightened his jaw, said, "I'm afraid there is something else. We need you to look at another video." The view on the monitor changed from the farmers market to a mug shot. "Daniel S. Strayer, aka, Stoner, is believed to be the ringleader in this part of the state. Calling themselves Stoner's Crew, they trade in all kinds of contraband and are part of a loose national affiliate of thieves and counterfeiters. Tobacco products are their primary target. Watch this." He activated the video and all three watched as the Hummer pulled up to a brick rancher on a neighborhood street. Two men got out of the SUV and were greeted by a woman with a small child shyly peeking from behind her. Ethan froze the video and zeroed in on the woman.

Louie's face expanded.

"We don't know how involved she is in this. She could be a victim or an active participant. We don't know yet."

Every nerve in Louie's body fired off. His feet and hands tingled. He tried to speak. "That's my," he whimpered, "my Jumpin' Bean."

"We need to find out if she's part of this crew or an innocent. Either way, she's in trouble," Ethan spoke softly. "And you need to help us."

Louie couldn't speak. He couldn't understand what his friend was asking. His life was moving into a space he wasn't entirely comfortable with, a space with no floor or ceiling, a space without dimension.

"Louie," Ethan said.

Staring at the wall just past Ethan's curly hair, Louie said in full monotone, "She won't tell me anything. Hell, I was the last person to find out I was getting a divorce. Came home one night, her clothes were gone and divorce papers on the kitchen counter."

The two lawmen gave Louie time to process the jarring news. His ex, the mother of his grown and indifferent children and grandmother to his precious Maddy, the Jumpin' Bean, was possibly up to no good. His whole world changed in an instant. Add this moment to his collection of memory stamps, like remembering the graffiti on his third-grade desktop when he heard President Kennedy had been assassinated or watching Dale Earnhardt's final-lap crash at Daytona. Here was the moment the Lisa in his heart vanished.

He blew out a tall breath and said, "What do you need me to do?"

Ethan got busy. "First, we need access to your business records. If she *is* involved, she's most likely laundering money through your business. And stealing from Gas N Go in the process."

Louie grimaced.

Sheriff Jones added, "Using legitimate businesses as a front is common practice for these clowns. Ms. Baskerville is a rat dog at ferreting them out. Who has access to your ordering systems and other electronic transactions?"

"Right now, just me and my guy who manages inventory and ordering," Louie said. "On the advice of the Basket-ville lady, I changed all the passwords." A memory of Lisa complaining about not getting access to the payroll system sparked in his brain. She'd made fun of his louieandlisa4ever password, which he hadn't changed in years.

"We'll need your guy's name so we can work up a profile on him," Jones said.

"Look here," Louie objected, coming out of his trance. Boyd Latimer was one of his second-chance employees on probation for a stupid mid-life crisis mistake. "My people ain't to be trampled all over 'cause some bone-headed boy wants to waltz right into my storage rooms and take whatever the hell he pleases. No, sir. You find another way around that circus tent, sheriff."

"Ms. Baskerville needs access to your systems," the sheriff insisted.

Louie turned to Ethan and asked, "On your word, that lady ain't going to wreck my business and steal my identity, is she?"

"I'm not in the business of absolute guarantees, Louie. But we'll do everything to make sure your business is protected." He pushed away from his desk to signal that the meeting was over. "I'll ask Ms. Baskerville to contact you. Do what she asks and we'll be in touch as to what else you can do."

They all stood. The sheriff shook hands with both men and said, "Ethan, I'll get back to you."

Ethan and Louie watched the stiff-legged sheriff leave.

"What is it you want me to do? Besides giving access to all my business to a complete stranger computer geek?"

"It's really more what I want you to *not* do. Stay away from Lisa. Do not approach Larry Baldwin or Kenny Wayne Young. Just go about your daily routine. We may need you, at some point, to talk with Lisa about Larry and this Stoner character, wearing a wire."

Pointing at the frozen picture of Lisa with Maddy beside her, Louie said, "But Ethan, my granddaughter and daughter are in that house. If these characters are as bad as you say they are, I need to get them out of there."

He placed his hand on Louie's shoulder to assure him. "Trust me, if there is any sign that those two are in any danger, we'll get them out."

Reluctantly, Louie agreed to Ethan's orders and left the center with feelings of helplessness. He'd just given an officer of the court his word that he'd stay out of the way of the investigation. To Ethan, Louie insisted that nothing could happen to Maddy and Jessica. And, again, Ethan assured him everything was under control.

CHAPTER **TWENTY**

Louie gripped at the steering wheel as he drove back to the store. He had to keep his wits intact. Yet his mind was spinning out of control like a skidding car heading toward a Daytona 500 pileup. His frustrations toward the shiftless, no-account degenerates who were getting away with stealing from him had been surpassed by learning about Lisa's involvement. Little Maddy and Jessica could be in danger. He bit his lower lip so hard it bled.

While Louie was learning about hillbilly contraband cartels and being told he might have to spy on his ex, he'd received a voice mail message from Jonnie Bailey. Apparently, her client, Turks McGraw, wanted to meet with him. No reason for the meeting was given but he was fairly certain it wasn't to tell him he'd won the Mega Millions jackpot at Speedy's. First Lisa and now a mega-store competitor was closing in on him and he was supposed to act like the day was full of boat rides and hot dogs.

Before he dealt with McGraw, however, he called Log Heaven. Kiara answered with Betty Doris in the background butchering the song "Raindrops Keep Fallin' on My Head."

"Were your ears burning?" she asked.

"Mama found out about Mr. Contento?"

"That would be an affirmative," Kiara said.

"Alex told her?"

"That would be another affirmative," Kiara said.

"I guess that blows my status as best son a mama could have that she laid on me the other day." Kiara's laughing at his joke soothed his anxiety. "Did you take her phone away from her so she won't bother Sheriff Jones?"

"We can't find it anywhere," Kiara said, and quietly giggled. "She's convinced Mr. Contento is going to blow up Log Heaven. Right now, we're playing Name that Tune from a songbook Mr. Morris gave me."

Louie heard Betty Doris call out, "Is that my son? Let me talk to him."

"Here's your mom," Kiara said.

"Son, what were you thinking? Allowing that man to come into our home and terrorize us."

"Mama, he's not bothering anybody. Leave it alone."

"Leave it alone? You've lost your ever-loving mind if you think I'm staying here another minute. Maybe I'll go down there and tell him what I think of him."

"Mama, I think that's a bad idea," Louie tried. But years of living as Betty Doris's son had taught him that persuasion was pointless when she made up her mind about something or someone. "Look, I've got something important going on at work. I'll be home as soon as I can to straighten this out."

"What's to straighten out? Either he goes or I do!" She started crying.

Louie hated to hear his mama cry, even if it was only one of her fake cries she used to get her way. "I'll talk to him tonight. Why don't you and Kiara and Donnie go sit on the dock and have some ice cream. Put Kiara back on the phone."

She sniveled. "And you'll tell him to leave? Tonight?"

"We'll talk about it when I get home," he promised.

From the parking lot, he saw Lupita standing in front of her office, talking to a client. He waved and, to his surprise, she waved back. Confused by her behavior, he tried to recall what he'd said or done to make her go from wanting to help him with the Speedy's invasion, to throwing him a cold shoulder at his house, and, now, back to being a friendly neighbor. Since her abrupt departure from his house a few days earlier, she hadn't called or emailed or texted or visited the store to buy her funny cigarettes. Whatever had her riled, he didn't have time for her coy distancing at the moment. He waved again and went into the store.

Thinking about Lupita's exotic cigarettes gave Louie an idea. Because cigarette sales taxes in Virginia were lower than in other states, stealing them was a popular criminal pastime. Petty thieves and organized crime syndicates alike stole or purchased tobacco from Virginia stores and sold it in other states, making tidy profits. He'd read somewhere that cigarette cartels earned millions on every truckload of the smokes. But that happened in the big metropolitan areas, not Fallam County. Louie decided to dig around in Gas N Go's sales and inventory history to see if Kenny Wayne and Stoner were targeting his cigarette inventory. However, after an hour or two, he was completely lost. He thought he had the answer but the data weren't there to prove his theory. He needed Yippies's sales logs to compare against his purchases to prove his theory. Without knowing who the police had identified as suspects, he was hesitant to call his contact at Yippies. He sat back in his chair and said out loud, "Louie, you're going to have to trust the Basket-ville lady." He emailed her the file on his sales and inventory history with a note suggesting that she compare them to Yippies's sales reports. As soon as the email was sent, his flip phone pinged.

A text from Talia Baskerville read: Thx ☺ Will be in touch ☺

"I guess this means she's on it," he mumbled. This new world moved too fast for Louie. Maybe it was time to hang it all up and start working on his retirement plan.

Returning Jonnie Bailey's call, he waited on hold for what felt like forever. Lawyers perplexed Louie. They were constantly reminding everybody about their precious time and their hourly rates but never hesitated to trample over other people's time. He was about to hang up when she came on the line and said her name in that tight, efficient manner of hers.

"You called me?" he asked her.

"Ah, as I explained in my phone message, Turks McGraw has hired me as counsel in his business endeavors as they relate to Fallam County. He's interested in sitting down with you to discuss a proposition," she said. "He's available tomorrow morning at 10:15 for a videoconference." She said in that talking up way people did nowadays. He didn't know if she was asking a question or stating a fact.

He asked, "A proposition for what?"

"I can't tell you," she said. "He prefers to talk with you himself?"

Getting information from a lawyer was like getting caught in one of those automated answering services everybody was so fond of using. How about press "0" for a straight answer? Louie was about finished with this day. The further he got into it, the less it made any sense. After agreeing to meet with McGraw the next day, Louie decided it was time to go home and take a nap. But, he was reminded of what was waiting for him at home when he saw an email from Kiara. She'd sent a photo of Betty Doris with her back against the kitchen hutch, a strained look on her face.

Driving home, Louie passed Lisa going in the opposite direction, in a direction away from her house. He waved but she appeared to be looking at something on her phone. In spite of Ethan's warnings to stay away from Lisa, Louie took a sharp left and headed for her house. Ethan didn't say anything about him talking to Jessica.

He found Jessica taking an afternoon break from her work-at-home job. To his disappointment, Maddy was down for a nap.

"You know, Dad," Jessica said, "you were right. I can work just about anywhere I want. It's been amazing being back in Fallam County. Although, Maddy gets a little restless while Mom's out all day and I'm in online meetings."

Lisa had lost her part-time job at Girl Curls because of the business closings and he saw very little of her at the store. Only she and God knew where she spent her time these days.

"Sweetheart, anytime you need a break, Maddy can come hang out with me," Louie offered. However, judging by how Jessica reacted to Log Heaven's new residents, she was not likely to allow her baby to spend any time there.

"I can't. I can't do that. I couldn't imagine what I'd do if she died from this horrible disease. It would be my fault."

Louie said, "I understand, you want to protect your baby.

But you know I would never put Maddy in a situation where she could be hurt. You've got to know that." The frozen video of Lisa and Maddy standing in the doorway and Lisa talking to a criminal compelled him even more. He needed to get his granddaughter out of a potentially dangerous situation. "Heck, Log Heaven is cleaner than any place on the planet. Your Gran Betty sees to that."

"But all of you guys, you and Alex and those two scary men you have living in our basement, you all come in contact with God knows who every day." Her eyes teared up as she pushed away her snack.

Louie ignored the character assassination of Sal and his grandfather and focused on getting Jumpin' Bean out of Lisa's house. "If you spent any time with me and Alex and the others at Gas N Go, you'd know the COVID ain't got a chance." He reached into his jeans and pulled out a pocket-sized Gas N Go hand sanitizer bottle and quietly placed it on the table. "We're handing these out to everybody." Trying to make her laugh, he added, "I wanted to print 'COVID whop-ass' on the bottle but I could hear your Gran Betty saying, 'It's not polite to cuss.'"

She gave up a tiny lopsided grin, the one she got from her mama.

"Maddy is as safe at Log Heaven as she is here. Your mama works at the same place as Alex and me." Here was his chance to find out what Lisa was up to with the Baldwin fella. "I suppose she's still running around with that dude Larry. With his job selling cars, he comes into as much contact with the public as we do."

"It's not the same," Jessica objected.

"How so?"

"It's just not."

Her lame answer prompted him to keep going. "Honey, has your mom said anything to you about what she's been up to with Larry?"

"No, why?"

"I came over one day and she was smoking weed with him and I'm just wondering if they're doing drugs around Maddy. You know how I feel about that."

"I know, Dad. You don't care if we smoke or drink, just don't do it around our kids."

"That's right. And if your mama is smoking in front of Maddy, or worse, dealing it, and you allow it, they could take Maddy away from you."

"Are you saying you'd call the police on Mom?

"You know I'd never do a thing like that. But somebody could. Alex seems really worried about y'all's mom. He says she smokes all the time."

Jessica's eyebrows shot up "Really, Dad? Alex worries about food contamination if an ant crawls across the table while he's eating. You know how he exaggerates everything."

Fearing he'd say something to mess up Ethan's investigation, Louie waited for Jessica to continue.

"What's going on? Is Mom in trouble?"

"Why do you ask that?"

"You're acting all weird about her."

Taking a cue from Jonnie Bailey, speaking and saying nothing, he said, "You have to admit, she has been acting strange lately."

Jessica got up and poured herself a glass of tea. Sitting back in her chair, she said, "She made me promise not to tell anyone.

Especially you." She hesitated then went on, "But she said that Larry is into some shady stuff."

"What kind of shady stuff?" Louie asked.

"She wouldn't tell me. You know how defensive she gets," Jessica said. "Dealing, maybe? But who doesn't sell a little weed these days?" She ran her hand through her uncombed hair and tugged at her T-shirt. "He came by here with this other guy and they talked to Mom."

Anger and fear nipped at Louie. If anything happened to his family, he'd have to think about what he'd do to Larry Baldwin. "What did they want?"

"She wouldn't say. They didn't come in the house. Which I thought was odd because the first thing Larry does whenever he comes by is raid the kitchen and eat all Mom's junk food. She seemed pretty shaken up after they left."

He decided he couldn't tell Jessica about the police investigation and their suspicions about Lisa's involvement. If what Jessica was saying was true, Lisa might not be part of the scheme. He cupped his daughter's hands in his and said, "If they show up here again and you feel unsafe about being here, I want you and Maddy to get in your car and come to Log Heaven. You promise?"

She nodded and, with that nod, Louie sensed Jessica suspected something wasn't right.

CHAPTER **TWENTY-ONE**

After getting a promise out of Jessica to come to Alex's birthday party on Saturday, Louie left Mt Pleasant to make his county store rounds. Later, on his drive home, his mind worried over how he couldn't tell his daughter that her mama might be on her way to prison for aiding, or worse, participating, in unwarranted crimes. The old wounds of Lisa's abandonment were finally healing but her latest basket of drama was about to break his heart all over again. If she was arrested and convicted, his kids would lose their mother.

A determined Betty Doris stood on the front porch, Kiara at her side.

"Well?" Betty Doris asked, placing her hands on her hips. "Are you going down there and tell that man he has to leave?"

Any effort or plea concerning his need to take a minute to unwind from his stressful day, Louie surmised, was fruitless. He asked Kiara to join him but turned to his mama and said, "You've done enough. I'll handle it from here." He and Kiara walked around the house and knocked on the glass of the sliding door.

From inside, Sal pulled at the door and greeted them. "Are we to have family dinner tonight? I'm roasting a leg of lamb."

"We need to talk," Louie said. He signaled to Sal to sit at the patio table.

"What is it?" Sal asked with his ever anxious expression. "Is it the newspaper? I'm sorry. I keep forgetting to call to have one delivered for Baba."

"Relax," Louie said. He could hear Betty Doris overhead, scrambling for a position to eavesdrop from the deck above them. "Sal, when we drew up a vendor contract, you gave me everything I needed to get us started. Your ID and everything." Louie winced. He felt uncomfortable with what he was about to ask this man, someone he now considered a friend. But the alternative to not having this conversation was having a different one with Betty Doris and, quite possibly, with whatever federal agency developed an interest in his ex-wife's revengeful snitching.

"I understand. It's no problem, Mr. Louie. I get asked all the time. I become a naturalized citizen on my twentieth birthday. And I vote in every election."

"And your baba?" Louie asked.

Sal was silent as he rubbed at a signet ring on his middle finger. Finally, he said, "We took the test together and waited." He smiled broadly as he said, "We received invitation for swearing in ceremony. It was on the Fourth of July at Brooklyn Courthouse. I was so happy." He looked down at his ring and continued, "It was a glorious day." He wiped at the corner of his eye. "Baba refused to go. He refused to pledge allegiance to United States of America. Later, when I came home from celebrating my new citizenship with others, he told me his allegiance was to his family and the one true faith." Sal swiped at another tear.

They heard Betty Doris from above say, "Stubborn old fool."

Kiara asked, "Doesn't he realize he's making things harder on himself and on you?"

"I think he refuses to swear allegiance to America because, to him, he sees it as an abandonment of his own country, his old life. In his mind, he will return to Iran someday. And things will be as they were."

"You can never go home again," Kiara said.

Louie chimed in with, "And, he can't go through life hiding in other people's basements, either."

"When I tell him America is about freedom to do and say whatever you want, he berates me by telling me individual freedom is a rationalized feeling which has no basis in truth."

"Wow," Kiara said. "That's a heavy conviction."

"He's a man with strict principles who believes Americans are soft and spend too much time looking at themselves in their telephones."

"Can't argue with that," Louie said.

"He's reluctant to be around Americans, especially American women. This is why he never comes to our dinners."

Kiara offered, "We'll set up a separate table for the men, if that's what's worrying him. And, he can tell us his story."

"Don't count on him coming," Sal said.

"Until I can see some ID, I'll have to be honest with anyone who asks me," Louie said. "I don't lie for nobody. Especially about something as serious as this."

Sal nodded slightly.

"Tell him if he wants to stay here, he's got to explain why he hasn't finished what he started. The pledge, I mean."

“He’s a proud man, Mr. Louie. I think he will leave here before doing what you ask.”

Looking at the decked ceiling above, Louie said, loud enough for Betty Doris to hear, “Either way, our problem will be solved.” Facing Sal, he added, “It’s his choice. He can stay and explain how we can help him or he can leave. Tonight.”

“Please don’t ask us to leave,” Sal pleaded. “I’ve tried to find a home for us in Fallam County but no one will rent to us. Because Baba is Muslim.”

They all heard Betty Doris call down, “They can’t do that. That’s discrimination.”

The irony of Betty Doris calling foul on Sal’s potential landlords while she was in the process of evicting him wasn’t lost on anyone, except maybe Betty Doris.

In frustration, Louie said loudly, “Mama, didn’t I tell you that you’ve done enough. I said I’d handle this.” To Sal, he said, “She means well. Ask Mr. Contento to join us for dinner tonight and we’ll get this figured out for the two of you.”

Later, Betty Doris set up the portable craft table from Lisa’s scrapbooking days at the opposite end of the long deck and set a place for Kiara and herself. Sal appeared with his roasted lamb and placed it in front of Louie. He was alone. Betty Doris threw her lightning bolt stare at Louie and Sal.

They found Mr. Contento sitting in lotus pose in the center of the reclining sofa, his closed eyes revealing tiny skin tags on his darkened lids.

“What is it?” he asked, his eyes still closed

A combination of layered odors, Alex’s old sweaty socks and scorched curry, hung in the air. Louie cleared his throat to hold back a cough.

"Baba, Mr. Louie has come to ask you to join him for the evening's meal."

Mr. Contento opened one eye.

"Mr. Contento, it would be an honor to have you eat with me and Sal and Donnie Tyler and my son Alex." He made a point to keep Betty Doris and Kiara's names out of it. "I've found that sharing a meal has helped us all cope with the uncertainty we are all going through. Why don't you join us."

Mr. Contento closed his eyes as if to dismiss his landlord.

Louie licked his dry lips before going forward with his ultimatum, "I know Sal has shared with you our concerns about your situation. And, I have no doubt he's also shared with you, many times, our invitation for you to join us for supper so we can all get to know one another better."

Mr. Contento barked at Sal. "You fool." Waving his hands in the air, he mimicked his host, saying, "Sharing, sharing! What is all this sharing? Why must I be compelled to tell you everything about myself? It's none of your concern. We work for you. You repay us with a place to live."

"Baba, they want to help."

Louie interrupted Sal. He'd had enough. "Listen here, Mr. Contento, or whatever your real name is, this is my house. And in my house, I have every right to expect common courtesy from a man who's taking advantage of my fairness. But you're not showing that courtesy." He pointed at the ceiling and went on, "Right now my mama's up there scared out of her mind that you mean to harm her and her family. All's I'm asking from you is to show a little respect to her and this family. And show her she's got nothing to worry about from Sal's baba, whatever the hell that is." Louie felt his blood pressure spiking.

A motionless Mr. Contento apparently had no response to Louie's rant.

"If this is how it's going to be, I need you to leave. Sal is welcome here but after supper, I expect him to take you away from this house." Louie left the room.

No one said anything as Louie sliced into the juicy lamb shank Sal had prepared. As he plated the meat, Sal returned with Mr. Contento at his side. Like his mama taught him, Louie stood to welcome his guest. They made room for Mr. Contento between Donnie and Sal.

As the meal progressed, the mild spices worked their magic. Louie felt everyone relaxing. Finished with his dinner, he pushed his plate away and said, "Sal, that was some mighty fine eatin'."

"My name is Rayan Omid Zadeh. In America, I'm known as Ray Contento."

From behind his napkin, Alex said, "He speaks."

Louie jabbed at Alex.

"My life began and ended in Iran. Our capital." He lifted an eyebrow at Alex and asked, "Which is?"

"Ah, Bagdad? No, no, Tehran."

The deck fell silent as everyone waited for Mr. Contento's story.

"I worked as energy engineer for the Shah. When he abandoned us in 1979, I lost my position. I was thirty-nine and married to my beautiful wild rose, my Nasrin. Forty years are between me and her death yet I still mourn."

A pitying sigh floated over from the craft table, "Aww."

"The details of my departure from my homeland are not important. I wandered north and found myself in what is now the small country of Montenegro." Tilting his chin upward, he asked Alex, "Which is where, young man?"

"That's an easy one. One of the Balkan states on the Adriatic Sea right across from the heel of the Italian boot."

"Impressive. Americans are just like Iranians. You keep your most gifted children under a bush, hiding their light."

"Where was I? Oh, in the capital city, I found work but kept to myself. I lived alone up in the hills. One night while traveling home, a young woman appeared in the middle of the road, covered in blood, and flagging me to stop my car.

"I have to say, it was the early nineties and not a proud time for the Balkan states. The U.N. had imposed embargoes for their torturing of refugees, calling it ethnic cleansing. Being right on the Adriatic, Montenegro became the trading center for all the wartime smugglers. Italians from across the sea quickly took over the black markets."

"I remember listening to NPR every night when that was happening," Donnie offered. He shook his head as he said, "Them was some dark times in that part of the world."

"I couldn't keep all the players straight," Louie added. "Bosnians, Croatians, Serbians, Christians, Moose-lums. Glad we didn't send our boys into that mess."

"Dad, that's somebody else's business you're always talking about," Alex joked.

"Will you boys pipe down and let the man tell his story," Betty Doris called from the crafting table.

"Actually, your government did make it their business, Alex," Mr. Contento offered. "If not for the Dayton Peace Accords brokered by your secretary of state, many more civilians would have perished because of their beliefs." He sat quietly, tenting his fingers in his lap.

"And the woman with all the blood?" Betty Doris nudged. She'd found herself a seat at the men's table.

"If you haven't guessed already, the woman was Sal's mother, Maria. When I offered to take her to a doctor, she refused and begged me to hide her. And I did, in my one-room stone house with no running water. The next day while in the city, I learned that smugglers had killed a militiaman. That night I asked my uninvited guest about it as I tended her wounds. She cried until dawn, then I never saw her cry again. That night, she told me the entire story. The woman and her husband were caught bringing in tobacco and liquors. Their captors forced her to watch as they tortured her husband to death. They tried to do the same to her but she managed to kill one of them and fled. 'No one expected a woman to fight back,' she told me. The next morning she threatened to turn me in if I didn't drive her to Bar, a coastal town about fifty kilometers away." He asked Alex, "Which is how far in your American miles?"

"Around thirty-one," Alex said.

"Brilliant child," Mr. Contento said. "Tell me, Mr. Louie. Why is this boy's mind wasted spending days placing things on store shelves?"

"I've asked myself that question a thousand times," Louie said.

"We've counseled Alex enough for an entire lifetime. He's got to make up his own mind about what he wants. Now, did you take her to the shore?" Betty Doris asked.

"With trepidation, I did," he said. "And, fearing the militia would discover my complicity in helping her, I followed her to Italy and stayed. The coffee was better." He faced Sal and said, "As I've said to you before, I wish I could say your father died honorably, smuggling medicine and other humanitarian aid, for instance. But it wasn't so. Your parents, they were opportunists looking for their fortunes. From that night on and for the last twenty-eight years, I posed as that woman's father-in-law. I'm sorry I lied to you, Salvatore."

"I knew you loved me when you insist I call you *baba*," Sal said. "Besides, how can I miss a father I never knew? I was a baby when he died. You are my baba, *mio nonno*."

The others looked on, in their front-row seats, witnessing a powerful forgiveness and reconciliation between the two men.

Sal continued, "You are my teacher, baba. My hope is you will remain so. You are the one person who cares for me." The two men stood and embraced.

"Not anymore," Betty Doris said, "We *all* care about you, Sal." She wiped at her runny mascara. "Who's next? Does anybody have a funny story?"

But the mood for storytelling had passed.

Louie's phone buzzed in his pocket. Seeing Ethan's number, he excused himself and took his call in the kitchen, hoping tomorrow would be the day police busted Kenny Wayne Young.

CHAPTER TWENTY-TWO

Louie was pouring kibble into a bowl for his three-legged cat, Possum, as Kiara came out on the deck with her morning coffee. He said to her, "Sometimes when I see Possum, I think about the three-legged dog who walked into a bar."

"What's the three-legged dog's story?" Kiara asked.

"A three-legged dog walks into a bar and says, 'I'm looking for the man who shot my paw.'" He grinned at Kiara.

She stuck her tongue out at him.

"I got an extra-long day today." He wasn't about to go into all the details about Operation Rattlesnake, the sheriff's name for the sting they had planned for Kenny Wayne Young and his bosses. The night before over the phone, Ethan told Louie something was going down today but wouldn't give him any logistical details. "Can you manage things here? Make sure we don't have another international incident?"

"No problem," she said. "I'm glad you were able to resolve things. You're good at that conflict resolution stuff. Uncle D and Mr. Contento are acting like two long lost brothers. They plan to go fishing on the dock today."

"Ain't that something," Louie said. "Who would imagine a man from Virginia and one from Iran finding so much in common to talk about?"

"I believe Betty Doris may be a little jealous of Mr. Contento giving all his attention to Uncle D," Kiara said. Imitating her uncle, she added, "Know what I'm sayin'?"

"That's my mama. Making it all about the Betty Doris Show."

"At her age, she's earned the right to get a little self-centered sass going on," Kiara said. "Is there anything I can help you with today?"

"You watching over Betty Doris leaves me fancy free to worry about everything else. I'm calling Iris Lee this morning to see if she knows of any houses for rent on Eastend Street for the Contentos."

"The way Uncle D and Betty Doris were fawning over Mr. Contento after he told his story last night, they might not want them to leave now. Did you hear the part about him and Maria posing as father-in-law and daughter when they immigrated to America?"

Louie reflected, that part of the storytelling must have taken place while Ethan was updating him on the state's investigation. With the help of the efficient Miss Basket-ville and Lupita's financial reports, Lisa's tampering with company business records, laundering Stoner's ill-gotten money, and dipping into Gas N Go's checking accounts was confirmed. He winced when Ethan told him that Lisa, at a minimum, would be arrested for embezzlement, but most probably would get caught up in the state's dragnet when they took down Stoner for racketeering. Suggestions of a charge of impeding a police investigation convinced Louie not to tip Lisa off with news of her imminent arrest.

"No, I didn't hear that part," he said to Kiara.

"And when Maria's brother did that thing to his wife with his boning knife," she shivered, "and Maria and the other brother abandoned Sal. In New York. With no money, no nothing. She's bad news, that Maria Contento. I say 'good riddance.'"

"I think it's high time Sal and his baba have a place to call their own," Louie said. "They were only supposed to be here for a week or so. And, as soon as this pandemic mess is over, Betty Doris is going back to Elder Home, where *she* belongs. Me and Possum are going to have us some peace and quiet." He reached down and scratched the feral cat's head. "Ain't that right, Possum?"

"Oh, so we're all cramping Possum's style?" she joked.

"No! I didn't mean it like that," Louie said. "Think you'll be sticking around after things get back to normal?"

She said, "I'm kind of liking the vibe of this place. Most of my mom's family is here in the county. And Uncle D's not going to be around forever. I'd like to spend some more time with him." Changing the subject, she asked, "What can I do to help with Alex's party on Saturday?"

AT THE TOWN STORE, a quick knock was followed by Chunky sticking his head inside. "Boss, there's somebody out here who wants to talk to you."

Abruptly, Turks McGraw brushed by Chunky and removed his oversized straw cattleman's hat. "Partner, you're a tough man to track down. Thought I'd try your store before I left town." He extended his hand.

As he stood, Louie asked Chunky, who was acting every bit like he planned to stay for the conversation, "You got a customer to tend to?"

McGraw dropped his un-shook hand to his side and waited for the offer of a chair as they watched Chunky leave.

Louie waited for the man to speak, something he'd learned from Mr. Henry when negotiating with an adversary: He who spoke first, lost. He waited silently for the man to say why he felt he had the right to barge into another man's office. This man was full of self-importance, which probably explained why he had hundreds of stores and Louie had four. Louie figured he had something this guy wanted. Until he figured out what it was, he wasn't saying anything.

As if he was reading Louie's mind, Turks asked, "You don't talk much do you? My wife, my ex-wife, my *third* ex-wife, says I talk too much. Maybe it's because I got a lot to say. Anyway, I'll cut through all the usual cordialities. Mr. Pyle, I want to buy you out. Your stores, the properties, all of it."

Practicing his tough guy squint, Louie asked, "Did you see a 'for sale' sign when you come in?"

"No, but I'd like to offer you a fair price." McGraw rubbed at his chin as if in thoughtful deliberation. "See, if you don't agree to sell to me, it's out of my control. My people launch what they call an annihilation plan. They're like an army of ants. In a matter of a few months, they buy property right next to yours, build a store all shiny and new with cheaper prices, hire away your best employees. All your customers will drive right by Gas N Go to get to their favorite Speedy's. And all you end up with are four rundown buildings full of trash and rats."

McGraw had just described Louie's greatest fear but he

stayed strong, not saying a word.

"How old are you, Louie? You've worked hard all your life. Time to relax, kick back in that lake house of yours. Go fishing. Play with all those grandkids you got."

"My family is none of your business," Louie said.

"Louie, we can do this the easy way," he pulled from his shirt pocket a business card and a pen and wrote on the card then tossed it on Louie's desk. "You can accept my offer. There it is. Or, you can be stubborn and lose a chance at real happiness." Lifting his stubby hands, he mimicked a pair of scales. "What's it going to be? Sleepless nights and heartache or whiling away easy times with those grandkids."

Louie said in a calm manner like his favorite bad-ass movie character, "Gas N Go is not for sale." *Punk.*

"Suit yourself," McGraw said. Pointing at the card he'd tossed on the desk, he added, "Let's think about it overnight before we give a final answer. What do you say?"

"I say the answer will be the same."

"I'll call you tomorrow." He left Louie's office. In spite of the self-service coffee station, Louie heard McGraw order Chunky to make him a coffee, cream and two sugars.

How dare that short-legged pea shooter, with his dyed black mustache drooping over his lips, assume he knew what Louie Pyle wanted. Without looking at what McGraw had written on the card, he tore it in half and tossed it on the floor. He turned on his oscillating desk fan to cool his brow.

"At least look at the offer."

"I don't have time for your nonsense. If I wanted your two cents, I would have asked for it," Louie said. He felt Mr. Henry behind him.

"You're right, you don't have much time. And, I agree with you, the man's repulsive. But that doesn't make him wrong. Life isn't all about cash receipts and making payroll. You need to learn some new tricks. To learn how to enjoy what's been given to you. Go ahead, at least look at what he's offering."

Louie picked up the two pieces of the card and placed them on the desk. On the front was a grinning Turks McGraw looking like a troll doll and his goofy Speedy's logo. On the back was a hand-written number. It had more zeros than he'd expected.

To Mr. Henry, Louie said, "He's blowing smoke, throwing in a high-ball number to get me thinking about it."

"It's an attractive offer," Mr. Henry said. "But I agree with you. I'd call Ms. Bailey to get a real number. Too bad Mr. McGraw has hired the only competent lawyer in Mt Pleasant."

"I guess that's why they call him Speedy," Louie joked.

"You'll need a lawyer. Ask Iris. She's got a few on retainer."

"Anything you need me to tell her?" Louie asked as he turned in his chair.

Too late. Mr. Henry had faded into the shelf of Gas N Go operation manuals.

As Louie searched for Iris Lee's number on his phone, he recalled that he needed to talk to her about finding Sal a house to rent.

"Mr. Louie?" a crisp voice asked.

Louie heard noisy city traffic in the background but it wasn't his place to ask the woman about her business. Instead, he asked, "Miss Lee. I'm calling to ask if you have a house for rent. You got anything over on Eastend Street?" Years earlier, Vinnie Quinn, Ethan and Lupita's son, and Iris Lee had renovated several rundown houses her father owned, creating starter homes for low-income homebuyers.

"Not really. We finished up the Eastend project years ago. Vinnie might know of something. He and Ludie are building a house on Ethan's farm. Maybe he's got his Eastend bungalow up for sale or rent. Call Quinn Building Services, I'm sure they'll know of something."

"That's a good lead, thank you," Louie said. "By the way, about your lot on Main Street? Are you going to sell it to McGraw?"

"I haven't decided. I don't think he's serious about the lot because he offered a really low price."

"Don't share this with nobody, but he just breezed into my office offering me a mega lottery-winning amount of money for my stores. From your dealings with him, do you suppose he's one to renege on an offer?"

"I couldn't say. I've never worked with him," she said. "You thinking about selling?"

"Maybe." He laughed and repeated Mr. Henry's assessment, "But first I've got to find a lawyer, and, as you know, he beat me to the only competent one in Mt Pleasant. Can you recommend one?"

She laughed, then said, "That sounds like something Mr. Henry would say. There are plenty of others in Mt Pleasant. Let me get back to you."

Chunky knocked at the door again. "Boss, Alex called me on my cell. Says he needs you to call him right away."

Louie rang off with Miss Lee and called Alex from his cell phone.

"Dad, Dad, Dad," Alex said in his nervous voice. "The police were here. They took the Yippies driver away in handcuffs and that creep Kenny Wayne."

"Let me speak to Thor," Louie said.

"They made him go with them," Alex said. "Is Thor in trouble, Dad?"

"I don't think so. He's probably just helping the police out."

"What's going on?"

Chunky poked his head into his boss's office for a third time that morning. "Call on the store phone for you. Jonnie Bailey. She says the ten o'clock call with you and her client is canceled."

"Tell her I'll call her back." To Alex, Louie said, "Son, don't go nowhere. Keep the store open. I'll let you know what's going on as soon as I find out myself." Before he could slide his phone into his pocket, it rang. Lisa was calling. "Leese?"

"I'm being arrested for spending my own flippin' money. They said I *stole* from Gas N Go. You need to fix this." She was crying. "You need to get over here and tell them I'd never do what they're accusing me of." The call disconnected.

Louie's day just caught on fire.

CHAPTER **TWENTY-THREE**

Louie took his time getting to the jail, which was in the basement of Mt Pleasant's public safety building. On the radio, a talk show host warned of gloom and doom. He noticed for some reason that whenever he played the radio, Mr. Henry didn't care to join him.

However, the old man's visits were getting more frequent and longer each time. Mr. Henry was usually waiting for him in the truck every morning like a faithful hound dog. The first time Louie saw him in the truck while it was parked outside the store, he worried that others might have seen him, too. If asked, Mt Pleasant folks proclaimed they believed in God *and* in science. For many these beliefs extended to horoscope predictions, extra-terrestrials, and time travelers. Seeing a likeness of the man, the one reported dead and buried who had lent them money which they never repaid, sitting in Louie's truck could scare off Gas N Go's customers, he feared. Louie eventually reasoned that he was the only one who could see and hear Mr. Henry. At least until the other night, when Donnie Tyler saw his lifelong friend. Donnie never brought it up again with Louis. He hoped Donnie had forgotten it or chalked it up to a bad dream.

Now, the radio shock jock was wandering too far afield so he changed the station to his favorite country music channel. A tenor voice yodeled through the speakers.

"Oo, oo, oo. My dog's gone and left me
for the arms of my ex-wife,
Now I can live my real truth, live my best life.
Oo, oo, oo. Randi, that's my name, I spell it with an 'I,'
But I'm still the same guy, still the same guy."

Louie chuckled as he switched off the radio.

"You call that music? Sounds like a dog caught in a rabbit snare," Mr. Henry complained.

"It's ah'ite," Louie responded. Feeling as if he'd lost all control of the day, he decided he didn't care if the entire town saw him talking to himself while riding around in his truck with the ghost of one of Mt Pleasant's past patrons. "I been meaning to ask. The other night, did you appear to Donnie on purpose?"

"It's been nice seeing him. He was always the sensitive one among us. He was more like his sister Vee than he cared to admit." Straightening his tie, he went on, "One must have an open mind to let the idea of me appear."

"Just like one has to have an open mind to accept a guy named Randi who spells his name with an 'I.'" Louie said.

"Where are we going now?"

"You know where," Louie said as he waited for a small crowd of young people, holding up signs and screaming "No justice, no peace," to get out of the way so he could enter the police station's parking lot. "Lisa's been arrested and I need to help her."

One of the protesters threw a plastic water bottle at Louie's truck.

"What are those young people so upset about?" Mr. Henry asked.

"You know the answer to that, too," Louie said. "They're miffed because their summer's been canceled by the pandemic."

"I suppose I'd be angry about that, too," Mr. Henry said. Watching Louie get out of the vehicle, he added, "You know they are not going to let you see her. Talking to her won't do any good, anyway."

"I want to look her in the eyeballs and ask if she knew what these crooks were up to."

"You mean was she complicit in the illegal acts?" Mr. Henry asked.

"Something like that," Louie mumbled.

"Time to turn it around on you. You know the answer to that, son."

Louie ordered, "Why don't you make yourself useful and spook those kids if they try any funny business with my truck." He slammed the door and went looking for Ethan.

He found Mt Pleasant's police chief grabbing a vending machine lunch in the station's break room and talking to Lupita Quinn.

"Ethan, tell me what's goin' on," Louie pleaded. "Hey, Lupita."

Lupita nodded hello.

Ethan appeared reluctant to share what he knew about the arrests. "We're still gathering evidence. But I will say that with the help of Lupita here and the Yippies's people, we have evidence of Lisa making deposits and transferring money to bank accounts not associated with Gas N Go. That's all I can say."

Lupita smiled as she readjusted her heavy purse on her shoulder.

A panicked Louie asked Ethan, "How do I get Lisa out of this?"

With that question, Lupita's smile froze. "Ethan, do you need me for anything else?"

Ethan shook his head no and she left. Then he motioned for Louie to follow him outside. Brushing at cracker crumbs on his shirt, he planted his hand on Louie's shoulder. Amid the noise of the chanting teenagers, Ethan explained, "We've got evidence to indict Kenny Wayne Young, the ring leader Stoner, the driver of the Yippies van, and Lisa and Larry Baldwin on a cigarette trafficking ring. When Christmas comes around, you owe Lupita an extra-large bonus. She proved you were not part of the operation. She saved your bacon, amigo."

"Wait a doggone minute. You guys thought I was involved? In stealing from myself?"

"Businesses commit fraud for the insurance every day. We had to be sure you weren't in on it. When you came into the station the other day to tell us about your suspicions, we had to rule you out. And, as you know, we stumbled on the other operation and your story fit with what the other agencies were discovering."

"You didn't believe me?" Louie asked. "That hurts, Ethan. That hurts deep."

"I believed you. But I had to prove to a whole lot of others that you weren't in on this scam. I'm sorry but that's just how the system works. I hope we can still be friends."

"I'm going to have to think on that one," Louie said. "Can I at least get Lisa out? You know she didn't willingly have anything to do with those thugs."

"They have proof to the contrary, I'm afraid."

"At least, can I drop the charges against her stealing from me?"

"You know it doesn't work that way. These are criminal charges and she'll be lucky if she doesn't do serious time at the Goochland Correctional Center down in Richmond."

"Good Lord, almighty," Louie swore. "Can I see her? Can I talk to her?"

"I'd advise against it. Anything she tells you, you'll most likely be asked to repeat in court." He removed his hat and scratched behind his ear. "If you really want to help somebody who just stole thousands and thousands of dollars from you, you could hire them a lawyer. But I'd advise against that, too. It could throw suspicion on you, again. And your insurance company might not like it when you put in your claims for losses."

The desk officer called from the doorway, "Chief, mayor's on the phone."

To Louie, Ethan said, "I got to get back to this mess. I'll keep you informed."

Sitting in his truck, alone for a change, Louie decided on the path he had to take. He was done trying to save Lisa from herself. If he continued to interfere on her behalf, he'd be dragged down with her. He had to walk away from his crazy ex, once and for all. The time had come for him to think about himself.

He watched as a sheriff's deputy shouted through a bullhorn for the small crowd to disperse or face getting arrested for being a nuisance to him and their parents. Jessica's orange compact ran the protestors' gauntlet. Her car window opened as she pulled up beside him.

"What the hell, Dad?" she asked.

He waited for a better, more informative, question.

"Why did the police arrest Mom?" she called out.

"Get in the truck and we'll call Alex and I'll explain," he said. "Where's Maddy?"

"She's with the Andersons," Jessica said. The Andersons were Lisa's retired neighbors. As Jessica climbed up into the cab of the truck, she said, "I was on a work call and these jerks burst into the house and arrested Mom. They scared Maddy and made her cry. I'm complaining to the mayor." Jessica's face was red from annoyance and panic. Dressed in a T-shirt, gym shorts and flip flops, she scratched at a tattoo of her alma mater above her ankle.

"Did the police say why they were taking your mom?"

"No. Do you know why?" Jessica asked. "Does this have anything to do with the conversation we had the other day? About us coming to Log Heaven?" She punched him on the shoulder. "Why didn't you say something? We could have warned Mom."

"I couldn't tell you because I'd be accused of impeding police investigations. I could go to jail for that."

"So, you just let these swine trample all over her? One of those assholes felt her up while they were putting handcuffs on her. Handcuffs! My God, what's wrong with this country? Fuckers treating a defenseless woman like she's chattel."

"Jessica, your mom and I didn't raise you to talk like that."

"I can't believe you. You're admonishing me for bad language while the mother of your children was hauled into jail like a common criminal?"

"Lisa has got herself mixed up with a gang of felons. There's evidence she took money from the stores. A lot of money," Louie said.

Jessica's face expanded. "You're abandoning my mother because of money? Because of that stupid store?"

Louie grabbed at her wrists as she tried to pound on his arm and shoulder. "Listen to me. I *can't* help her even if I wanted to. Your mother broke the law and she's got to face up to her actions."

Crying, Jessica jerked free of Louie's hold.

"I'm sorry as I can be about this but it's been a long time coming. Lisa Woods Pyle's been acting wonky ever since she left Log Heaven. Maybe you didn't see it because you moved away, or maybe you just didn't want to see it."

"We've got to help her. She's my mama," Jessica said. Her face scrunched up like her daughter's when Maddy didn't want to take her nap. Jessica planted her weeping face onto the side of his upper arm. "This sucks so much."

Louie reached with his other hand to pat his daughter's head, his fingers getting tangled in her messy bun. "Sweetheart, sometimes the truth is ugly. But, because it's ugly don't mean you don't face it. This is something Lisa's going to have to face on her own. She needs to stand up and account for what she did."

Wiping her eyes with the hem of her shirt, Jessica said, "I don't understand. Why did she do it? I mean it's not like she's homeless or anything."

"Who knows? Only she can say why she did what she did. I hope you understand why I can't go in there and demand they let her go."

"I guess so," Jessica said. She'd calmed down and was fidgeting with her hair. "You know, sometimes I'd get mad at her for being mean to you. You're a good dad and I'm grateful you're mine."

Until this moment, no child of his had ever said those words, not even in a Father's Day card. Louie wanted to cry. Not having a lot of practice at weeping tears of happiness, he wasn't sure what to do. He pressed his hand against his shirt pocket but refrained from grabbing his notepad. He held back from telling her that he loved her to the moon and back, as Leese used to say, for fear of blubbering all over her. Instead, he pointed at her phone and said, "Let's give Alex and Ken a jingle to let them know what's going on."

CHAPTER **TWENTY-FOUR**

Sitting in his truck with Jessica, Louie watched as she connected her brothers on her phone. Then he did the hardest thing he'd ever done in his life, harder than telling them that he and Leese were getting divorced. He explained to them what their mother was accused of doing.

"Dad, Dad?" Alex interrupted for the third time. "Is Mom going to have to sleep in the jail tonight? She can't sleep without her medicine."

"Alex, will you be quiet so Dad can finish?" Ken, the oldest, said.

"Your mom is going to need all three of you to keep her spirits up. She'll need your support. Like I explained, I can't be involved. Not anymore."

"But you just said she has to figure things out for herself," Ken said, highly irritated with his family's inconvenient phone call. "I mean, what am I supposed to do? Drop everything and drive over there? And do what, actually?"

"Ken, stop giving Dad a hard time. He's doing the best he

can," Jessica said.

And to Louie and Jessica's surprise, Alex said, "Why are you even on the call, Ken? You're not even part of the family anymore. You left."

"As usual, re-tard, you don't know what you're talking about," Ken said.

"Shut it down, boys. You two need to get along and help your sister figure out how you are going to help your mom."

"Do I need to come there, Jess?" Ken whined.

"Let me see what's going on. I'm at the jail now. I'll call you later," Jessica said. When she ended the call, she snarked, "Thanks, Dad, for putting me on the spot like that."

"I don't put anything on you that you can't handle. You're our responsible one. You got this." He reached for her hand and squeezed it and then looked away to swipe at his weepy eyes. As his daughter climbed down from the truck, Louie reminded her again to bring Maddy to Alex's birthday party on Saturday.

Before Louie left the safety center, Boyd, the Gas N Go West manager, called to say the police had raided the store. A second Yippies' driver was taken away along with Kenny Wayne's younger brother Arnold. Louie gave Boyd the same instructions he had given Alex earlier. "Don't close the store. Keep things moving along."

"Jasper, he claims he's traumatized. His word, not mine," Boyd said.

"Is he physically hurt?"

"Nope," Boyd said.

"Tell him to go home. Report the rest of his shift as sick time. You ah'ite?"

"Little shook up, is all," Boyd said. "Didn't expect to be in a police raid when I came in this morning."

"All in a day's fun," Louie said. Knowing Boyd favored those micro-brews the college kids liked to pay twice as much for as a regular beer, Louie said, "How about you take home a four-pack of that stump water you like so much. On the house."

Louie closed his eyes to reflect on what had happened in the last three hours. A man he barely knew had walked into his shop and offered him an insane amount of money for his stores. Two of them had been raided by the police to arrest thieves in the act. Lisa got arrested as a known associate. And people he thought were his friends suspected him of being involved, of robbing from his own company. He drew in a deep breath as if taking a hit on a cigarette. He'd stopped smoking when an oncologist found a small patch of nasty cells on the inside of his lip a few years back. "I sure could use one right about now," he said out loud as he started the truck. The smoking had helped with anxiety he'd experienced most of his life. After quitting, he'd learned to cope with everyday aggravations by closing his eyes and taking in deep breaths. A lady friend, whom he dated briefly right after he and Lisa divorced, called it meditative interpretation. Whatever it was called, the breathing exercises helped him cope with daily stress like belligerent customers and a crazy ex-wife.

Mr. Henry was back. "You don't need to start smoking again," he offered. "I personally can testify that smoking makes for a painful end." After he suffered a major stroke brought on by decades of smoking, Mr. Henry had hung onto the physical life for a few days, long enough for his wife, daughter, and niece Bert Swanson to say their goodbyes. "Where to now?" he asked.

"I have to get Alex's birthday present," Louie said. "Then go to the county meeting about the right-of-way for the East store's new loading area." Glancing over at his mentor, Louie asked, "Don't suppose you have any insight on how the supervisors will vote?"

"I expect I can figure it out. Let's see."

By the time they reached Stuff Mart's parking lot, Mr. Henry had laid out how the vote for the rezoning of the property beside Gas N Go East would go down. "They'll be persuaded to follow whatever that environmental fella wants. You know, the one who owns the solar panel company? Unless there's a bribe under the table or a horse trading quid pro quo deal in the works, you can be pretty sure the property will stay zoned for farm use. Or, not." He flashed an open-mouthed grin. Then he added, "There's a hundred percent certainty that you got a fifty-fifty chance of getting the rezoning passed."

"You're a useless puff of hot air," Louie said, surprised at himself for talking so uppity to his elder. He got out of the truck, heading for the store.

Trekking across the hot, sticky parking lot, Louie questioned whether he was doing the right thing regarding Alex's gift. He had wanted to give his youngest a hunting rifle when he turned twelve, the age most boys in Fallam County began hunting with their dads. But Lisa wasn't having any of it and she'd violently objected. Her fear of guns bled over into her child-rearing rules. No child of hers was ever going to touch a gun much less use one, she swore to her husband. Each time Louie went hunting with Ethan and his son Vinnie, he realized how much he'd missed out on special bonding times with his boys. He should have been more insistent.

To make up for lost time, Louie decided he'd give Alex his first hunting rifle on his twentieth birthday. Earlier, he'd cleared things with Iris to allow them to use her farm's firing range for gun safety lessons and target practice. Anxious about his gift choice, he hoped Alex would like it.

"It's about time you taught Alex some useful skills," Mr. Henry said, joining Louie.

As they strolled the store's tall aisles, teetering with inventory Louie felt could crash down on him at the slightest disruption, he encountered a handful of his own customers wondering about the goings-on at Gas N Go. News of the raids and Lisa's arrest had traveled quickly. Drawn to others' misfortunes, they wanted to know if anybody got hurt. They needed details so they could form their own opinions on how much jail time should be handed out. One fellow had already prosecuted the case, passed his own judgment, and slapped the verdict right down on Louie in aisle seven.

"I heard the feds shut you down for selling illegal whiskey out of the back of your stores. Pretty stupid gettin' caught, brother," another man said as he hooked his thumbs in the bib of his denim overalls.

"Not that it's any of your business, but that ain't what happened," Louie said. His idea of shopping for a gun at the Stuff Mart was turning into a bad one.

Mr. Henry blew a raspberry at the man. "Tank Turner, you got as much sense as a basket of hair." As Tank walked away, Mr. Henry said to Louie, "Don't waste your money in this godless place. Go over and see Iris. Tell her what you're up to. There's a blue steel Remington in my gun safe that would make the perfect first gun for Alex. Don't offer more than fifty bucks." He pointed at the ammunition showcase and added, "Pick up a couple boxes."

A notice on the front door of the county administration building informed Louie that all public meetings such as the zoning decision were canceled because of the state health mandates. He tugged on the locked doors for confirmation.

The display on his phone informed him that Betty Doris wanted to talk to him. He ignored it. But Mr. Henry reminded him that there was no need to cause his mama endless worry.

"Are you going to pester me the entire day?" Louie asked Mr. Henry as he opened his phone to answer Betty Doris's call.

"Am I going to do what?" Betty Doris asked. She didn't wait for his answer. "I got an earful from half of Elder Home calling me and asking if you've been arrested," she said.

"The police arrested some guys for stealing inventory off of one of the delivery trucks." Maybe this explanation would satisfy her curiosity. He didn't need his own mama spreading gossip all over the tri-county area. Let a judge and jury try the case.

"Alex said Lisa's been arrested. Son, what's really going on?"

"Don't worry, I'm fine, the store's fine, Alex is fine."

"When are you coming home? Kiara said you'd be late getting home tonight. What aren't you telling your mama, Louie?"

"Gotta go. By-sickle." He slapped the phone shut before hearing the next accusation.

Iris met Louie at her front door. She was on her way out but insisted on inviting her visitor into the airy foyer. "We don't see each other for years, then twice in just a few days," she said. After her father passed on, she had renovated the old Arts and Crafts-style home. The minute Louie stepped inside he felt like he'd entered one of those high-end fancy mansions on the home show channel Kiara and Betty Doris watched. The place felt as chilly as his walk-in beer coolers. He removed his ball cap and explained to her his plans to present his son Alex with his first hunting rifle at his birthday party on Saturday, only two days away. "While I was at the Stuff Mart buying some rounds, I got an idea." He added, hastily, "Don't hesitate to say 'no' because I'll understand completely." He pulled back, thinking what a stupid idea.

"What is it?" Iris asked.

"I … I thought you might be willing to sell me one of Mr. Henry's guns. I mean we were friends and we hunted a few times together. And …."

"Of course," she interrupted. "Dad kept a gun log. Let's take a look at it and see what might work for Alex."

"A gun log?" Louie asked. This elevated his view of the old man's eccentricities to an entirely new level. But who was he to criticize? He collected ball caps and displayed them on a wall in his bedroom.

"Follow me," she said and led him up a fancy staircase. Inside a small, stark room at the end of a skylighted hallway, she said, "This is Damian's room when he comes to visit me. My second cousin," she explained. "And my father's before that. Damian and I both agreed it needed to be kept the way Mr. Henry lived in it." She walked to the far wall of the room and tumbled through the combination lock on the gun safe.

Glancing around, Louie imagined the old man occupying the uncluttered room. It suited him, Louie thought. The old man had lived a simple life.

The essence of gun oil and powder erupted as the door to the safe swung open.

"Here we go," Iris said. She reached in for a yellowed composition notebook, the kind the kids used in school, and opened it up on a desk in a corner. She pulled the chain of a banker's lamp and said, "Let's see." The notebook had homemade tabs made with paper and clear tape. Each tab was labeled in neat cursive. "As you may know, Mr. Henry kept records of everything." She went to the tab labeled shotguns and rifles and pointed at the first page. "He kept track of every firearm he purchased, the purchase date, how much he paid for it, when he used it, cleaned it, the game he killed." Scrolling down the lines of the page, she noted, "When he sold it and to who."

"He was particular about details, that's for sure," Louie said. He told Iris about the time that Mr. Henry had loaned him money for land and new store. "My lawyer said he'd never seen so many contingencies and exceptions."

"Here's one," Iris said. "Remington Model 700 bolt-action." Her finger moved across the lined page. "Says here he got it from Waddy Woods to cancel a debt he owed. Doesn't say how much money. Looks like he used it for target practice but never hunted with it."

As Iris pulled the gun from the deep safe, Louie said, "Waddy Woods is my ex-wife's uncle. He most likely traded the gun for money to cover a gambling debt. Man bet on anything, didn't matter."

"Did he have any children?"

"None that I know of," Louie said, "Not claimed, anyway." Embarrassed, Louie averted his eyes from Iris. "I mean, he never married." He rushed to change the subject, "Mr. Henry and me talked about his guns and hunting when I visited him in the hospital there at the end."

Iris smiled at her guest. She hefted the rifle in her hands as if she was weighing her choices. But her thoughts seemed elsewhere as she said, "I wish Mr. Henry could have stayed awhile longer. You know, stayed long enough for me to have realized that I needed to ask forgiveness for all the judgmental and childish things I said to him. Enough time for us to reconcile." She handed the rifle to Louie and said, "I reckon Alex is a descendant of Mr. Woody. Let's give it to him."

"How much can I pay you for it?" Louie asked.

"I'm not sure how much Mr. Henry would have asked for it, but he's not here. Consider it a gift." She winked at him and then led him back down the stairs. At the front door, she said, "It hasn't been fired in a while. You might ask a gunsmith to look at it before Alex fires it. Let me know when you plan to go to the range and I'll join you."

"Thank you," Louie said. "And on that other thing, take it from me as a dad, you got nothing to ask forgiveness for. You being his daughter is all he ever wanted."

CHAPTER **TWENTY-FIVE**

Kiara filled Louie in on the day's events that evening. Uncle Donnie and Mr. Contento had spent the morning fishing from the dock while Betty Doris supervised. The day had worn out her uncle, so he'd decided to turn in early. Sal and Mr. Contento were still out looking at a house to rent. Betty Doris had retired to her bedroom to watch *Wheel of Fortune* and was asleep in Louie's bedroom easy chair. Alex texted her to say he was spending the night at Thor Bear's. Next, it was Louie's turn to share with her the news of the police bust and Lisa getting arrested.

"What a rotten day," she said. "Can I fix you something?"

"I'm good," he said. Actually, he was exhausted. Upon leaving Iris's house, Louie got a call from the manager of the East store saying a second-shift employee had been exposed to the coronavirus and wasn't coming to work. Louie drove over to cover until a new hire, Bart, showed up. He spent the next two hours notifying the entire staff of the exposure and instructed them to follow the procedures they had set up to get tested. Louie suspected the kid, a high school part-timer, didn't really have the virus, he just wanted the time off so he could go to the beach with his friends. Foot traffic was heavy for a weeknight so Louie stayed until closing time.

He was tired to his bones, yet, the minute his head hit the pillow, his mind revved into overdrive. Worrying about the stores and the thefts, about his employees getting sick, and about Lisa's arrest kept him from much-needed sleep.

Before today, he'd never seriously thought about selling the stores. He'd always assumed Alex or Ken would one day take over and he'd settle down at Log Heaven with a fishing pole. That was the plan, anyway. But, in his life experiences, plans never seemed to actually happen.

Someone was banging around in the kitchen. Downstairs Louie found Donnie standing at the sink, staring out the window into the moonless night, and clutching his picture of Mr. Henry and him as kids. He was sleepwalking again. Gently, Louie led a mumbling Donnie back to his bed.

"Hank! Where you been at?" Donnie called out.

Louie felt the familiar coolness at his back as he tried to help Donnie into the bed.

"Hank, tell about the time at Honey's when that punk tried to coldcock your brother after Ben told him to leave Vee alone." Donnie guffawed. Abruptly, his temperament changed as he shoved Louie away and said, "Get your hands off me, sucker." He sat on the bed on his own.

"He's hallucinating," Mr. Henry said.

"You being here ain't helping none," Louie whispered from the side of his mouth as he stepped away from Donnie.

"Hank, sit down here." Donnie patted the space beside him.

"I got a whole stack of questions I need to ask you. Like, why did you leave a baseball bat with dried up blood all over it under Bert's house?"

"Go to sleep," Louie said quietly. He turned to Mr. Henry and said, "You need to leave."

Louie left Donnie talking to the shadowed walls and made his way back to the loft. In his own bed, he punched at his pillow and tried to get comfortable on his back.

Mr. Henry appeared at the foot of Louie's bed. "I never told anyone, that I can recall, where I hid that bat, I don't know how Donnie found out," he said. "Since everyone is telling their stories. I'll remind you of one of mine, the one I told you on the day before I died. The one about my brother killing a young man."

"I don't remember you telling me this," Louie said. He propped up on his elbows.

"Yes, you do. Stop denying it. As you will recall, I told you I wasn't witness to the actual event, but I believe the man who told me about it. Reuben Young, the great-grandfather of the fellow messing with your stores, told me a story I couldn't deny because I knew what my brother was capable of. Ben was a flawed and tortured man. His jealous rages were boundless.

"My brother clubbed a college boy to death with the baseball bat of Reuben Young's son. The student had called Ben's mistress a whore. Ben and Gus Young followed in Gus's truck as the inebriated boy drove away from Honey's. The roads were frozen, slick as glass, and the car skidded down a steep embankment and into a tree. When they found him, he was still alive. Ben sent Gus for help. And while Ben waited for the police and ambulance, he took Gus's bat, which was on the truck's gun rack, down into the ravine and bashed the boy's skull in and tossed the bat into the thickets.

"Gus went back and found the bat because it had his name on it. He gave it to his paw because he didn't know what to do or who to tell. Scared him all the way to Kentucky to live with kinfolk."

"Seems like I remember you telling me that you helped Gus out with his school tuition so he could play ball at Tech," Louie said.

"The tuition bought Gus's silence in the matter," the old man said.

"Why didn't you take it to the police? Report the murder?" Louie asked.

"At the time, I reasoned that my brother had seen to it that the police and the hospital and the parents believed his version of the truth. That the boy died of head injuries from the car crash. Besides, I told myself, it wouldn't have done any good. By then, Ben had the judges in his pocket for bribes they had taken from him. Shortly after I confronted Ben about Reuben's story, he left. Moved out to California."

"Great day. All this time, I thought you was the mean one," Louie said.

"Not telling anyone about Young's confession is the one thing I regret doing. At the time, I thought I was protecting my family. I reasoned that reporting it years later would have forced the boy's family to relive his death and no good would have come from that.

"Eventually, retribution was made. When Ben died, I hired a private detective out in Los Angeles to find out what happened, how he had died. The sweet irony is that Ben Lee was bludgeoned to death with an L.A. Dodgers baseball bat."

Pulled in by the morbid story that he vaguely recalled Mr. Henry telling him years earlier, Louie wanted it to go on. He asked, "Do you believe in coincidences?"

"No," Mr. Henry said, "I do not."

"So why did you put the bat under Bert's house?" Louie asked.

"Insurance. After I told him what Reuben Young had revealed to me and that he'd shown me the evidence, Ben got angry with me for not getting the bat and destroying it. His anger proved to me his guilt. I told him it was safe, stashed in the one place he'd never look."

"How's that?"

"He'd never visit his daughter. Never claimed her as his own and that's what killed her mother Vee Tyler. I'm sure of it."

"That's one sad story," Louie said as he drifted off to sleep.

LOUIE GOT A LATE START the next morning.

Mr. Henry was waiting in the truck. "Donnie is getting ready to pass over."

The pair drove to the town store in silence. At the store there was a man loitering around the coffee service area. Louie asked Chunky to follow him into the cramped office.

"Who's the guy by the coffee station?" Louie asked.

"How should I know? Says he wants to talk to you," Chunky said. "Are you going to say anything to us about what happened yesterday? I got everybody calling me wanting to know what's going on. One of the part-timers asked if she was going to jail for working here."

"The only thing that person would get arrested for is asking such a dumb question," Louie said, annoyed at himself for thinking Chunky Brown was capable of being a competent convenience store manager. "When employees ask, tell them that the police busted up a cigarette cartel and Gas N Go was one of their targets."

"Dawg!" Chunky exclaimed. "Who was it?"

Feeling his blood pressure spike, Louie spoke softly, saying, "I'll put out a message to everyone in the next hour or so. Ask the guy to come in here."

The scruffy young man introduced himself as Duncan Shane, freelance reporter for *Fallam County News Online*. In his mind, Louie translated this to a local college student working for some media corporation for free. Duncan's clothes were wrinkled, like he'd slept in them for a couple of weeks. A smattering of facial hair covered his jaw and upper lip. His tangled hair was piled at the back of his head with a blue rubber band, the kind supermarkets used to bind broccoli stalks.

"Mr. Pyle?" the reporter asked as he leveled his cell phone in front of Louie. "I'd like to get your side of the story on the arrests made at your two stores yesterday."

"I really don't have anything to say about it," Louie said, fearing that Lisa's arrest would bring shame to his children.

"Sources tell me that the Kentucky Mafia has infiltrated the region and is robbing places like yours for cigarettes and selling them in larger markets for a profit. What do you think of that?"

"I'll keep my opinions to myself but I'll state the facts as I know them," Louie said. "Fallam County sheriff's office has arrested a group of people. The charges are stealing Gas N Go inventory as it was being delivered. They have also questioned two Gas N Go employees about the incidents."

"So, it was an inside job?" the reporter asked.

"I didn't say that," Louie said. "You can leave now because

I have no further comments." He opened the door and elaborately swept his arm and bowed, inviting the reporter to leave. Watching the guy buy a pack of smokes and a handful of beef jerky sticks, Louie realized he needed to get in front of this mess. If he didn't let everyone know his position, the town would do it for him. He called the one person he'd grown to trust over the last few weeks. "Kiara? How's Betty Doris getting on?"

"She's resting. Yesterday really wore her out," Kiara said. "And I'm worried about Uncle D. He doesn't want to get out of bed this morning. I talked to my cousin Bert on the phone earlier and she said she never knew him to want to stay in the bed all day."

Recalling Mr. Henry's warning, Louie asked, "Think we should take him to the doctors?"

"Let's give it a day," she said. "Maybe yesterday was too much for him."

"Say the word. I'll call his doctor and get a home visit for him," Louie said. "I was wondering if you'd do me a solid." He stroked his beard as he waited for her response. When she didn't say anything, he said, "I need to get an email out to all my employees about what happened here yesterday. Can you write it for me? Lisa was in charge of employee communications but …."

"What do you want me to write?"

Louie rubbed at his eye, the one with the dark spot in the center of his vision. "A memo about the police raid. I want to lay out the facts so employees won't get all worried about how it might affect them, you know, let them know they ain't gonna lose their jobs or nothing like that. Let them know Gas N Go is not getting shut down."

"That's the 'what'," she patiently said. "And how about

instructions? Do they need to act on anything?"

"If anybody, official or otherwise, asks them about what happened, they should say the store was robbed by an organized band of shiftless thieves and the police have arrested them. End of story. They need to pitch in and go about the business of selling coffee and doughnuts and beer and cigarettes."

"'Two of Gas N Go's stores, South and West, were robbed of large amounts of Yippies inventory. Please be vigilant and double check behind all vendors. Verify items received to items listed on shipping documents. Refer all inquiries about the incident to Louie. Keep up the great work and stay safe.' Something like that?" she asked.

"That's really good," Louie said. "Send it to me and we'll rock 'n' roll."

IRIS LEE WAS TRUE TO HER WORD and referred Louie to one of her attorney friends. The lawyer had agreed to meet Louie the following week to discuss possible strategies for protecting Gas N Go's assets from the greedy clutches of Speedy's and Turks McGraw. Having someone in his corner created a sense of relief for Louie. Yet, he wouldn't allow himself to trust the feeling. He'd learned the rules early, life wasn't fair and the final score was always a zero-sum game. Most of his life was spent preparing for whatever bad luck eventually came his way, like never having the chance to spend time with his father and losing the respect of his wife and children.

However, failure at keeping his business, something of his own creation, afloat and his workers employed wasn't going to be his life's story. He wouldn't allow it.

CHAPTER **TWENTY-SIX**

At noon on Friday, Louie sat at his desk and watched the local news from his computer while eating one of Sal's lamb pita pockets. Amid the gloom and doom of confusing pandemic statistics, protesting and rioting, and a heated national election, the Stoner crew story emerged. Roanoke's TV station anchor was interviewing Duncan Shane as he stood in front of Louie's store.

"Sources close to the case say Lisa Pyle, owner of Fallam County's Gas N Go convenience stores, was arrested on charges associated with a complex network of gangs selling contraband throughout the region. Pyle's ex-husband and co-owner, Louie Pyle, had no comment about the break-ins but confirmed that two employees were involved."

"Lies!" Louie yelled at the monitor as Shane spoke of nefarious cigarette cartels and the implications of his store and employee's involvement in organized racketeering.

His chair crashed into the wall as he jumped up from his desk and rushed outside to where the reporter and a cameraman were broadcasting the story. He shouted at Shane, "You! What you are saying is untrue! If you are going to make it your business to meddle in somebody else's, son, the public expects to hear the truth. If you'd done your homework and checked public records, you'd know that Lisa Pyle ain't the owner of Gas N Go. She was a part-time employee. I'm the sole owner and I didn't say anything about my employees being involved in criminal shiftlessness. What I *said*," Louie jabbed at the air in front of the reporter's chest, "is the police *questioned* employees. Get your facts straight, son, or consider another line of work. And get a haircut, for crying out loud."

Tittering from the cameraman was most likely broadcast for the entire tri-county audience to hear as Louie walked back into the store.

By six o'clock, Louie's tirade, in spite of the day's blistering headline news, had been viewed by thousands, local and elsewhere. People were calling him with their own opinions regarding his commentary on the competence of the county's newest chronicler, from high praises to threats of burning all his stores to the ground.

"Dad! Dad!" Alex exclaimed when Louie answered his son's call. "You've gone viral. You're blowing up the internet."

"I'm guessing that's a good thing?" Louie asked as he entered Log Heaven. "Are you coming home tonight?"

Ignoring his dad's questions, Alex explained, "Me and Thor snagged the video from the broadcast and loaded it onto our Gas N Go video channel. It's trending. It's got more likes than Sammy Hagar and her swinging hammock. Last I checked, it's got over five thousand hits and climbing. We've got over a thousand new followers on our channel."

“That’s great, son,” Louie said, not completely understanding why his success at making a fool of himself on TV created such excitement for Alex and, apparently, most of Fallam County.

“People are reacting to what you said. The video’s got three times as many likes as dislikes. Thor Bear says we need to have you go commando again.”

Shuffling through the day’s mail left on the kitchen counter, Louie asked, “Why would I want to make an ass of myself on purpose?”

“That’s it!” Alex squealed. “Saying things like that! People love it when old guys say stupid stuff like that.”

“Are you about finished offending your dad?” Louie asked.

“You don’t get it. The more people watch the video, the more they’re likely to come into the store and buy stuff. It’s free advertising.”

“I never spent a dime on advertising,” Louie said. “I expect a video of me sent from Mt Pleasant to Nigeria and back won’t affect store sales one way or the other. Do you plan to come to your own birthday party tomorrow?”

“Duh! Of course,” Alex said.

“We can’t have a lot of people swarming around Gran Betty and Donnie so we’ll have to keep it low-key. How ’bout we invite the Log Heaven supper club? You can ask Thor if you want to.”

“Thor Bear can’t come,” Alex said. “Marsha Ann said her mom says she can’t come, either. But, that’s all right. Birthday parties are for kids and I’m not a kid anymore.”

Surprised at his son’s proclamation, Louie said, “That’s a mighty grown-up way to look at it.”

“Know what I want for my birthday? I want mom to come over. This might be the last time she’ll be with all of us for a while."

Louie loved his third child. Alex wasn't as self-absorbed as his brother and sister. Whenever he asked for anything, it was usually for someone else's benefit. The Most Edible Weenie Roast was launched when the popular girls at school had gone out of their way not to invite Marsha Ann to a birthday party at The Happy Pizza. Alex had asked his mom and dad for a birthday party so his Sunday school friend didn't feel left out. When Thor couldn't get a job, Alex had insisted that he and Thor Bear were a packaged deal and Louie had to hire Thor. Every time Alex pushed him to an uncomfortable place, a place he didn't want to be, he'd discovered his son knew what was best. Nature had made up for the boy's lack of interpersonal instincts by gifting him with an innate sense of fairness and purpose. Alex seemed to always be right about the things that mattered. But this last request, having Lisa in his house after what she'd done, was something Louie didn't want to do.

"Dad? You there?"

"I'm here. Let me think on it and we'll discuss it when you get home."

Louie sat on his deck having a glass of iced milk, waiting for the noise in his ears to settle down. He worried about Alex's latest request. Unlike most people, Alex judged no one. His mother was his mother and what she'd done to the store was something he was unable to measure. To Alex, physical space mattered. Feelings and emotions played only a minor role in his world.

Louie loved his son and, up until now, he denied him nothing. But this time he'd have to put his foot down. There was no way he would allow Lisa into his home, not after what she had done to the store, to their lives, and to him. It hurt too much.

As he'd done on other summer nights, Sal quietly rounded the corner of the house and sat next to Louie. He waited for Sal to say whatever was on his mind.

Sal reported that their latest house hunting venture had failed. Once the landlord had met Sal and his baba, a better offer appeared on the woman's phone. They'd been outbid, again.

Louie didn't have the energy to explain to Sal what was really happening. He decided to take the conversation in another direction. He asked, "Would you be interested in going into the restaurant business with me?"

"How do you mean?" Sal asked.

"I'm thinking about opening a restaurant, featuring Gas N Go's star chef. The finest pizza chef south of the Mason-Dixon Line: Sal Contento."

"I'm flattered but do you think it wise to open a new business when so many are closing because of the pandemic?"

"I'm thinking of a spot on a county road with mountain views and a place for a garden for tomatoes and herbs."

"It would be madness to open a restaurant now," Sal warned.

"Someone told me once that to be successful in business I should do the opposite of what everybody else is doing. By the time this bug settles down, everybody will want to go back to eating out, having somebody else do the cooking for their families."

"Would I be cook or partner?"

"Let's take a drive on Sunday and I'll show you the spot I have in mind."

The headlights of Alex's truck beamed through the shadowed woods. Louie and Sal sat quietly as Alex trampled through the house then appeared on the deck with a package. He had found his birthday present on the dining room table.

Holding up the colorfully wrapped box, he asked, "Is this for me?"

Louie nodded as he scooted his chair aside, allowing Alex to place the gift on the table.

"What is it?" Alex asked.

"Open it up and see," Louie said. The timing of this couldn't be better, Louie thought. He worried about presenting the gift to Alex at the party in front of everybody, and by everybody he meant Betty Doris.

Alex eagerly ripped the paper from the box. The young man's silence confirmed that Louie had hit the bull's eye with this year's gift.

"Wow! Can we shoot it now?"

"Let's wait 'til we have a gunsmith check it out. It belonged to your mom's Uncle Waddy."

"I can't do it in the morning. Me and Thor Bear are installing our first security system at the lake." After the successful capture of the Stoner gang on the Gas N Go videos, Thor Bear and Alex had proposed to Louie that they be allowed to offer installation services to other stores and homeowners. Louie thought it a good idea and lent them seed money to get their operation started.

"Who's covering for you at the store?"

"Normal and Betsy are pulling a double. They said it's my birthday present."

"Sounds like you've got it covered."

Alex draped his arm around his dad and said, "I'm going to be an entrepreneur. Just like my dad."

"You are?"

"So you know what that means? I can't work for you anymore," Alex said.

"I see," Louie said. He looked away to hide his amusement and pride, secretly hoping his son's declaration would come true.

Alex stood and stretched. "Can Thor follow you around next week to get some B-roll for the podcast?"

Louie laughed and said, "As long as it don't hurt."

"Trust me. It'll get more customers in the door," a confident Alex said. He waved at them as he went inside.

In his quiet voice, Sal said, "Your son is becoming a man."

"I expect so," Louie said.

LOUIE'S EYES WOULDN'T CLOSE. Staring at the steep ceiling, he strained to hear whether Mr. Henry was haunting Donnie in the kitchen again but the noise in his ears was too loud. He sat up and switched on the bedside lamp. Mr. Henry was standing at the foot of his bed.

"What is it?" he asked the ghost.

"You've been dragging that lovelorn torch for your ex-wife for too long. It's what's keeping you up at night."

"Don't put the blame on somebody else, you're doing a fine job on your own," Louie said. He got out of the bed and went over to the side window, the one overlooking the path to the boathouse.

Mr. Henry's likeness appeared in the window. "You tell yourself you're over her but you're really not. Believe me, I know about attachments. I became so fixated on loving my Vee I couldn't see the truth. She never cared for me. She wanted my brother. I had spent my entire life believing my love was enough for the both of us."

In the window's reflection, Louie's dark eyes glistened with tears. "I can't get her out of this mess she's in. What's going to happen to her?"

"What's going to happen to her is none of your concern. In fact, you need to stop meddling in her life and start thinking about your own. What's your mother always saying? Leave it with God?" Then he said, "Follow me."

At the dock, the boards of the dock glowed silver from the light of a waxing moon. The waters were still.

"Go ahead, do it."

"Do what?" Louie asked.

"Throw yourself into the water. Cleanse off all the salty distain that woman ever put on you. Wash away the petty scorn she threw at you for everything you ever did or didn't do for her. Wipe from your mind this notion that you are obligated to be her savior. Force every thought of her from your head and make way for a new life."

Before he could catch his balance, Louie found himself immersed in the clear water. With acute calm, he allowed his body to sink into the deep, the water cooling his skin. The ringing in his ears stopped and his mind became still. Millions of effervescent bubbles swirled around his arms and legs, their energy pulling him to the surface. When he broke through the water, he cried out with joy as the bubbles rushed to join the stars in the night sky.

CHAPTER **TWENTY-SEVEN**

Like the rest of the country's summer celebrations, the Most Edible Weenie Roast fizzled like a dud firecracker. On the lakeside lawn of Log Heaven, Louie lit the grill coals while Alex sat at the picnic table noodling on his phone. Down on the dock, Donnie and Mr. Contento sat under an umbrella, talking quietly while neglecting their fishing lines. Betty Doris had yet to make it outside, blaming the summer heat. Sal and Kiara beelined from house to picnic table, preparing the late afternoon birthday feast.

"Alex," Louie called out, "text Jessica. She said she was going to be here an hour ago." He worried because when he called his daughter to remind her to stop by the new Mt Pleasant bakery to pick up her brother's birthday cake, he also requested that she not bring Lisa with her. Jessica had hung up on him. His daughter was still mad at him because he refused to give her money to post Lisa's bail. His mind was made up, Lisa was no longer part of his life.

"Poppy!" Maddy squealed from the deck of the house.

“Jumpin’ Bean,” Louie called out. “Did you bring your swimsuit?”

Jessica waved from the deck as Betty Doris leaned against her.

“Alex, set up a nice shady spot for your Gran Betty to sit,” Louie instructed. “And roll out Big Bertha.” Together, Louie and Alex had rescued an abandoned industrial floor fan from the county dump. Twelve-year-old Alex named it after they had replaced the chewed-on wiring. Big Bertha had been stirring up air ever since. Lisa had complained about where the fan came from, saying she felt like she was living in TV character Fred Sanford’s junkyard whenever they dragged it out of the gardening shed and unreeled the orange extension cord across the yard.

Maddy rushed at Alex, stretching her arms for him to pick her up. “We bought your birthday cake. It’s got a dragon on top. Mommy says you can’t blow out the candles because it would give us germs and we might die.” Then she cried out, “Swing me! Swing me!”

“Maybe later. Come help me set up Big Bertha for Gran Betty,” Alex said.

Jessica guided her Gran Betty to a lawn chair and helped her sit.

“Alex is setting up the fan for you, Ma,” Louie said.

“I don’t want that thing blowing on me,” she said. “It makes me cold.”

“We’ll set it up just in case it gets too hot for you,” Louie said. That woman was never satisfied about anything. Too hot, too cold. He was never able to make it just right. When he thanked Jessica for getting the birthday cake, she stuck her nose in the air and mumbled something about helping Kiara in the house.

Betty Doris shook her head. "She's just like her mother. Something gets in her craw and she broods for days."

"I might have said something to upset her. Alex wanted Lisa to come to the cookout but I told them both this morning that it was probably not a good idea. You know, the situation and all."

"I expect Lisa has convinced her that this whole mess is your fault."

"I'm partially to blame. I should have paid closer attention to what was going on."

"Son, the only thing you're guilty of is catering to Miss High and Mighty's every whim, even after she left you. It's time your kids learned you can't take on their mother's mistakes anymore. Especially this one. How much did she take?"

"Lupita's still looking into it," Louie said. He didn't want to tell his mama that Lisa's little embezzlement scheme was going to cost Gas N Go a hefty sum. He'd have to borrow money from Travis English's bank to cover this year's retirement contributions. He could forget about drawing down funds for himself for the rest of the year.

As soon as Betty Doris finished the blessing and everybody said, "Amen," Lisa paraded down the sloped lawn as if she had never left the place.

"Ah, Queen Lisa, the Malevolent," Betty Doris called out. To Louie, she said, "Looking more and more like her driver's license's picture every day."

"Mama, don't start," Louie said.

"Broom-Hilda," Lisa responded to her mother-in-law's greeting.

"Mom, what are you doing here?" Jessica asked.

"Maw-mee," Maddy yelped. She crawled down from her spot

at the picnic table and rushed to her grandmother. Lisa squatted and hugged her. "Sweetie, did you have cake?"

Louie motioned to everybody to continue with their meal and then stood. "How'd you get here?" he asked. He'd heard through Betty Doris's Elder Home gossip line that she'd hocked her car, the like-new one he'd bought for her a year ago.

"Larry brought me. I sold my car."

Gently taking her arm, Louie tried to steer her away from the others, saying, "Thought he was in jail."

"That's why I sold the car. Needed the money to bail out Larry."

"Leese, I don't think it's right for you to be here," he whispered.

"Why not? This is where we raised our kids and one of them is having a birthday party," she said, loud enough for even one-good-ear Donnie to hear.

"Stop playing around. This ain't your home no more. You left."

She flipped her hair away from her neck in that way that used to drive him wild. "Larry's waiting for me. We came to get my coffee table." Then, directing her scorn at Kiara, she continued, "The one your girlfriend shoved out onto the front porch for the raccoons to gnaw on. And my kitchen buffet and my bedroom furniture and the sofa in the living room and the trundle bed in the loft. Plus my china. I want Jessica to have it. With all the oddball creeps you have living here, there's no telling what will happen to all my stuff."

"Enough with the insults. I want you to leave now. Call me next week and we'll set up a time for you to come over and get whatever it is you want."

"I'll leave when I'm good and ready." Lisa stepped around

Louie and sat next to Alex at the picnic table and planted a sloppy kiss on his cheek. "Hey, you. Happy birthday to my baby boy." Throwing Louie a sour look, she said, "Lookee what we have here. Enough food to feed the entire neighborhood but your dad didn't want me to be here on your special day."

"Mom, don't," Jessica pleaded.

"Can the Hollywood theatrics, Lisa. You're no Meryl Streep," Betty Doris said.

Sal tittered.

"Stay out of my business, you bag of bones."

"Oh, no she didn't," Donnie said under a cough.

"That's enough with the name calling," Louie said. He walked over and stood behind her. Gently tugging at her elbow, he said, "You've wished Alex a happy birthday. Time for you to leave."

Lisa brushed Louie's hand away. "Get your paws off me, you lunkheaded Neanderthal." She rose from the table and commanded, "Alex, come help Larry and me get my stuff?"

Indifferent to his mother's plea, Alex stated, "I'm eating my birthday dinner." Then he opened wide for his first bite of a fully dressed Log Heaven hot dog.

While Alex and Maddy munched on weenies, the rest of the party watched as Lisa marched up the hill to the house. Trying to hide the ugly awkwardness, Louie laughed nervously then said, "Y'all go ahead and eat. If I'm not back in fifteen minutes, wait longer." He found Lisa on the driveway where the Hummer was parked. Larry sat in the passenger's seat, flicking cigarette ashes on the tarmac. "Lisa, don't show up here again without calling me first. You hear me?"

Her bleached curls bounced as she whipped around and

pointed her finger at him and hissed, "You lied to the police. Told them lies about me." Tears mixed with mascara formed a mask around her eyes. Since her ex-husband was denying her accusations by not responding, she went on, "You can't tell me where I can go. I can come here whenever I please."

"Then I'll get a restraining order so I can call the law on you."

Rubbing her elbow, she said, "And I'll make a complaint about how you assaulted me in front of my children just now. And everybody will have to say they saw it."

Louie snorted. "You go right ahead, sugar britches." Something inside had released its hold on him. The pressure from all the years of trying to be a good husband fell away. Laughter erupted from his belly. He felt freer than he had in a long time. The laughter felt good, earned.

Furious with her ex-husband's reaction to her threat, Lisa called out, "Larry! Come and help me get this table."

Louie watched as the couple struggled with the oversized coffee table. Eventually, they got it into the back of the vehicle. When he offered to get them bungee cords to secure the back hatch, Lisa reeled on him and spat, "I'm coming back for the rest of it. I'm coming back to get even with you. Mark my words, Louie Pyle. You'll rue the day you laughed at me."

Louie followed the vehicle as it backed out of his driveway and down the road, the back hatch bouncing up and down with every bump.

"Good luck, Larry!" Louie yelled. He had been released.

As Louie approached the picnic table, everybody stopped talking. He straddled the bench and said, "Kiara, everybody, I apologize for Lisa. She's going through some pretty rough times right now. I'm inclined to say she ain't herself but that would be a lie. Anyway, I'm sorry if she upset y'all."

"Stop apologizing for her. All her life Lisa insisted she was in the right and everybody else was wrong," Betty Doris said. "But she'll learn different when she meets the judge."

"Is she gone?" Jessica quietly asked.

"She left," Louie said. "But, hey, this party ain't about her. We're here to celebrate Alexander Woods Pyle's twentieth birthday." He raised his red cup of sweet tea and said, "To the best son a father could ever have."

"You're the most brilliant when you're with me," Alex joked, holding up his own cup.

"Hey?" Louie asked. "Did y'all know that studies have shown that birthdays are good for your health? People who've had the most lived the longest."

"Burn," Alex said as he high fived his dad.

"Happy birthday, sweetie," Betty Doris toasted.

"Love ya, bro," Jessica said.

The rest added their birthday greetings as they raised their own red cups.

After the cake had been sliced and eaten, Alex said, "Dad, you haven't told a single story since we started telling them. It's your turn."

"Let's see." Stalling, Louie refilled his red cup. All these weeks of listening to others' storytelling, he'd yet to come up with an idea for his own. He tried a joke instead, "I think the worst time to have a heart attack is during a game of charades." He bugged out his eyes and stiffened his arms.

"Har har," Jessica said. "That's so old."

"And lame," Alex chimed in.

But they both laughed with their dad.

"Tell us a story, Poppy," Maddy insisted as she played with a flower appliqué on her bathing suit.

Directing her eyes at her daughter, Jessica said, "And make sure it's G-rated."

"OK, one time I was hunting over in the western part of the county."

"Were you looking for Bambi?" Maddy asked.

"Bambi's cousin Otis," Louie said. He paused then went on with his story, not sure where it was going to take him. "Anyway, I was about to crest a grassy hill when I stumbled on a bevy of quail. All of a sudden they were flapping all around me."

Without warning the memory washed over him now as if he was back on the hill. He'd gone there because he'd wanted to get away, to forget about Lisa's note he'd found on the kitchen counter the night before. Time slowed as the energy of the rising quail swirled about him, creating an eddy of current and grass and feathers. His arms rising from weightlessness, he watched his orange stocking cap as it floated in front of him. His rucksack floated weightlessly on his back. A noisy cloud with hundreds of wings spun around him as they ascended toward the infinite blue sky. He hovered over the brown field, able to see over the next crest. As time caught up with him, he felt the weight of his body lightly touching the earth. The torrent of noise had left as fast as it had come.

Now he realized the meaning of the rapture from that day. He had been set free of the bonds of commitment to his marriage.

Louie had never shared with another living soul that day's experience, of being lifted by a flock of birds, each weighing no more than a pebble. Talking about it meant it actually happened. That wasn't a story he wanted to tell. He needed to switch gears lest his children would force him to take a room at Elder Home next to Betty Doris.

"Those quails were so noisy I almost didn't hear it."

"Hear what?" Maddy asked after pulling her thumb from her mouth. By now she'd climbed into her mama's lap.

"Somebody was calling for help. I sat quiet and listened." He paused, raising his eyebrows at Maddy. "And there it was again. Some tiny voice was crying, 'Help me, help me.' It sounded like somebody was trapped in the thicket that ran along the pasture I was walking in. So I pulled back a handful of briars and got the fright of my life."

Now Maddy's eyes were getting big, "What was it?" she asked.

"It was Otis, Otis Whitetail, Bambi's cousin. He was crying out 'Help me, help me.' His antlers were all tangled up in briars and rusty barbed wire. The more he fought, the tighter the hold got," Louie said. "He told me he was on his way to the North Pole to be with Rudolph and the other reindeer but he got stuck in the briar patch."

"Did you help him get out?" Maddy asked.

"Yes, ma'am, I did. Afterward, Otis said he'd tell Santa what a good boy I was by helping him out."

"Did you get to talk to Santa?" Maddy asked, impressed that she was only three degrees of separation from The Big Guy. Not waiting for her poppy's answer, she asked, "Was Thumper there, too?"

"Rabbits don't work for Santa, Maddy," Alex schooled her. "And Dad, the Virginia white-tailed deer is not the same species as the North American caribou."

"You're right, Mr. Smarty Pants. But Otis can be Santa's

helper if he wants to," Jessica said to Alex while shifting a nod at Maddy.

"Mr. Smarty Pants," Maddy repeated and giggled.

"What happened next?" Sal asked, fearing the story was getting off track.

"Well, as soon as that barbed wire turned loose of Otis's antlers he started glowing. Not like Rudolph with his red nose but Otis's entire body glowed. A bevy of quail rose up out of the thicket and started circling him, spinning around his antlers." Louie drew his face closer to Maddy's. "Then this big spinning circle of birds lifted him up into the sky and they all flew away."

No one spoke for a minute, allowing Louie time to realize that he'd just confessed to talking to a white-tailed deer. To detract from his revelation, he joked, "I'm aware that the voices I hear aren't real but sometimes their ideas are awesome."

The group laughed politely. Maddy's wonder glowed in her dark brown eyes, the eyes she inherited from her poppy.

CHAPTER **TWENTY-EIGHT**

Flickering light seeped into his closed eyes. Throwing off soaked sheets, Louie rolled over in his bed. In his groggy state, he wished the screeching in the nightmare he was having would stop. The room was unbearable, air-conditioner must be on the fritz, he thought. An acrid smell of burnt creosote stung inside his nose as he became aware of the dryness in his mouth.

"Loooouieeeee!"

Was that Betty Doris screaming like a banshee or some more of his bad dream? He opened his eyes to the trees ablaze in light. "What the …?" he asked as he sat up in his bed.

"Keeeeaaraaaa!" Betty Doris yelled. "The house is on fire!"

He fell out of the bed and then freed his feet from tangled sheets. The floor was as warm as the air. He grabbed jeans and T-shirt and opened his door. In the grainy light of dawn, a gauzy smoke crawled up the steps.

"Mama, I'm coming!" he called back to her.

As his bare feet hit the second floor carpet, he became aware of the smoke alarm. The piercing sound hurried him along the hallway. He found Kiara rousing Donnie from his bed. Donnie coughed as he pulled on his bathrobe over his pajamas. The coughing prompted him to grab at his chest as he leaned into Kiara.

"Go find Betty Doris and Alex," Louie shouted to Kiara as he pulled on his jeans. Then he handed his shirt to Donnie and said, "Here, breathe through this." Grabbing Donnie around his waist, Louie draped the frail man's arm over his shoulder. Lifting him, Louie carried Donnie down the stairs and into the thickening smoke.

"Louie!" Betty Doris cried out. "Back here!" He followed her voice and found a frazzled Kiara and Betty Doris out on the deck. Both were hacking and coughing.

"Where's Alex?" Louie yelled. "Call 9-1-1!"

"He wasn't in the den," Kiara said. Pointing to the other end of the house, she added, "The fire is coming from the front. We can't get off the deck. The steps are on fire."

"Move the hutch," Betty Doris wheezed. "We can get out through the basement."

Louie set Donnie in a chair and went back inside. With seemingly little effort, Louie pushed the oversized hutch away from the kitchen door leading to the rec room. He tried the knob but it wouldn't turn. Pounding on the door, he shouted, "Sal! Wake up!"

Dense smoke was finding its way into the kitchen from the great room. He went to the great room threshold and shouted, "Alex!" The only response was the crackling of wood. Back outside on the deck, Louie asked Betty Doris, "Where's the key to the basement door?"

Frantically, she replied, "I don't know. You've got to get Alex out of there." She sobbed while pulling at her nightgown.

A loud twang sounded from the front of the house, then, in rapid succession, more twangs popped and hummed at various pitches.

"It's the piano," Kiara cried. "The fire is in the front room. Do something! We've got to get to Sal and Mr. Contento."

Breathing in what felt like heat from hell, Louie went back into the kitchen and opened one of the hutch's drawers, searching for the door key with no luck. His eyes watering from stinging smoke, he blindly searched through the second drawer but it wasn't there either. All the while, he called to Alex and to Sal and to Mr. Contento.

"The key is in the lock," a calm Mr. Henry whispered inside his head.

Louie pounded on the door again and shouted for Sal. In the smoke-filled room, his hand searched for the doorknob and then the deadbolt right above it and, as Mr. Henry had said, the key was in the lock. Panicking, he tried turning the key both ways but the lock wouldn't budge.

The popping and cracking of the great room's beams were getting louder.

"Stand back," someone from the other side of the door called.

"Sal?"

"Stand away from the door!"

Louie did as he was instructed then called out, "Ready on this end!"

Amid the swirling smoke, shattered wood exploded into the room. In a matter of one-two-three mighty swings of the woodpile axe, the door had crumbled into large splinters. Holding the ax with the confidence of a brawny lumberjack, Mr. Contento stood in the doorway with Sal at his back.

"Help me with Donnie," Louie shouted. Louie and Mr. Contento carried a frail Donnie down the basement stairs and out into the back lawn. Sal and Kiara followed behind with Betty Doris.

"Where's Alex?" Betty Doris cried out.

"He isn't in the basement," Sal said as he tried to calm the shaking woman.

"Louie, you go back in there and find him," she demanded.

Disobeying his wailing mother, Louie rushed to the front of the house. Alex's truck wasn't in the driveway. He breathed out a small prayer, thanking God for removing his son from harm's way.

Kiara joined him, her face glowing from the light and heat of the flames. They watched in silence as tall flames engulfed the north side of the house. Pointing at the phone at her ear, she said, "Alex. He's at Thor's." She finished the call and stood with her arms around her tiny waist. "He went to Thor's last night after we all went to bed."

"Thank the Lord for small favors," Louie said as he watched his life's dream being consumed with flames. His son was safe, that was all that mattered.

Kiara pointed at the side of the house where the steps to the deck and the first floor bedroom were, she said, "It looks like it started there."

"Right outside of Mama's room," Louie said.

"I'm no fire expert but it looks that way to me," she said as she took a picture with Betty Doris's phone.

Flames were overtaking one of the center beams in the great room as the fire truck pulled into the drive. Firefighters doused the house as an EMT worker placed an oxygen mask over Donnie's face. Another EMT patiently waited as Donnie insisted on getting on the gurney under his own steam. Kiara hovered close by.

The rest of the band of Log Heaven residents stood in the driveway. A bare-chested Louie had managed to get his jeans zipped and to find some flip flops. Sal sweated in his buttoned-up striped pajamas as Mr. Contento, in his ankle-length kaftan, adjusted his sooty skull cap. Alex, who had arrived shortly after the fire trucks, held his Gran Betty's hand while she sat in a plastic lawn chair, crying at the loss of her son's home. Mesmerized, they all stared on as Log Heaven cracked and hissed then spit out red hot wood coals. Log Heaven had transformed into Log Hell, morphing into a giant blazing jack-o'-lantern with the front bay window's shards of glass appearing as a mouth filled with jagged teeth and the flames from the smoky second-floor windows staring at them like evil eyes.

"This is arson," Mr. Contento said to Louie. "I've seen plenty of destruction in my life. And this is the devil's work."

"Everybody made it out alive. That's all that counts for now," Louie said as he watched the EMTs lift Donnie into the back of their vehicle. If what Mr. Contento said was true, who would do such a thing? Alex, his mama, Donnie, Kiara, and the men downstairs, any one of them could have died a gruesome death. He felt his familiar anxiety creeping up from his gut.

Sal joined his baba and Louie and asked, "Mr. Donnie will be all right?"

"He's tough, he'll pull through," Louie assured Sal. "Kiara's going with him to the hospital. We'll have to find a place for them when he's discharged."

"And you? Your son? Sal and me?" Mr. Contento asked.

"Where will we go?"

Still disoriented by the blistering destruction, Louie spoke absentmindedly, "I've been known to sleep under the stars. Y'all are welcome to camp out with me and Alex." The spasm in his lower back reminded him that carrying an eighty-seven-year-old peanut, who didn't weigh a hundred pounds soaking wet, down two flights of stairs was probably a bad idea. And shoving Lisa's kitchen hutch all by himself wasn't a smooth move either. He discovered that he'd grown too old for playing Superman.

His home and all the stuff he'd accumulated during his lifetime had vanished in minutes. Some things he could replace, like his phone and keys. But pictures of the kids when they were babies were gone, homemade Christmas gifts, a family painting Jessica had created in art class her senior year of high school that hung in the great room, all now in a mound of everlasting ashes.

"Has anybody seen Possum?" Alex asked as he joined the other men. "I've been calling for him but he's not answering."

"He'll show up when he gets hungry," Sal said.

The morning sun's rays streamed through haze as firefighters went about packing up their gear. Louie joined the fire marshal and Sheriff Jones as they stood by the steps leading to the deck on the side of the house. The sheriff squatted to get a closer look at Louie's overturned grill.

"I believe I found your culprit, Warren," the sheriff said to the fire marshal. "Looks like grill coals spilled out onto the steps."

"Maybe," the fire marshal said.

"Louie, did y'all grill out last night?" the sheriff asked.

"We did. But I keep the grill …." He stopped mid-sentence. Someone had moved the grill.

Living in an all-wood house, Louie was a stickler for fire

safety. When he built a brick patio down by the dock specifically for the grill, Lisa had fussed at him because she'd wanted a firepit on the back deck instead. At the time, he'd tried to explain to her how firepits were a bad idea on a wooden deck. He'd reminded her of his mama's story about how her grandparents died in their homestead one winter night because a rogue spark from a fireplace had jumped onto a rug. Lisa had pouted for days, called him a meanie and accused him of being selfish, not caring about what she wanted. Another one of their domestic disagreements, he resolved.

"Why is the grill up here?" Alex asked as he joined his dad and the others.

Standing, the sheriff brushed sooty dirt off his hands and asked, "Where do you usually have it?"

"Down by the boathouse," Alex said. "We roasted hot dogs on it yesterday for my birthday. And later we made s'mores."

As Alex reached for the grill to stand it upright, the fire marshal said, "Wait. Leave that right there, son." He looked at Louie and said, "We'll have to rope the house off to complete our investigation."

"Can I go in the basement and get a change of clothes?" Alex asked.

"No, son. It's not safe for anybody to be in there. Those giant beams are still smoldering. One could fall on you." To Louie he said, "I swear, Louie, I know how much you love this place but we'll probably have to condemn it. I'm sorry as I can be, man."

Louie found Possum lounging on the fishing bench he'd made for Ken and Jessica when they were in middle school. He sat next to the cat and cried until he didn't have any tears left inside.

CHAPTER **TWENTY-NINE**

The smoldering heat of July droned on as Louie and the others recovered from what Alex had dubbed The Great Log Inferno. The refugees set up camp down by the boathouse. In the evenings, Big Bertha whirled hot air around as Louie, Sal, and Mr. Contento sat on the dock, swatting at bugs. Alex, who had escaped to Thor Bear's house, dropped in for dinner a few nights each week. He'd named the three homeless men The Burnt Log Gentlemen's Club. Louie joked with Alex by adding, "Membership is free to anybody who ever lived in a burned-down log house."

Miss Wanda's Home for Ladies, over in the next county, was happy to make room for Betty Doris. But Betty Doris hadn't reciprocated the sentiment. Miss Wanda reported to Louie that Betty Doris reminded the caregiver every day that her stay was temporary and that she'd be moving back in with her son once he rebuilt his log cabin. Miss Wanda also reported that his mother spent her entire two-week quarantine on her cell phone telling folks about her family's ordeal.

News of the catastrophe spread as quickly as the fire had raged on Log Heaven's timber. People Louie had never met approached him, insisting on details of the misfortune. And, they wanted to know, did Betty Doris really push a three-hundred-pound kitchen hutch out of the way so she could save y'all? To which, Louie replied, "Thank the good Lord and Betty Doris, everybody got out."

Kiara and Donnie dropped in on the Burnt Log Gentlemen's Club one evening in early August. After Donnie's release from the hospital, the pair moved in with Donnie's niece Bert. In a slow shuffle down the path to the boathouse, he pushed a lightweight walker with neon tennis balls on each leg. A small oxygen tank, tucked inside a denim bag, swung from a cross bar on the walker.

"Look at you. You need some NASCAR racing stripes on that thing," Louie said as he helped Donnie get comfortable in a chair.

Donnie laughed and said, "It helps me get where I'm going."

"One of the nurses gave him the bag to carry all his stuff," Kiara offered.

"It's my man-bag," Donnie joked.

Kiara asked Louie, "When are you going to start rebuilding?"

"Waiting on the fire marshal to say it's all right to take down the yellow tape."

They gazed up the hill at the charred heap.

Louie's insurance agent assured him that smoldering barbecue coals from a grill fell in the accidental category and that his house was covered. But, the agent cautioned, if the fire was ruled intentional, Farmer's Surety and Life would deny his claim. They frowned on policyholders submitting claims caused by arson, the agent had explained.

"What're they waiting on?" Kiara asked. "It's been a month. Doesn't the county realize you're homeless right now?"

"I don't think The Man cares about anybody's housing situation, Kiara," Donnie said.

Louie wasn't sure how he felt about the insurance agent's explanation or the fire marshal's theories about how the fire had started. Warren Hardy, the fire marshal, explained to Louie that the presence of the grill indicated the fire was accidental but he had to talk it over with his crew. Over many sleepless nights Louie fought with himself about what he should do. That grill had been moved from the brick patio. The fact that the grill had been moved pointed to arson and Louie had watched enough TV cop shows to know he'd be crazy to incriminate himself by insisting someone else had moved the grill. His silence ate at him. If it was arson, the suspect list was short, a list of one. He was torn: Should he share his suspicion about his ex-wife burning down his house with the fire marshal or let the man figure it out on his own.

Real life was too gray for Louie. Sometimes he wished life could be like the black and white TV shows he watched as a kid where all the conflict was resolved in thirty minutes. By the end of each episode, a man knew where he stood with everybody and everything.

Kiara followed Louie up the hill to his truck to get the day's camp supplies. "Let me help you with that," she said as Louie lifted a bag of ice and a grocery bag.

"How's Donnie really doing?" Louie asked her.

"He's not recovering as quickly as the doctors would like. Bert is beside herself with worry. He told us last night 'It's time for me to go on *eternity* leave.'"

"That's sad. You think it's depression or something else?" Louie asked.

"When Bert asked him why he said it, he told us he saw Mr. Henry while he waited on the deck before you and Mr. Contento rescued him."

"Really? He thinks seeing a dead friend is a sign of dying?" Louie asked. On reflex, he flattened his beard with his wide hand. Mr. Henry visited him every day and he was still on the grassy side of the ground.

"I think the smoke from the fire robbed his brain of oxygen and caused him to have hallucinations. That's what the doctor suspects, anyway."

"That's probably what happened," Louie said.

"I saw Lupita at Stuff Mart yesterday. She asked about you," Kiara said. "You need to talk to that woman. She thinks you're mad at her about something. Are you mad at her?"

"Naw! Why would I be mad at her? She cracked the case on how they were laundering their money through my accounts," Louie said.

"How did she do that?"

"She found where Lisa was depositing and withdrawing money from our accounts." Ethan had shared with Louie that Lisa had set up dummy accounts and skimmed money off the top of the laundered money and transferred it to another account. She'd played the Stoner crew. Louie suspected that's why Stoner paid Lisa a visit, confronting her about it. Not wanting Fallam County to know he'd been played, too, he said, "Don't repeat what I just said to anybody. Ain't nobody's business to know."

Kiara stopped halfway down the hill, readjusted the grocery bag on her hip, and turned to Louie. "Oh. My. God. She burned down Log Heaven. Didn't she?"

"I didn't say that."

"But it all makes sense. She was here that night. All worked up about getting stuff out of the house. But really, she was pissed at you and Lupita for messing with her boyfriend's playbook. What a sick-o. And you were married to that woman? Unbelievable."

"You're giving Larry Baldwin way too much credit. Leave it alone. The police will figure out what happened," Louie said, hoping Kiara would let it go.

"You're kidding, right?" Kiara went on, "If it was me, I'd call the cops and…."

Louie interrupted, "Did you see or hear anything that night?"

"No, but it doesn't take a genius to figure it out."

"I don't know if Lisa or anybody else came to my house that night to set fire to it. Let's let Warren and Sheriff Jones do their jobs."

"But if she was the one who did it, she's guilty of arson." Kiara's eyes lit up. "She tried to kill us all!"

"Hey, this ain't an episode of one of those true crime shows you and Mama watch." Pointing at the house, Louie said, "If they rule it as arson, meaning somebody intentionally burned this place to the ground, I might never get money to rebuild."

"That explains why they're taking their time getting back to you. Do you think they suspect you had anything to do with it?"

"Me and Alex already told the fire marshal what we know. It's up to them to decide. Unless it's the police asking, don't talk to nobody about this. And especially don't talk to Betty Doris. You know how she likes to hear herself talk, telling stories to anybody who'll listen."

Kiara laughed. "Somebody said to me the other day that they heard Betty Doris carried Uncle Donnie out of the house."

"You see what I mean?" Louie asked, relieved they'd moved onto another topic. Leading the way back to the dock and the others, he asked, "Y'all staying for Sal's kebobs?"

Setting the groceries on the picnic table, Kiara placed her hand on his arm and said, "You need to call Lupita. She's all worked up about you not talking to her."

The evening passed with everyone sitting around the picnic table nibbling at Sal's latest creations, which were scheduled to debut the following week on the Get N Go dinner menu. They laughed as they suggested funny names for the dishes like COVID Croquettes for the fried tuna cakes and Louie's Lockdown Salad for the tabbouleh and lamb bits. No one spoke of fire or arson.

When Kiara and Donnie left, Louie dragged his droopy air mattress from the boathouse and spread sheets over it. He groaned as he squatted and rolled onto it. He'd never again take for granted the simple pleasure of a firm mattress. There was no telling how long it would be before he got the rubble cleared out to rebuild on his most favorite spot in the world. To keep his mind from overheating, he tried to find the Big Dipper and other constellations.

While a shooting star flew across the dark sky, Mr. Henry appeared at the foot of the air mattress, illuminated from within. "I'd take your friend's advice and tell Jones about Lisa coming to the house that night. As my Elizabeth used to say, 'He's not the sharpest rock in the box.' He could use the help."

"I don't know who moved the grill," Louie insisted.

"They're not going to stop with their investigation until they're satisfied that all the pieces fit together. What if you are their primary suspect? Telling them about her visit is self-preservation."

Louie considered his advice. "But telling them I think somebody else done it, my vindictive ex, for example, puts a spotlight on me. Like, I'm telling them to look somewheres else."

"As you've said, tell them what you know. Tell them she was here earlier in the evening," Mr. Henry suggested.

"Mr. Louie?" Sal called out. "You have problem sleeping?"

Louie whispered to Mr. Henry, "I never thought of it that way. Let me sleep on it." He burrowed down into the sheet and drifted off to sleep.

Mr. Henry was waiting for Louie in his truck the next morning. After a rough night on the air mattress, Louie still hadn't decided if he was going to tell the fire marshal and the county sheriff about Lisa showing up uninvited to Alex's birthday party.

"At least call Ethan Quinn and tell him," Mr. Henry suggested.

"I ain't in the mood to deal with you this morning," Louie said. He started his truck and switched on the radio to listen to his morning tunes. A young Texan crooned:

"How can you say I have it all
When you've taken everything from me.
You stole my money, my truck, my dog,
And now my self-respecting dignity."

CHAPTER **THIRTY**

Louie circled Mt Pleasant's command center, twice. He couldn't make up his mind about telling Ethan or Sheriff Jones about Lisa's visit the night before his house burned to the ground. So, he drove to his town store. Thinking about what Kiara had said the night before about Lupita wondering why he hadn't called her, he parked his truck next to Lupita's car.

He hadn't called Lupita because, since he had bungled his last attempt at asking her out, he dreaded approaching her for fear of another rejection. However, that day at his office, the day he learned that a convenience store giant planned to crowd him out of business, she had offered to help save Gas N Go from Speedy's imminent siege. In fact, she'd sent him an email stating she'd agreed to help Louie's lawyer with his inquiry into Mr. McGraw's offer, upon his approval, of course. Then, later, she'd helped the law catch the criminals who were stealing from him. "Louie Pyle, you ignoramus, she's looking out for you. Lest you can do is thank her," he said to the windshield of his truck. But his self-doubt and fear of rejection weren't giving up that easily.

Chunky greeted Louie with his morning grunt.

Louie asked, "Has that reporter fella been in this morning?" Since their first encounter, Duncan Shane visited Louie every few days asking for a quote on the Stoner case and his ex-wife's involvement. Louie responded by offering him a free cup of coffee. Now, he hoped the reporter might have something to say about the fire investigation.

"Ain't seen him," Chunky answered. "Probably chasing after another scoop. Heard on the police band this morning that they was bringing in the driver of an Army-green Hummer for DUI and reckless driving. My money's on Larry Baldwin."

Louie froze. The last time he saw Larry Baldwin's Hummer, Lisa was in the driver's seat.

"No rest for the lovelorn," Mr. Henry said. "Let her go, son."

Feeling Mr. Henry's presence follow him into his office, Louie mumbled to his mentor, "It's gonna take some time, boss."

"I say go for the saucy Mexican gal," Mr. Henry said. "A couple of spins around the dance floor with her will cure your first-love blues in no time flat." His arms raised and wrapped around thin air, the old man shuffled in a tight circle in front of Louie's desk.

"I do owe Lupita a thanks for helping Ethan out on the investigation."

"What are you waiting for? Take her out for a nice dinner," he insisted.

"Not that it matters to you, but for those of us still living, everything's closed down. That makes dating kind of a problem."

"Let me think," Mr. Henry said after he stopped spinning. "For our first date, I took Elizabeth up on the Skyline Drive for an afternoon cruise and a picnic."

Louie glanced at his desk calendar and noticed he had an appointment scheduled with his new attorney, Carter Jackson, in half an hour. At their first meeting, Louie had explained about Turks McGraw's offer to buy Gas N Go. When Jackson learned how much McGraw had offered Louie, the attorney sat a little straighter behind his desk's plastic sneeze guard, like the ones over the salad bar at Charlie's House of Beef on Route 220 near the Roanoke County line.

"Lupita's office is on the way," Mr. Henry said. "If you leave now, you can pop in and invite her on a midweek picnic and be at Carter Jackson's with five minutes to spare."

"Yeah," Louie said, rubbing his chin. "Midweek. Picnic over in Matilda Park. That might work."

"Go for it! My mother will be happy to learn you're spending time with a beautiful woman in the park named for her." Slowly, Mr. Henry's image faded into the framed business certificates on the gray wall.

Mr. Henry's plan for Louie didn't work. Lupita's car was gone from the parking lot. On the three-block walk to the attorney's office on Court Street, Louie called Lupita but got her voice mail, so he hung up.

Upon seeing his new client, Jackson rose from his desk and welcomed Louie from behind the sneeze guard. "Take a seat," he muffled as he adjusted his face mask.

Louie wedged his long body into a narrow wingback chair as Jackson resettled into his and shuffled through a stack of folders on the corner of his desk. "Let's see. Pyle. Pyle. Pyle. Here it is." He placed the folder on his lap and opened it.

Louie waited while Jackson read.

Eventually, Jackson laced his fingers atop the folder and said,

"Well. We've had a real adventure researching your question, Mr. Pyle."

"Is that good or bad?" Louie asked. "Call me Louie."

"If you take our advice, it's good news." He leaned in and went on, "Our efforts may have saved you from financial ruin, good sir."

"Tell me more," Louie said, mocking Jackson's cornball sincerity.

"You know the expression 'too good to be true'?" Without waiting for Louie to respond, he continued, "I'm afraid that adage applies here. Based on what we've managed to find on this company, I'd strongly advise you, as my client, to avoid this man and his offers. Avoid him like the plague." The lawyer tittered at his playful reference to the current pandemic.

"Why's that?"

"In short, he's a thief." Jackson removed his reading glasses from his masked nose and planted them in his shabby hair. "With the help of your accountant, we've managed to uncover some irregular things about Mr. McGraw. He has yet to honor the full obligations on his agreements with the last three retail operations similar to yours." Looking up from the file, he asked, "Did he insist on a handshake deal?"

Louie shrugged. "I don't recall it even getting that far."

"Good news for you. According to his own company's financial practices, spelled out in their annual reports and on its website, it places new Speedy stores in metropolitan areas with populations of fifty thousand or larger." Peering up at Louie, he added, "Which Fallam County isn't, thanks be to God."

"What does that mean for Gas N Go?" Louie asked.

"Turks McGraw is probably running some kind of side

hustle." Raising his hands in the air, he proclaimed, "Full disclosure here. This is only my opinion."

"If a man offers to buy something of mine, I'd expect to get paid. How does he get away with taking over the stores and not paying for them?"

"Easy. He's got more lawyers than you," Jackson joked. "Seriously, without seeing an actual contract, I'm speculating that he's got clauses buried in them that are tied to performance objectives. One of the store operators we spoke with handed over the deed to his store. Then, oops! Business slowed down and sales objectives stated in the contract weren't met. McGraw was no longer obligated to make payments. At which point, the legal fees the store owner would have incurred to get his business back would have been more than the business was worth. This gentleman lost everything, his entire life's work. But I have to admire McGraw's legal team's handiwork. Genius. Devilish, but genius."

"I was born at night but not last night," Louie said. "I'd want my money up-front before I handed over any deeds."

"We believe that wouldn't be what is offered."

Louie considered the attorney's comments.

"Again, I advise you to not do business with this person. If you do, you do it at great peril to your business. Is there anything else I can do for you, Louie?"

"Not for now, but I appreciate your help."

"Talk to your accountant. She did the research on three other businesses similar to yours and spoke with their owners." He stood, signaling a dismissal, and said, "Your bill will post today. Thank you for coming in."

Outside, Louie heard shouts coming from the front of the courthouse. Young people were climbing all over the Confederate memorial statue, holding up signs and yelling at pedestrians, "Silence is acceptance! Silence is acceptance!"

His phone raised above his head, Duncan Shane was posing in front of the crowd and talking into its camera. Louie headed to the back of the courthouse. At the entrance to the parking lot, he found more protesters waving signs and flags so he kept walking down the sidewalk toward the Grove Street side of the command center entrance. He found Ethan Quinn standing by the front door talking with two Mt Pleasant police officers. As he approached, they left Ethan and strolled through the parking lot toward the protesters.

"All in a day's work?" Louie asked Ethan.

"They're just kids blowing off steam," Ethan said. "With all the closings, most of them don't have anything to occupy their time."

"Send them over to see me," Louie said. "I'll find something for them to do. My store needs a power wash."

"Right," Ethan said. "Hey, if you're serious, I'll mention it."

"I'm serious as a tax collector. When one of my employees gets the sniffles, they have to stay in quarantine for two weeks. I'm always shorthanded these days."

"Jonnie and I are so sorry about what happened to Log Heaven," Ethan said. "Y'all need anything, let us know."

Louie removed his sunglasses and clipped them over the back of his ball cap. "I need to ask you something if you have a minute. Something personal."

The police chief motioned Louie to join him on the wooden bench by the front doors. They sat together and, for a minute, watched the two officers chatting with the protesters.

Louie took in a gulp of warm air, then slowly let it out. "I'm not sure what to do about something and I thought you could help me. As a friend."

"Shoot," a distracted Ethan said.

"Warren still hasn't completed his investigation into the fire."

Ethan sat quietly, his thumbs hooked over his utility belt, waiting for Louie to go on.

"I need some advice, as a friend," Louie repeated.

"If you know something about the fire or its cause, I suggest you tell Warren."

"It's concerning the fire, but not exactly," Louie said. "That's why I need your advice." Louie stood and walked out three paces and turned around. "Ahhhh, I just don't know what to do!"

"Spit it out, Louie."

"Lisa was at the house the night before." Then it all poured out, "It was Alex's birthday cookout. I'd asked the kids to tell Lisa *not* to come because of all the stuff, well, you know, all the trouble she's gotten herself into. I didn't think it was smart her being around me is all."

"That makes sense," Ethan said. He retrieved a handkerchief from his pocket and wiped sweat from around his neck.

"She was gettin' mouthy. You know how she gets when things don't go the way she wants them to. Like that time she called the law on me for not giving her the keys to her car. Told one of your deputies I hit her."

"Yeah, I remember that. She was madder than a wet hen when I relayed to her that your mama told us that it was her that was doing all the hitting."

"Before she got in Larry Baldwin's Hummer to leave that night, she said she'd be back. She said it like she meant it, real mean like." Louie sat next to Ethan on the bench. "I just don't know what to do. Should I tell Warren what she said?"

Ethan's eyes told Louie that he understood his friend's dilemma. If Louie reported the incident, he'd be seen as deflecting blame on his ex-wife. If he didn't report it, he'd be seen as a conspirator. He placed his hand on Louie's bouncing knee and said, "Alex came in this morning and told Warren about Lisa crashing his party. He was pretty insistent when he said the grill wasn't on the steps when he left around 1 a.m. I don't think telling Warren what you just told me matters one way or the other."

Louie focused on the protesters to keep his hunting buddy from seeing his weepy eyes.

FALL
2020

CHAPTER **THIRTY-ONE**

One September evening, Louie stopped by Gas N Go South on his way home. Both Alex and Thor Bear were on shift. Thor helped customers while Alex led Louie into the stock room. All the inventory was pushed to one side, piled to the ceiling. Several large monitors were mounted above an oblong folding table. Two leather gaming chairs, one blue with "Thor Bear" embroidered on the back, and one red, with "Alex," were in front of the table.

"Welcome to The Bear's Den," Alex said. He swiveled Thor's chair around, offering it to his dad, then slid into his own as it rolled away from the table. "Not including Gas N Go, we've got four security customers and one marketing content customer, Marsha Ann's aunt's business, Butterfly Migrations. We shoot and edit videos for her. Mostly for realtors showing houses."

"Wow, that's impressive. When do you find the time to do all this?" Louie asked. Just thinking about Alex and Thor's endeavor exhausted Louie and his arthritic knees.

"When we go off shift," Alex said. For the next half hour

or so, Alex demonstrated a monitoring application he and Thor had designed for businesses and homeowners. "We've signed up for an online cybersecurity class at Southwestern Poly. I want to be certified to help people keep their data safe."

"I hear that's where the future is," Louie said. "You really did some growing up this summer."

"I'm rocking this adulting thing, Dad," the boy boasted.

"I guess all that computer gaming paid off," Louie said, clearing his throat.

"You're not mad at me for not wanting to run Gas N Go, are you?"

"Son, I'm so proud of you. Look at all this," Louie said as he swiveled in the chair. "You've done all this on your own without anybody telling you. In my eyes, you're carrying on the Pyle tradition by working hard for yourself. Don't you worry about Gas N Go, it'll take care of itself. But I gotta ask. Can you and Thor Bear keep yourselves in rent money running this outfit?"

"You bet," Alex said. He proceeded to show his dad the accounting software he'd installed and The Bear's Den's bank account. "I set up the bank account when our video *My Dad Owns a Convenience Store* went viral."

Louie whistled. "Don't look like you need any business advice from the old man." He ruffled the kid's dark curls. "But you know where to find me," he added. "Door's always open."

"As soon as you get a house built to attach it to," Alex joked. "Dad, I got to tell you something. It's something I did."

"Telling Sheriff Jones about the grill?" Louie asked.

Alex stared at his lap.

"You did the right thing. You told the truth," Louie assured him.

"They still don't know who did it. If I had installed cameras on our house, we'd know who did it," Alex insisted.

"Coulda, woulda, shoulda. A man can't rely on those cheaters," Louie said. "Let the law do their job. We've told them everything we know. It's up to them to figure it out."

"I guess," Alex said. He was silent for a minute then confided, "Mom's been catfished."

"Come again?"

"You know, 'Hello, my beautiful dear. I'm in a Nigerian prison and can't get out. Please help by sending me your debit card number.'"

"I don't follow," Louie said.

"I forgot, you don't do social media," Alex said. Rubbing his hands on the tops of his thighs, he appeared to be thinking about how to explain his mother's predicament. "Scammers troll social media sites and find gullible people to rob. Most of their targets are lonely widowed or divorced women. Me and Jess finally got it out of her. Mom's been sending money to some guy she claims she met on Just Friends. Claims he's from Austin, Texas, and got arrested while working in Africa on an oil site. She fell for it hook, line, and sinker."

"Guess that's why they call it catfishing, huh?" Louie asked.

"She's not sorry about what she did," Alex said.

"What exactly did she do?" Louie asked.

"She took money from Gas N Go accounts and sent it to the scammer."

"Did she report it to the police?"

"No! She still thinks he's real. And she threatened to never talk to us again if we say anything to anybody about him, especially you. She says when he gets back to the States, he's gonna come and get her and take her back to Austin. That's why she's so mad at you for taking away her access to Gas N Go bank accounts."

"Good grief," Louie said, pushing his ball cap to the back of his head. "I missed that one. Didn't I, buddy?"

"You tried to help her. But, like you said, she's got to fix her own mess. Jess is trying to get her to see a psychologist. She really, really thinks this guy Marshall Pinto is a real person."

"So she wasn't taking the money for herself," Louie said.

"She swears she doesn't know anything about Larry Baldwin stealing from Gas N Go," Alex quietly said.

"You can't believe what your mom tells you about all this mess. Think about it. Does Baldwin strike you as being a mastermind of *anything?*" Louie placed his hand on his chest and said, "Your mom was a good mom and she loves you and Jessica and Ken but she also manipulates people to get what she wants. And if she wanted a date with this Pinto fella, whether he was real or not, you know she'd go to great lengths to get it."

"Then this avatar Marshall Pinto is some righteous karma, man," Alex said.

"I expect so. When you see her, tell her I'm praying for her," Louie said. As he stood, dizziness overtook him. He placed his hand on the table and waited for Alex to lead the way out of the stock room.

Mr. Henry was waiting for him in his truck. "You ah'ite?"

Louie nodded and turned on the radio, full blast. He needed to be alone. The sweet voice of a young woman crooned:

"I'm gonna get a tattoo
A picture of me and you
Stamped right over my heart..."

THE NEXT WEEK, ALEX TOOK his drone to Log Heaven. Louie was tired of waiting for the fire marshal to tell him how his house caught on fire. He hired Alex to video the ruins in case the fire marshal needed another look around.

Over the loud beeping of an excavator rolling off its flatbed, Alex said, "Dad, taking video of the crime scene is an awesome idea. We can go to the county sheriff's office and offer to do this for their crime scenes."

"There you go, thinking like an entrepreneur," Louie said. "Better go make some hay with Sheriff Jones before somebody beats you to it."

Earlier, his insurance agent had called. Based on discussions with the Fallam County Fire Department, the company was confident Louie didn't set fire to his own house, on purpose or otherwise. Louie took this conversation as a signal to move ahead with demolition. The rubble of half-burnt timbers and exposed bathroom fixtures weren't doing anything for his state of mind. The past had been buried inside the pile of cold ashes. He was ready to move ahead with a new way of living.

Colder weather was on its way. Louie needed a place to live while his house was being rebuilt. Along with Sal and his baba, the three were still camped out in the boathouse with the canoe and lawn furniture. Sal's everyday chickpea dishes had given Louie eternal gas and he'd eaten enough lamb to last a lifetime. He didn't look forward to telling the Contentos that it was time for them to move on.

Josh, the son of one of Louie's fishing buddies, walked down the driveway as Louie and Alex watched the loud excavator scoop up debris and empty it into a dump truck. Josh was hired to build a smaller version of Log Heaven. Alex had already named it

Two Dot Oh. Louie's goal was to be back in his house for his annual Super Bowl party.

Louie shouted to Josh, "Since it's just me and Possum, I figured I'd downsize in place."

Josh politely smiled at his new customer's corny joke. "I saw Jessica in town the other day. Has she moved back home? I had a secret crush on her in high school."

Louie chuckled, "Son, I have no idea what *any* of the Pyle women are going to do from one day to the next. You'll have to ask her yourself because I'm liable to get it wrong."

Amid the noise of the excavator, Louie felt something tugging on the leg of his blue jeans. He looked down to see Maddy. She squealed, "Poppy!"

Louis picked up his granddaughter and gleefully shouted, "Jumpin' Bean!" He hadn't seen her since Alex's party in July. She wrapped her tiny arms around his sunburned neck, gibbering on about going fishing with her Poppy.

Jessica appeared at Louie's side. He noticed right away that something was wrong. Her eyes were red with black half-moons underneath. It was a mid-morning Tuesday and she wasn't at her work-at-home desk.

"Can we talk?" she asked. "In private." To Maddy, she said, "Stay with Uncle Alex. Mommy needs to talk to Poppy."

Louie followed her back to her car, which was parked behind Josh's work truck.

"They've arrested Mom," she squeaked. "Took her away in handcuffs."

Louie swept his daughter up into his arms and hugged her as she sobbed into his shoulder. In a muffled tone, she repeated, "They took my mommy away."

Louie tried to absorb his daughter's grief by squeezing tighter. Helpless worry threaded through him because he was unable to protect Jessica from her own pain.

Pushing away from him, she blew her nose then said, "The lawyer said he'll try to get her bonded out but we shouldn't get our hopes up."

"What is she charged with?" Louie feared the answer to his question.

"Conspiring to commit arson," Jessica sniffled. "And … and …. attempted murder." She planted her forehead on Louie's shoulder again.

"Jess, be strong. For Maddy," Louie said. "What proof do they have?"

"Her lawyer says her dipwad boyfriend Larry confessed to setting the fire and that Mom told him to do it."

"But why?" Louie asked. "Why would she do this?"

"I don't know," Jessica said. "Lately, she's not been making any sense. She's lost it. She's got this crazy notion that some guy from Austin is coming to get her and take her away."

"Alex told me about the catfishing scheme. It fits with all the money she stole."

"Dad, she's not well. She's sick. She needs help." Her pleading eyes told Louie she was waiting for him to say something, to fix it, to clean up the mess and make it all better.

Having just learned that his ex-wife was arrested for trying to kill him, had wanted him dead, what could he offer his daughter? For the first time in the long years of knowing Lisa, Louie wasn't compelled to offer a helpful solution to her problems. He was done. Really, really done. As the old troubadour's song went, he had been released.

CHAPTER **THIRTY-TWO**

Because of Louie's recent distractions—avoiding a takeover by Speedy's, catching thieves who were robbing the store, and his house burning to the ground—his weekly business meetings with Lupita had taken a summer hiatus. Passing each other in the parking lot one day in late September, they awkwardly agreed that it was time to get back into their weekly schedule of reviewing Gas N Go's income and expenses.

On the day of the meeting, he parked his truck and turned off the radio. Mr. Henry's image flickered in the passenger's seat as Louie dialed Kiara's number on his phone.

"Why are you calling her?" Mr. Henry asked. "You can handle this on your own."

"Be quiet," Louie said to the old man. "Kiara, I'm seeing Lupita about some of my business. Do you think it's OK to talk about that other thing?"

Kiara yawned into the phone. "What other thing?"

Mr. Henry smirked. "See?"

Louie waved the old man off. "Be quiet."

"Why you telling me to be quiet? You called *me*," Kiara said.

Louie turned the radio on, causing Mr. Henry's image to fade into the car seat. "Tell me what to say."

"You can begin by apologizing for not calling her. Then, thank her for helping you catch Lisa with both hands in the cookie jar."

"Right," Louie said. He patted his shirt pocket, searching for his notepad to write down Kiara's instructions. Not finding it, he repeated them to his friend, "Apologize for not calling her then thank her for helping me. Do you think it's too soon to ask her out? Maybe I should wait a day or so before I do that."

Kiara insisted, "Stop overthinking it, bra. Ask her already. Then you'll know if she's interested or not. Either way, you can stop obsessing for crying out loud."

Inside the building, a nervous Louie found his way to Lupita's office. There she was, even more beautiful than ever. Her dark glossy hair emitted an exotic perfume as she swept it up into a messy bun with one of those talon-like clips of hers.

"Have a seat," she said while gazing into her computer screen. "We've got a lot of catching up to do. I'm seeing a positive up-trend in net income."

Standing with his cap in his hand, Louie said, "Before we get started, I wanted to thank you for pitching in with Miss Basket-ville. Ethan said you figured it all out for them."

"*De nada*," she said, waving him off. "It's what you pay me to do."

"I'm serious. Thank you," Louie said. He gulped at dry air and ruffled up his hat hair. "I'm not the brightest guy around. And I don't know how to ask for help when I need it. You saved Gas N Go. Thank you."

Folding her hands on her desk, she looked up at him and said, "Sit."

He had her full attention now, he thought as he slipped into the chair.

In a discontented tone, she said, "I don't want to hear your 'I'm sharp as a marble' excuse. You can't fool me. You're not *estupido*. Because men are incapable of asking for help doesn't make them lacking in intelligence. Not asking for help is hardwired into your genes." She placed her palm on her heart. "It's part of your macho trait to protect others. It's your most endearing quality. It's what I like about you." Pointing her slim finger at her temple, she said, "Your real shortfall is you are too busy *not listening*."

"But, I …," Louie started.

Lupita raised an eyebrow, conveying that his objection confirmed her point. "Several times I told you somebody was stealing from Gas N Go. Did you listen to my advice? No. Instead, you hired someone three hours away who doesn't understand you or your business. Your Miss Baskerville is billing you three times what I charge. You want to see the bill?" Not waiting for a response, she continued, "I told you about *eSpeedy* McGraw. I pleaded with you to let me help. I even came to your house. But did you listen? Or act on *any* of my recommendations I sent to you on email? No. Instead, you hired a lawyer and *he* came to me to do all the research."

Louie sputtered. What good would it have done to try to explain his decision to trust no one until the thief was locked up? Better he kept his mouth closed, zipped, and locked.

"I thought it was understood in our business arrangement that you would heed my advice. Advice backed by years of training and experience." Holding up an index finger, she went on, "I'll say this only once, Louie Pyle, please show respect for the advice I give to you."

"You're right. I've not been listening. From now on, I'm all ears."

"Good," she said. She swiveled the monitor so he could see it. "Tell me. Why is Sal buying enough flour to make a cake big enough for the entire county?"

The meeting ended without Louie asking Lupita out for a Matilda Park lunch. After her lecture on her professional abilities, he feared he'd offend her should he end the meeting on such a personal level. Sadly, he thought as he left the building, their partnership was destined to remain one of commerce and not one of the heart.

IN SPITE OF THE CONTINUED pandemic shutdowns, Gas N Go was projected to have its best fourth quarter ever. Since Alex and Thor's *My Dad Owns a Convenience Store* video channel was discovered by foodie trollers from as far as Vietnam, folks were coming into the store to take selfies with Louie and to buy what Kiara called "merch," Gas N Go ball caps, T-shirts, and face masks.

"You have to promote your brand," she told him when she'd pitched her idea to be Gas N Go's digital marketing manager. In a matter of weeks, the three young entrepreneurs — Alex, Thor, and Kiara — had expanded Sal and Angel's Get N Go Dinner ordering website to include a page for purchasing hats, T-shirts, face masks, and sanitizers all stamped with the Gas N Go logo and funny expressions from the Louie videos. Videos of Sammy Hagar swinging in her hammock over the chip aisle and two girls wrestling over a store clerk were tied for second place for the most "likes."

In the video with the most likes, Louie commented, in reference to the ready meals for the stay-at-home customers, "We're making hay while the sun shines!"

"What does baling hay have to do with anything in this century?" Alex had asked.

Louie laughed at his son's ignorance of the agrarian reference. "You millennials are supposed to know everything."

Rolling his eyes for the camera, Alex whipped out his cell phone and read aloud the phrase's meaning, "Make the most of a favorable situation while it lasts."

"Exactly," Louie said. "See, farmers need to mow and bail hay before it gets rained on. Horses can't eat moldy hay, son. It gives them gas and causes them to fart."

Egging him on, Alex asked, "So we're feeding our customer's hay so they'll fart?"

"Stop playing around now."

After the camera was shut off, he said to Alex, "What I'm telling you is if we don't get these ready meals out in the deli cases, we'll miss an opportunity to make some hay. Get it? Hay equals money."

Alex rebutted, "Your analogy makes no sense, Dad. Today, people say you're 'making bank.'" As an afterthought, he joked, "Maybe the internet trolls are laughing at you, thinking you're a *hayseed*."

Keeping the joke going, Louie said, "Hey! Look who's laughing all the way to the bank, sunshine."

Louie Pyle had finally become the star of his own life.

FALLAM COUNTY SIGHED IN exhausted relief as the first day of fall arrived. Earth's subtle shifting into autumnal light had brought with it an easing of the endless worry. Many of the state-ordered restrictions on social interaction had been relaxed. And, praise to all His Glory, the congregation at Mt Pleasant Methodist church celebrated its first in-person communion since Easter, albeit with fewer congregants.

However, in those waning days of the pandemic, the air's ions felt out of balance. A quiet uncertainty tugged at everyone. Some waited patiently for the great reset while others nervously planned for a different future. One thing was certain. The world had changed and Fallam County had changed, too. No longer did the residents view themselves as a single entity, a secluded tribe hidden from the harsh realities of a modern world riddled with inequities. Time, a river polluted with contagions, had washed their virtuous solidarity away. Exposed, they had no place to go except forward.

Louie was working the cash register at the town store one morning when Duncan Shane showed up for his free breakfast of coffee and a beef jerky stick.

"Today's my last day on the Fallam County beat," Duncan offered. "I got a job in D.C. working for an e-rag called the *Political Mite*." He handed Louie a business card. "Call me if you have any news you want to share."

Louie noticed the spelling of the name of the publication. "I'm not the smartest guy in town but ain't a mite an itty bitty parasite? I mean, if I was an aspiring journalist such as yourself, I'd want to work for somebody like *The Washington Post*."

"Believe me, I've tried," the young man said as he pushed up the sleeves of his flannel shirt so Louie, and anyone else in the store, could admire his tattoos. "*The Post* is a lame newspaper. It's a dinosaur."

Louie wanted to say to the young man that maybe if he lopped off the lice nest he called a man bun, he'd have a chance at working for the revered newspaper. Instead, he said, "They still call them newspapers? Nowadays, people get their news online, don't they?"

"Are you ever going to give me a quote for the Stoner story?" an irritated Duncan asked.

"How about this," Louie said. He offered the reporter another jerky stick and said, "No comment."

"What about the Speedy's story? You got anything to say about Turks McGraw and his plans to build a Speedy's here in town."

"I read in one of your competitor's reports that Speedy's has opted not to come to Fallam County," Louie said. In fact, Louie had received a phone call from his attorney Carter Jackson saying the McGraw family had reached out to him and stated that McGraw was not authorized by the company or the McGraw family to make offers to purchase competitor's operations. They were not responsible, nor legally bound, to any offers Mr. McGraw had made or will make at any time in the future.

"Is it true that he offered you several million dollars for your stores?" Duncan asked.

"Mr. McGraw and I had a nice chat about the convenience store business in Fallam County. That's about all it amounted to. How 'bout the protesters? If you ain't here to cover them, who's going to keep the public informed of their grievances?" Louie asked.

Duncan waved the question off. "They all went back to

school or Philadelphia or wherever they came from. Anyway, the oppression here isn't as bad as it is in places like Richmond."

"Is that a fact?" Louie asked.

Frustrated with not getting anything out of his best possible source for news in Fallam County, Duncan thanked Louie for the coffee and waved good-bye. Louie wished the young man luck in his new endeavors and invited him to come back anytime.

CHAPTER **THIRTY-THREE**

On the fourth Saturday of October, a full week before Halloween, Louie hosted an afternoon fall barbecue for his staff and their families at Gas N Go West. The day before Sal and Angel roasted pork and lamb on the West's oversized spit for the occasion. The stone patio behind the store was decorated with pumpkins, gourds, orange and black paper ribbons, and bundles of dried corn stalks. The picnic tables offered a front-row seat to Bear Mountain's ridge of red and brown oaks interlaced with a pop of yellow maple and dark evergreens, all framed by crystal blue skies and green pastures.

In preparation for the big day, Kiara and Angel worked hard at rearranging work shifts so everyone had an opportunity to participate at some point in the festivities. Lupita insisted that Louie establish a designated driver system to aid those who drank too much beer or hard cider. Earlier in the month when Lupita had offered to manage Gas N Go's H.R. responsibilities, Louie handed them over with wild exuberance. Both seemed happy with the arrangement. Louie now had time to focus on new business ideas while Lupita seemed energized by managing a large work staff.

Sitting at one of the picnic tables, Louie watched as Lupita got out of her SUV and walked toward him, her bangles jingling. Her brown skin glowed from the warmth of the midafternoon sun. When she noticed him watching her, she twirled around in her marigold dress as it floated over the tops of her bare knees. She boldly plopped beside him and propped her elbows onto the table. Tilting her face toward the sun, she closed her eyes and said with her Latina passion, "I love this time of the year. Don't you? Leaves are exploding everywhere in their final gasp of color before they die."

He wasn't sure how to get excited about dead leaves exploding but he certainly was excited to be this close to her with a view of her elegant neck and locks of hair swirling about in the calm breeze.

She opened one eye. "You were right, Louie. This is the perfect spot for a picnic destination. But I'm not sure how you can pay for all the enhancements you expect to make since you bought that property across the road."

"The farmhouse is part of the plan," he said. "Artie Three's bank said they'd loan me the money."

The two sat side by side for a quiet minute and watched an eagle ride the afternoon's warm drafts.

Calmly, she asked, "Why don't *we* go on a picnic together?"

"I'd like that," he said. His heart picked up its pace as he heard Kiara's advice from weeks before, "Let the lady lead the dance." Then, he said to Lupita, "And afterward, we can go for a dance."

"Oh, I'd love that. I'll teach you how to dance cumbia."

She closed her eyes again and smiled as the sun illuminated her face.

Kiara arrived next, dressed as a sexy pirate barmaid. Louie got up from the picnic table and helped her set up her photo booth complete with Halloween-themed paper masks. "This is going to be so much fun. We'll get a lot of shots for the website," she said as she posed with a pirate mask and snapped a selfie. "Jessica said she'd pick up Betty Doris from Miss Wanda's."

"Don't you think the air might be too chilly for her?" Louie asked. At Miss Wanda's Home for Ladies, Betty Doris showed no signs of slowing down. She'd found a new cast of extras for the Betty Doris Show and, fortunately, the hourly phone calls to Louie had dwindled to once a day at sunrise.

Kiara assured Louie, "We'll make sure she sits by the firepit. That'll keep her warm and she can regale everybody with her fire rescue story."

They both watched as Jessica's bright orange car bounded into the gravel parking area and slid to a quick stop.

Louie observed, "Jess drives like her mother. Two speeds. Sixty mile an hour or both feet on the brakes."

Shading her eyes from the sun with her hand, Kiara asked, "Have you heard anything about Lisa's situation? I read online that she's being charged for the arson and is in jail until the trial."

"That's some of her business I don't need to know about," Louie said.

"Lupita's happy she's in jail," Kiara said. "Did you know that Lisa threatened her?"

"What?" In Louie's head, Mr. Henry whispered, "I told you your ex-wife was unhinged."

Kiara frowned. "She told me yesterday that a few days after

the day the piano was delivered and we were all at Log Heaven, Lisa barged into Lu's office and told her that if she ever showed her face at *her* house again, she'd have Lu's head shaved and her fingers broken. That she knew people."

The news stunned Louie. All he could say was, "I didn't know."

"You better make it some of your business," Kiara mocked.

"Kiara, I swear, I didn't know. That explains why she turned down my invitations to come over for dinner or come to Alex's weenie roast."

"I'm sure it was," Kiara said. "Have you asked her out on a date yet?"

"I'm working on it," he said.

"What are you waiting for? Get a move on!" Kiara said. She rubbed Louie's arm and added, "I didn't mean to bum you out. I thought you knew about Lisa's threat. I'm sorry."

"I'm glad you told me," he said. Watching Sal's beat-up commuter car pull in beside Jessica's, he added, "I got something I need to look after. Help Jess with Betty Doris, will ya?"

As Sal, his baba, and Angel crawled out of the tiny car, Louie waved at the pizza chef to follow him. The pair walked across the county road, approaching the long, dusty driveway of the house across from the store.

The empty house sat on a knoll amid a field dotted with dried corn shocks and crows picking in the red clay. The crows and the shocks foretold the fate of the land; it had produced its last crop of corn. The farmer's son, Ben, was selling the two hundred-acre spread. Rumor around Mt Pleasant had Gus and Augie Young building a tract of starter homes on it.

Ben had worked for Louie while he was in high school but,

like many of Fallam County's youth, he moved away for a different life. When Louie learned the farm was going up for sale, he called Ben and offered to buy the house and surrounding yard complete with chicken coop and driveway.

"Augie plans to put the community pool where Pop's house sits," Ben had explained over the phone to his first boss. Then he grumbled, "I really don't want to sell but I need the money to cover Dad's Elder Home bill. Sure you don't want to buy the whole farm?"

"Nope, just the house and the driveway," Louie said.

"Screw it. I went to school with that jerk. He bullied me until I was big enough to punch back. The house is yours, Mr. Pyle."

"I heard Iris Lee was looking for some land out that way to build one of those, what do you call them? A solar farm?"

"Oh, yeah? Maybe I'll give her a call."

Louie and Sal stopped at the entrance to the farm and took in the view across the road, watching as Angel and Kiara scurried around with their party preparations. "Remember that proposition we talked about the day before the fire?" Louie asked. "How would you like to open a pizzeria at this store? We could extend the other side and move the store over there and make the current area a restaurant. Alex already has the name picked out for you." Louie stretched his arms into the air like a carnival barker and shouted, "The Montenegrin Outback. In honor of your baba." Facing Sal, he went on, "How's that sound? Mr. Contento could sell cigars for me in the store and you could spin your pizza dough in the new restaurant."

Sal was wringing his hands, lathering up a heap of worry. "I don't know. Baba doesn't like to bring attention to himself."

"Don't you worry about that. Ms. Quinn is working on getting your baba's immigration papers straightened out." Tapping his nose with his index finger, he said, "She's an expert."

"Your generosity is too much," Sal said. "But where would we live? We would have to drive across the entire county twice every day."

"I like you and all, Sal, but I think it's time you and your baba moved out of my boathouse." Louie grinned. "People are starting to talk about us spending so much time together." He placed his hand on one of Sal's shoulders and spun him around. Pointing up the dirt road to the shabby little farmhouse, he said, "Welcome to your new home. It's yours. You can rent it month to month or rent to own. Your choice."

"But?" was all Sal could say. Since the blessings in his life were so few, he was unsure of how to react to such a generous offer. "Am I dreaming?"

"No, it's not a dream. It's a lot of work is what it is," Louie noted. "What do you say? Are you in?"

Grinning, Sal nodded vigorously. "I'm in, Mr. Louie."

They watched as Jessica took something from the trunk of her car.

Out of the blue, Sal said nervously, "I'm in love with your daughter. Do I have your permission to ask her to marry me?"

Louie didn't see that one coming. He chuckled as he thought of Josh, his home builder who asked about Jessica every time they spoke. "Get in line, Sal. Get in line."

Together, they laid out the fall feast for the guests. With everything at the ready, they stood and watched as Angel topped her pumpkin pie tarts with whipped cream. Maddy watched, her big eyes level with the picnic table, as Angel squeezed and swirled the thick cream from her pastry bag onto the pies.

"Seeing Maddy there," Betty Doris said, "reminds me of the time Louie and I were visiting my mother at her boarding house."

"Mama, you don't need to tell this."

Ignoring her son, Betty Doris continued, "My mother's cherry pies were famous. Louie was barely tall enough to see over the kitchen table, four or five. His little eyes lit up when he saw a cherry pie, just out of the oven, sitting on the table. He said, 'Grandma, is that you pie or we pie?'" She wrapped her frail arms around her son's waist and hugged him.

Louie blushed. "Mama, you love telling that story to embarrass me. Don't you?"

She continued as the others laughed. "We laughed so hard it made you cry because you didn't understand what was going on." She softly patted her son's belly and said, "We were laughing because we loved you so much. After that, my mother baked Louie his own little pie whenever he visited. She called it Louie's pie." She pulled a tissue from her sleeve and dabbed at her eyes.

"Thanks, Mama. I'll never hear the end of this," Louie said.

Angel said, "I can make some of those for the Get N Go Dinner menu. You Pies can be the tarts and We Pies can be the regular sized pies."

They all laughed again. The collective joy was a sign that the day was going to be a successful one. And it was.

CHAPTER **THIRTY-FOUR**

In spite of promises of pandemic closings ending by Labor Day, in time for back to school and football games, the accursed virus wasn't abiding any government mandated schedules or waving its white flag of surrender. With a readily available vaccine months away, Mt Pleasant's volunteer community wasn't sure what to do about hosting the annual Thanksgiving dinner held at the American Legion every year. Fallam County's destitute were in jeopardy of not receiving their autumn feast of turkey and giblet gravy and cornbread dressing and mashed potatoes and collards and green beans and pumpkin pie.

The second week of November, Iris Lee invited Louie and his son Alex to her farm for her annual turkey shoot. The event raised money to fund the community's Thanksgiving dinner.

As they stood around waiting their turn to shoot at the paper turkey targets, they discussed what could be done to feed those in need on the occasion of their showing of gratitude and brotherly love. More than any other year, the event was needed to help the community weather a dark and sad time, they all agreed.

Jonnie Bailey said, "We've got to figure out a way to host the turkey dinner. Families rely on us to help out this time of year."

Ethan asked his wife, "How many meals did we serve last year?"

"Over five hundred," she replied.

Louie let out a low whistle and said, "Whoa, that's a lot of green beans."

"We could set up a voucher system and give out a free turkey in our stores," Oral Sams, the owner of Food Markets, offered.

"That's a good idea but it doesn't help those who don't have access to a kitchen," Jonnie said.

"And what about those who just can't cook," Iris Lee chipped in.

"I suppose Gas N Go could make up some Get N Go turkey dinners," Louie offered. "Somebody else would have to pick them up for distribution." And turning to Oral Sams, he added, "I expect your kitchen could handle double what I could make."

Sams nodded. "Our take-out food business has tripled since the lockdowns started. We could create a packaged dinner for donation. But who would decide who gets them?"

Travis English, the community banker, said, "Penn runs the food pantry at our church. I'm sure she'd know somebody who could organize the distribution part."

"I know what let's do!" Jonnie said, changing the direction of the discussion. "What if we still held it at the American Legion but held it outdoors? In the parking lot. Get some of those standing propane heaters the restaurants are using. Move the tables and chairs outside."

"Build a bonfire," someone suggested.

"We'd have to get fire and rescue involved if we did that,"

Ethan said.

"Let's do this!" Jonnie proclaimed. "Iris, why don't you and Louie take lead on this. The rest of us will follow your direction."

Louie wasn't sure he liked where this was heading.

But before he could object to somebody else volunteering his time for their own priorities, Alex nudged him. "Dad, it's our turn to shoot."

"You go ahead. I got to nip this in the bud before they got me running the entire show." His phone vibrated in his pocket. When he pulled it out, he saw Kiara's number flash on the display.

"Louie, where are you?"

Recognizing the worry in her voice, he asked, "What's wrong?"

"Donnie's asking for you to come visit him today."

"I'm at Lee Farm's shooting range with Alex." Louie turned his back to the gathering and gazed out at the long view of gentle hills. He spied the lone oak tree on Lee Farm's cemetery hill, the one Donnie had described in his story about the moonshiners. Mr. Henry was standing under it, waving lazily.

"Is Miss Lee there?" Kiara asked. "Donnie wanted me to call her, too." Kiara was holding back tears but staying strong.

After hesitating, he asked, "Is he?"

"Today's a good day. That's why he wants to see y'all."

Hearing whoops coming from the range, Louie made his way to Alex.

"Dad, Dad!" The young man exclaimed. "I won! I won! I won the turkey shoot. Mr. Quinn says I'm a natural. Can we set up a shooting range at Two Dot Oh? I need to practice before the spring competition. This is awesome fun."

"Congratulations," Louie said. "Let's talk about it later. Right now I've got to go and visit with Mr. Tyler." He grabbed his son and hugged him, whispering in his ear, "I love you, son. And I'm proud of you."

Excitement consumed Alex. Ignoring his father's tender declarations, he pushed him aside and said, "They said I could shoot another round. A victory round! This is the most ever victorious day in Fallam County target shooting history."

"You bet," Louie said. He found Iris Lee and repeated Donnie's request. He offered her a ride to Bert Swanson's house as he slid his hunting rifle into its canvas bag.

After speaking with her farm manager, Iris followed Louie to his truck. "This will work for me. I rode in with Jonnie and Ethan. Can you give me a ride to Grove Street afterward?"

He nodded.

"Thanks for including me," she said as she pulled herself up into the truck. "I don't know about you but I'm not too keen on being drafted into cooking dinner for half of Fallam County. If we'd stayed any longer, Jonnie would have us crafting napkin rings."

Louie was grateful that Iris had accepted his offer, occupying the passenger seat of his truck. He wasn't sure how he'd handle Mr. Henry's presence on this particular journey into Mt Pleasant. In the silence of the cab, he felt compelled to tell Iris about his recent conversations with her father, about how the old man's wisdom had guided him through his latest rough patch in his own life's journey. But the woman would think he was crazy and demand to be put out on the road.

"Alex seems to like his gun," she said to break the silence. "I don't know if I ever thanked you for what you did for my father in his last days. After his death, one of the nurses told me that you visited him every day while he was in the hospital. And that you were with him when he passed."

"I have little recollection of my own father. Mr. Henry tried to fill in as best as he could," Louie offered.

"When I was young, I was jealous of you. He was always talking about your successes. The implication being I had none. My father was a thorny man. It made it hard for his family to love him."

"Oh, he dished it out on me, too," Louie said. "I know he thought the world of your mama and was proud of you."

"So I've been told. It's a shame I never heard it from his own lips."

"I was hardest on my kids when I wanted them to be better. Maybe I learned that from Mr. Henry," Louie said, daring not to glance at the passenger side for fear of seeing the old man's face hovering behind Iris's head.

"Donnie Tyler told me the same thing," Iris said. "Listen to me yammering on about my daddy issues. Bert says the doctor told her he's in the end stage of COPD and his heart is failing." She reflected, "Too much ganja weed in his tobacco I suppose."

"I heard he liked his smokes," Louie said.

"Donnie Tyler is the humblest human being I've ever known."

Bert welcomed them into the cozy front room of her Eastend Street bungalow. She fussed over untidy lap blankets and imperceptible dust while offering them a seat and something warm to drink. Louie noticed that time had been good to Bert. Short heather gray braids framed her creamy pie-shaped face, not a wrinkle in sight. Her once portly stature had been replaced with a smaller version of herself.

Kiara appeared with a tray of coffee. Her grief bore down on her, her hair as frazzled as the oversized nubby sweater she was wearing. She said, "We can't get him to go to the hospital. He told us he wanted to die on God's terms, not by some white coat's schedule."

"He gets his stubborn streak from his mother's side, Kiara," Bert said. To Iris and Louie, she said, "The hospital sent over a palliative care worker and Donnie told her to set the morphine on the table and leave. He won't even let me call the preacher."

Iris laid her hand over Bert's to calm her cousin.

"Mr. Pyle, you know the Lord. Can you say something to Donnie? Help him understand we're trying to ease his burden of dying," Bert pleaded.

"Louuuie Pyle. Is 'at you?" Donnie called out from the back of the house.

Louie said to Bert, "I'll do what I can, Miss Bert. But it sounds like he ain't quite ready to take the final communion just yet." The sound of his friend's voice assured Louie that Donnie wasn't dying, not today anyway. However, Louie was not prepared for what he saw when he entered Donnie's room. In August he'd seen a bent but spirited Donnie Tyler shuffling along with his new lightweight walker, his humor still intact. But now the man lay on a single bed in the tiny bedroom that was covered in chintz and damask. His dark face had taken on a blue hue brought on by the chronic oxygen robbing ailment. As Louie entered the room, Donnie struggled to sit up in the bed. The motion ignited a coughing fit, the sound of which caused Louie to shiver.

Bert brushed by Louie and leaned in to straightened Donnie's bed pillows. She rubbed his back, quietly repeating a Bible passage Louie didn't recognize.

Finally catching his breath, Donnie said, "Bert, can you give us a few minutes? And close the door behind you."

Launching a stern look at Louie, she said, "Ten minutes."

Louie searched for a place to sit, finding a chintz chair overflowing with accessory pillows.

"Just toss them on the floor," Donnie said. "Bert and Kiara been fussing over me and I'm being suffocated by pillows. When can I move back to Log Heaven?" The hitch in his laugh brought on the threat of another coughing fit but he managed to calm his breathing. In a strained voice, he went on, "I ain't got but so many words left in me, so I'll get right to what I need to say."

Louie waited for Donnie to continue.

"First off, you're a good man, Louie Pyle. God graced Fallam County the day He let you come into this world. I want to thank you for saving me and your mama from the 'rona virus. Breaking us out of the nursing home. And for helping Kiara. She's finding her way 'cause of you. I know she's going to do big things."

Louie looked at his hands as Donnie rested.

Taking in a gulp of air, Donnie delivered a surprised punch at Louie, "I knowed Hank told you the bat story." Donnie wiped dribble from the corner of his mouth with a tissue.

"Bat story?" Louie denied knowing of Mr. Henry's claim, the one the old man had told Louie years ago and again this past summer.

"Gus Young's baseball bat. The one Ben Lee used to kill that college boy. Hank finally got around to telling me what actually happened. Boy was drunk, sniffing around my sister Vee and calling her ugly names." Donnie took a hit of air with his oxygen mask then continued, "Remember when Mr. Henry showed up at your house this summer?"

“I remember you sleepwalking and talking to yourself a couple of times before the house burned down,” Louie said. What with everything going on, he’d forgotten about the old man’s retelling of his account of his brother murdering a man because the pair were chasing after the same woman.

Donnie aimed his finger at Louie. “Don’t play dumb,” he wheezed. “Mr. Henry talks to you. I seen him riding around with you in that fancy truck of yours.”

To avert Donnie’s judgmental gaze, Louie picked at a fingernail. All this unease was Mr. Henry’s doings. The old man was dragging him into something that didn’t even concern him, something that happened to somebody he didn’t even know, something that happened too long ago to matter now.

“I can feel it. He wants us to see to it that the man’s family learns the truth of how he died.”

“Donnie, what does it matter how some drunk, smart-aleck college kid got hisself killed what, fifty, sixty years ago?” Louie paused, realizing he’d revealed his awareness of the story. No sense in lying now, Donnie was too smart to fool so he might as well argue his case. Leaning toward the bed, he said, “Telling the boy’s parents, if they’re even alive to hear it, won’t change a thing. The guy will still be dead after the telling.”

“What’s everybody yelling on the courthouse steps these days? No justice, no peace?” Donnie wiped at his mouth again. “How can that boy’s soul *k-n-o-w* peace? How can his family *k-n-o-w* justice until they hear the truth about how he spent his last minutes on Earth?” Donnie placed a feeble hand over his chest. “No, I got this burden in my heart. Hank put it there for a reason. He wants us to do this for him.”

Louie looked away. Why was life always so damned hard?

"Think about it this way, Donnie. Ain't no way we could prove it even happened."

"What about Gus Young? He was there," Donnie argued.

"You think Gus Young is going to walk into the jailhouse and tell Sheriff Jones how he was accessory to murder by holding back evidence? And where's the evidence? You actually seen this bat?"

"No, but Hank told me where he put it."

"Did you go looking for it?"

"I got Kiara to crawl up under the house where he said I'd find it," Donnie said.

"And besides cobwebs and spiders, what did she find?" Louie asked him.

The hopelessness of the case was beginning to sink in with Donnie. He lowered his head. His breathing became calm.

"That's what I thought. Nothing," Louie said, "You got no way of proving what Mr. Henry told you. Whenever he told you." Louie added, "Besides, he's got no right putting that burden on you. Or me."

"It troubles me. Ben Lee was the biggest bully there ever was. He should be burning in hell for what he did."

"Who's to say he ain't?"

Donnie didn't seem convinced.

"If we went digging around on this, the boy's family are the ones who'll suffer." Recalling Mr. Henry's own words, Louie repeated them now, "And don't you think they've suffered enough?" With this sentiment, Louie realized even ghosts needed to relieve their conscience, to ask for forgiveness.

"If it's any comfort," Louie went on, "Ben Lee got what was owed him. Somebody told me he was bludgeoned to death by an

L.A. gang. I'd say justice was served.

"I expect so," Donnie acquiesced.

ON THEIR RIDE TO IRIS'S HOUSE, she said to Louie, "At my father's memorial service, Donnie told me that Mr. Henry pushed me away because he wanted me to go out into the world and live life on my own terms." She sniffed then went on, "Today, Donnie told me my dad loved me deeply. I don't know, it felt like Donnie was talking to him, like Dad was in the room with us. Donnie said Mr. Henry was glad I found happiness here at home, here in Mt Pleasant."

"The little man is smart about such things," Louie said, not offering to share what he and Donnie had discussed. Then he proceeded to tell Iris about the progress his builder had made on Two Dot Oh. The roof was up but he wouldn't be able to move back in until after Christmas and before Super Bowl Sunday. He was renting a room from Sal Contento at his new home. He joked about how the builder Josh was dragging his feet on completing the rest of the house because it guaranteed the young man opportunities to ask about Jessica who had decided to move back to Fallam County.

When he rolled into her driveway and she got out of his truck, they agreed to go see Donnie together the following week since their visit seemed to lift his spirits. Louie hoped he had done the right thing by persuading Donnie not to mention the story about the bat and how he came to learn of it to anyone else. Yet, he grinned as he imagined Duncan Shane shoving a cell phone in Donnie's face, demanding to know what it was like to talk to a ghost.

Half wishing for Mr. Henry to show up on the ride home,

Louie turned off the radio and glanced at the empty passenger seat. Aloud, he said, "That young man's story doesn't need to be told right now. What was done was done. Talking about it will only cause heartache and resentment. Bury that bat and let it go. Move on, old man."

And with that, the radio lit up by itself and one of Louie's favorite songs blared from the surround sound speakers:

"I can be famous when I'm dead.
But, for now, I'll take to the dance floor
and make memories with you instead."

He sang along as he accelerated the truck's speed. He had to get home to feed Possum and check on the builder's progress. Later, he was meeting up with Lupita at the Under the Stars Dance at Lake Park Center for their second date. She was going to teach him how to tango.

Let the lady lead the dance, Louie. Let the lady lead the dance.

www.ingramcontent.com/pod-product-compliance
Lightning Source LLC
Chambersburg PA
CBHW051130190726
48290CB00006B/1777
* 9 7 8 1 7 3 5 0 5 8 2 2 1 *